The Death of CHARLOTTE WILSON

The Death of Charlotte Wilson

Beth Everett

This book is a work of fiction. Any references to historical events, real people, or places are fictitious. Other names, characters, places, and events are products of the author's imagination, and resemblance to actual events, places, or persons, living or dead, is entirely coincidental.

Copywrite © 2024 Beth Everett
All rights reserved, including the right to reproduce this book or portions thereof in any form whatsoever.

For information, contact betheverettauthor@gmail.com

Cover illustration © Edel Rodriguez

Cover Design by Jessica Jenkins

ISBN: 9798867704421

Fern Publishing

for Dina, friend of all friends

2005

◆◆◆

IN THE LAND of lenticular clouds and luminous moss sat an old red cedar. The tree grew on the edge of a farmer's field and spent years reaching toward the sun in ribbons and fans. As time passed and the world changed from cart to car, dairy cows disappeared from the clearing, and the farmer died without heirs. With the help of the crows and sparrows, the acres grew wild, eventually swallowing the tiny farmhouse. Left alone, the backside of the cedar's petticoat grew to touch the damp, sunless part of the woods, creating a secret unzipped place beneath her canopy.

Charlotte thought the tree was magic and hid beneath her skirt when her father raged. She snuggled into a nest made of fallen sprays and leaves and heard him call her name from the trail above the ravine with a pathetic attempt at concern. But his alcohol-fueled fire couldn't be smothered for long. He stormed down the muddy path, and his calls became threats, cutting through the pouring rain. The bruise on Charlotte's face pulsated as he passed. The tree warned her to be still.

Charlotte visited the cedar often as the years passed and still believed in its magic. Some days, she sat in the rain and read a favorite book without a drop of water touching the pages. When the weather broke and the afternoon sun touched the tree, thousands of sap drops lit the trunks like golden tears. Low branches provided seats to contemplate and steps to climb when she felt brave, but she mostly preferred the protection of the spongy ground, with the tree's pillowed bark as a backrest.

Charlotte spent three days under the protection of the cedar during the black, wet time after her mother died. She let cones fall into her hair, blanketed herself in fanned needles, and cried for her mother, who had promised not to leave her behind.

Sheltered from the wind and rain, young Charlotte dreamt the tree was her mother, wrapping her into its trunk. When she finally crawled out of the darkness to drink the water beaded on the flat sprays of the tree, Charlotte was alone in the woods, without roots or the ability to soar high enough to touch the clouds. She knew she must return home.

She entered through the screen door, which gave her away with a squeal before slamming shut. Her father fried an egg in a cast iron pan on the stove that Charlotte usually connected to her mother. He looked up but didn't ask where she'd been. She patted her hair to let him know she was aware of the mess and passed without speaking.

CHAPTER 1

◆◆◆

2013

CHARLOTTE SMILED FROM the passenger seat as the car wound through the wet forest. A verdant tree tunnel stretched overhead as the road curved along the ravine. She'd always loved her mother's house; now it would be hers again. Charlotte put her hand on her husband's leg and squeezed with excitement.

Lawrence Wilson couldn't remember the last time his wife touched him. A little fire traveled up his thigh. He kept his hands on the wheel, fearing even the slightest movement would cause her to withdraw. Lawrence didn't like the house but worshiped his wife like a stolen painting he knew he should give back. He'd been hoping the inspections would fail, the owners would change their mind and keep it, or the place would slide into the ravine to which it clung. But one touch from his wife erased his concerns. Mr. Wilson didn't look behind him. The future lay ahead.

But then it happened, and they spun once over the wet pavement, twice as mud and pine needles greased the street, before plunging over the edge, cutting through fern, wood, and earth, until a massive tree trunk stopped the car from falling into the ravine below.

CHAPTER 2

◆◆◆

FIVE BRIDGES STRETCHED across the Willamette River between the Portland Airport and my oldest friend Amy's house. Velveteen hills rose across the west side, and Mount Hood's glacial peak glowed from fifty miles to the east.

"Thanks again for picking me up," I said.

Amy gripped the wheel and leaned toward the windshield. Cars passed constantly, one flashing their brights before angrily speeding around. Using her car to pick me up when I could have taken the light rail said everything about how she felt about our friendship. "I'm both surprised and thrilled by your mysterious visit." She didn't take her eyes off the road for a second.

A campsite sat on a triangle of barriers along the highway. "There are even more homeless people than on my last visit."

"Everyone in the country is moving here," she said. "It's making it impossible to find housing."

"Like you did?" I laughed.

"I've been here for as long as I lived in California," she said. "That makes me a local." She laughed at herself, knowing you had to be born and raised in most places to be considered a local by the natives, especially the ones who never left.

We hugged the river, where one bridge shared a level with a train, another looked like a series of rainbows, and several vintage drawbridges hugged the water. Our crossing was a freeway that rose uncomfortably high over the river before dropping down on the west side.

"Sometimes I feel like a Jersey Girl," I said. "San Francisco is a city of strangers now, and the East Coast is where I raised my kids."

Amy exited the highway and stopped at a light. "I can see your tombstone now—Here lies a Jersey Girl." She erupted with laughter.

"Seriously! I love New Jersey. It's home."

"What do you love about it? Bon Jovi?" She knew I frowned upon big hair.

"I prefer Bruce. Have you seen how his body has held up?"

"You don't listen to his music. Ever," Amy said. The car behind us didn't honk when the light turned green.

"Not true," I said. "It's not getting any greener, Amy."

She drove on so slowly you'd think she'd run out of gas, and the guy behind us still didn't respond. In New Jersey, they honk at you for letting someone in a wheelchair cross the street.

"You'll always be a California girl to me, Lee."

"Ditto, Sister."

Our childhood homes were only a block away from each other on a foggy hill in San Francisco. Amy's father left her alcoholic mother for his secretary. He died a year later, leaving his estate to his new wife and giving Amy's mother another excuse to drink. My parents were dead before my eleventh birthday, and we'd been together through all of it.

"So, back to the house," Amy said. "I had a healthy down payment because I bought my condo eighteen years ago. It's a huge stretch, and I don't know how young people do it. Rents are sky-high, and wages are not, and it's hard to save a dime."

A tent sat under a highway onramp, and a woman in a lawn chair had a dog curled at her feet. "That explains the campers," I said. "How sad."

"There's a drug epidemic looming. But that's just part of it. Portland doesn't have rent control laws. Landlords jack the rates up by the hundreds of dollars at lease end." Amy drove the speed limit due to her agitation. "It's cheaper to buy, so everyone is trying. I made three other offers before I got my house; half of those I lost to someone with cash and the other half to the two incomes. It's hard not to be resentful."

A curvy, tree-lined street turned to a gravel road before we arrived at a mossy-roofed cottage nestled in the woods, and Amy parked in the driveway. "Finally, I was forced to hire Ellen."

"Who's Ellen?" I asked.

"If you want a house in my neighborhood, you must work with Ellen Robinson. Top producing agent in Southwest Portland for ten years in a row, according to her," Amy said. She opened her center console and handed me a clear glass tube with a joint inside.

I squealed, joyous. "You know I hate those plastic containers!" I opened it and sniffed.

She laughed and handed me a lighter.

"You really get me." I sighed. "Those Puritans in New Jersey won't even let me buy..."

"A sweater on a Sunday. I know," she said. "And just like that, you're a Jersey Girl no more."

We laughed.

"Guess how I got this house." Amy opened her car door and waited for an answer.

I couldn't keep my eyes off her forest-green cottage. "It's adorable, Amy. I love the rounded front door. Like fairies live here."

"Guess," she insisted.

"You wrote the world's best letter to the sellers about how the doctors said you only have one year to live?" I lit the joint and exhaled out the open door before passing it on.

"Wrong."
"Your agent knocked on the door and asked if they'd sell?" I asked. "People do that in my neighborhood, and I find it rude."
"I know. Don't come to my door unless you call first." She passed the joint back. "Wrong answer."
I left the car and spun around in the front yard. Green dripped from every surface, including the branches of many trees and Amy's roof. I stood in a sun patch and took a deep breath. "It smells like Christmas."
Amy pointed toward the end of the road. "That's a trailhead. Can you believe it? On my street."
"Street is an overstatement—more like a fire trail."
Amy smiled so wide her eyes squinted.
"I haven't seen you this happy since your lover redid the kitchen in your condo. What was his name?" I asked.
Her face turned sour before she shook it off. "You're never going to guess, so I'll tell you. The couple who outbid me drove off the road on their way to their home inspection. A hiker found them wrapped around a tree trunk.
"Whoa," I said. "Wouldn't have guessed."
"My real estate lady tried to get me to buy the house across the street as a consolation prize." She pointed to a cottage, overcome by a wild garden and gated by a chipping picket fence. The roof sagged, and there were twirling ornaments all over the garden.
"What did it sell for?" I asked.
"It didn't. The neighbors decided to stay." A crow flew from a tree and landed on Amy's brick chimney.
"Is your roof living on purpose?"
"I don't know, but it doesn't leak except in that one spot. And it is mine," she said. "Well, the bank's, but.... A long pause passed while the joint disappeared. Our gaze made the crow

5

uncomfortable, and it flew away. "I wish I felt sadder for that couple, but even though it has asbestos on the pipes and the roof needs replacing, it's my dream house," Amy said.

The property felt like a place light didn't visit often. The house fit right into the wooded setting, decaying and blooming simultaneously.

Amy pulled a few weeds along her driveway and threw them into a pile. "They grow overnight."

"The accident was a convenient tragedy," I said.

"What do you mean?" It sounded more like a warning than a question.

"Come on. You can't believe that couple died on the way to their home inspection? You know I don't believe in coincidence."

"You're looking for a motive in a car accident." She used her snotty tone, so I knew I'd scratched at something.

"I'm not," I said.

"You are, Lee. I can see it in your face. You'll make me walk around the neighborhood with a magnifying glass like you did when we were kids, so you don't have to deal with your problems." She dusted the dirt from the weeds off her hands with a clap.

"We never found anything but lizards, and that rock I'd convinced myself was an arrowhead," I said.

"And you dug up cat bones," she said. There were things she would never let me forget. "I guess I'm your prime suspect because I benefited most from their deaths."

"The cat bones weren't my fault," I said. "It's a great house, Amy. I'd kill for it too."

She opened the car door, and a suitcase popped out at us from the stuffed hatch.

"Why all the baggage?" she asked.

I changed the subject, talking about the kids while we carried as many pieces as possible to the door. Amy stopped in the vestibule so I could admire the brick and woodwork in the living room. We dropped my things in the guest room next to the kitchen, where she poured me a glass of wine and gave me a tour of the upstairs suite.

"All right, Lee. What's going on?"

We stood over her clawfoot tub, rusty around the drain but crowned with a new rod and a folksy, botanical shower curtain.

"You're a one-bag woman. You moving in?"

"Jack insisted we send the kids to camp again," I said. "You know I like to take that time for myself."

Amy could smell a lie, so I took the steep steps down to the wall of windows in the living room. Shades of pink and yellow sunset provided the backdrop for a wooded silhouette. "You live in a birdhouse, and I'd never have known from the road."

A sliding door led to a small deck overhanging the woods. I sat on a bench and watched the light fade.

"The couple I spoke about earlier... they skidded off the road and landed in the ravine right about there." Amy pointed across the way.

I imagined the sound of the car plummeting down the ravine and shivered. "How strange," I said. "Do they haunt you now?"

"Please. Ghosts don't come near me."

"You'd spray them with mace," I said.

"I would." She didn't crack a smile.

Amy kept a bowl of canisters on the table by her front door. "You should sell pepper spray for a living," I said. "You could write a blog on the uses of pepper spray."

The sun bowed out for the day, and an owl celebrated with a hoot from across the way. I thought of the dead couple. "What were their names?" I asked.

"The Wilsons," Amy said.

"Sad," I whispered.

"The weird thing is I'd been raging jealous of them that day. I thought they had a perfect life and would get my perfect house." Amy handed me a blanket and wrapped herself in another. "And then, poof! The house was mine. Maybe I'm a witch."

"Maybe I'm Big Foot," I said.

The owl hooted again, closer this time. Darkness reigned, causing small creatures to scatter on the forest floor, and the silence of the night began.

CHAPTER 3

◆◆◆

WE DRANK OUR coffee while the morning sun pushed through the trees, drawing patterns in spots and slivers on everything below the canopy. The deck swayed a little when anyone moved, and I wondered out loud when it would slide into the ravine.

"Stop stressing. The inspector said it has a year or two," she said. "What do you want to do today?" She promised the day would be warm.

We both wore pajamas, and my head hurt from too much wine the night before. I would have been thrilled to sit there all day, but I knew it wasn't Amy's speed. "It's your day off. What do you want to do?" I asked.

"I thought we could take a trail downtown and adventure from there. Maybe some live music after lunch?"

"Sounds good." I lit a joint, and we passed it until Amy broke the silence.

"So, you ready to talk about what's going on at home?" she asked.

"It's too early for therapy," I said.

"Whatever," Amy said. "I just know your kids have been going away to camp for a long time. You're bothered every year, but aren't they old enough to work there now?" She shook her head.

"You're not telling me something."

"Don't bring your work home, Amy. You're ruining my buzz."

"Okay. Okay." She raised her hands as if to surrender but smiled with one side of her mouth as she did when challenged. "I'm just going to ply you with booze all day until you cry. Then the entire bar can hear your problems, and you'll look like John Mayer when he plays guitar, except with snot and tears. It will be ugly," she said. "Don't say I didn't warn you."

I'd flown three thousand miles to forget about my problems, so I changed my tone and said, "Not now."

"Okay," she said.

We both knew it wasn't the end.

I leaned over the deck to see what was under Amy's house, curious if there were enough supports to keep us from sliding. Posts disappeared into a bed of ivy that might have been the only thing holding us on the vertical hillside. A padlocked set of plywood doors provided the only opening to an enclosed lower level. "You have a basement?" I asked.

"Not really."

"I see a door. What's down there?"

"I don't do underground spaces. Read my home inspection. The guy said there are pipes and beams and things that needed fixing." She sighed a weighty sigh. "How about we don't talk about house or husband problems for the rest of the day?"

"Agreed," I said.

◆◆◆

Amy walked briskly along the shoulderless winding road, then made a sharp turn onto a trailhead so hidden that Lewis and Clark would have missed it. Moments ago, I was sure I'd get hit by a car, but now we dove down a steep staircase into a quiet ravine where the crows ruled the airwaves and a dense forest of Douglas fir competed for the sun. A few miles (and blisters) later, we arrived downtown. Once we hit the sidewalk, I whined about my sore feet for the remaining four blocks to the pub.

Amy scolded me about my footwear over a Bloody Mary. I purchased the leopard print sandals because they looked cute *and* comfy. I glanced around the busy bar and found mostly hiking sandals and boots. Portlanders wore camping clothes to brunch.

"I'm no good at rugged chic," I said.

"New Jersey did that to you," Amy said.

"What?" I gave her my most evil eye and tapped my sore foot while awaiting her response.

"Nothing," Amy finally said. She could barely keep from laughing while she sipped on her paper straw. "Leopard print 'hiking' sandal." She almost spit her drink out laughing.

I liked my shoes and did not think she was funny. "My friend told me the workers spit into the giant vats of glue used to make those straws," I said.

Amy pulled the candy-striped straw out of her drink, and her face contorted with disgust. "I forgot what a bitch you can be," she said.

"No, you didn't." I didn't ask for a straw, so when I took a sip from the tall glass, ice cubes rushed down and hit my mouth, sending liquid out both sides of my face and down my shirt.

Amy almost rolled out of her chair, laughing. "Instant Karma."

"But seriously, can we take a cab to our next stop?" I asked. "No one should have to walk four miles for a drink."

Amy once hiked from the Southern California desert to the Canadian border on the Pacific Crest Trail. All her shoes were for climbing, and all her clothing looked water-resistant. "You've lived here too long," I said. "How is work?"

She shrugged, more resigned than I'd seen her in the past. "It's overwhelming. I lost several clients in the last month to overdose. We're handing out Narcan kits as fast as we get them in, but it's not fast enough. Each death hurts."

"What's Narcan?" I asked.

"It's the antidote to opioid overdose."

"I didn't know there was one. Why doesn't everyone have it?" I asked.

"Greed." Amy picked up her drink and sucked on the straw until her glass emptied.

When Max was little, she told him she'd give him an enema if he didn't stop jumping on her furniture. "Tell me a story I can scare my boys with," I said.

"My client is so crazy from doing meth that he thinks he saw a person cut in pieces and fed to people at a food truck pod." Amy paused while a waiter dropped two more Bloody Marys on our table.

"Maybe he did," I said.

She rolled her eyes. "He truly believes it, so he stands outside the food truck pod and warns people away."

"Uh oh," I said.

"This didn't go over well with the food cart owners."

"Meth is nasty," I slurped the last of my drink. "Does it ever strike you as odd that we can have two rounds of alcohol on a Saturday morning, and no one cares?" I asked. "Isn't alcohol a hard drug?"

Jack and I drank every night, and I had a reputation for hosting cocktail and weed-filled parties among our equally buzzed friends. The kids saw drinking as normal. People in the burbs of New Jersey smoke all their weed in the basement or behind some detached garage, and they treat it like sex—something they hide from the kids.

"Someone gave me a glass that says, 'Wine is Good Food,'" I said. "My kids see it every day when they open the cabinet."

"The kids are fine." Amy adored them from three thousand miles away and sent extravagant outdoorsy gifts to "buy their love," as she called it.

"The boys loved those hiking backpacks you sent, by the way," I said. "Did they thank you?"

"Better than that. They invited me on a week-long Appalachian Trail hike next year." Amy grinned from ear to ear. She could never reel me into her trail shenanigans, but she'd hooked my boys.

"Nice. I like how they didn't invite me."

"No leopard print sandals are allowed on the trail." She smiled shamelessly.

"So smug," I said. Do you ever see kids like mine on the street, Amy? With two parents at home?"

"All the time, Lee. This epidemic spares no family: Rich, poor, single parents, or married parents. You're all fucked."

"Are you trying to freak me out?" I asked.

"The boys are going to be fine. And if they aren't, we'll deal with it."

"We lost a kid in Forest Glen to heroin this year. I can still see his baby face from kindergarten. His poor parents." My eyes pooled with thoughts of the boy's parents. "His sister is Max's age. My God, it's too horrible to think of." I shook it off with a deep sip of alcohol.

"Imagine if a plane full of two hundred spouses, siblings, and children crashed into the ocean every day for over a decade," Amy said. "That's what's going on right now in the United States. No one cares until it's someone they love; shame and stigma keep them quiet even then. Like it's their fault."

"It's an amazing thing you do, Amy." I took my friend's hand and squeezed it. "How many lives have you saved?"

"Not enough, Lee," she said.

CHAPTER 4

♦♦♦

"I'M GOING TO WALK five miles today," I said aloud, so I'd have to do it. I dressed in jeans and stretched to get a happy reflection of my shrinking rear end through the window.
"I believe you," Amy said. She rushed about the kitchen making coffee.
"Also, I am not drinking alcohol today," I said.
"Okay." She pulled out a frying pan.
"Don't make me anything. I'm taking myself out," I said.
"Oh, thank you," Amy put the pan back. "I'm so late for work." She shuffled around the house, gathering bags, files, and lunch.
"Check out the Maplewood for breakfast. I think you'll like it," she shouted before the front door closed.
I cleaned the kitchen and mapped out my day before heading out. Many of the streets around the neighborhood were gravel and without sidewalks, and roads could turn into trails that turned back into roads. I counted seven houses with a Subaru and Prius in the driveway, three Little Libraries, two chicken coups, and a home painted in rainbow colors before arriving at the café.
The general store turned café bustled with young moms and silver-haired hippies in comfortable shoes. Cake plates full of fresh pastries at the counter held more calories than I could burn climbing Mt. Hood.
I thought about the text chain I'd discovered a week ago between my husband and a coworker and bounced between pain

and rage—mostly rage—while I waited in line. The betrayal might have been forgivable if it had been the first time, but the conversation between them had been long, as long as his history of fucking me over. Amy hadn't liked Jack from the beginning. I'd spent many years convincing her she'd been wrong after he had an affair while I was pregnant with our first child. Now I felt shame.

I growled a little, forgetting my surroundings. A boy in line heard me and wrapped himself tightly around his mother's leg. I ordered coffee and skipped breakfast. A snug spot awaited me next to a wall of paned windows in the back room. The chatter of West Coast accents rose and fell as I caught pieces of conversation from the air. A group of middle-aged ladies argued over a volunteer project. A hipster wore headphones and typed furiously on the keys of his laptop. Two women sat at the table next to me, and one went on about a house.

I wore headphones but hadn't turned the music on. Instead, I deleted dozens of Jack's texts without reading them. He'd filled my mailbox, so I listened to one of his desperate pleas. Hearing his voice left me soft, so I deleted the rest. Ignoring my husband felt like my only power. But communicating with him was a comforting habit, and I hadn't figured out how to fill the gap yet.

One of the women next to me had bright cheeks and wore a periwinkle dress. She refolded her napkin into squares, unfolded it again, and took a deep breath. "I fear I may have done something bad."

"What do you mean, dear?" The woman across the table let her glasses drop to the tip of her nose.

I pretended to casually glance around the room until I accidentally stopped at the tiny, intimidating woman who stared back at me. Oversized sunglasses rested on her severely bobbed head, and she wore an impeccable linen shift dress and frosted salmon lipstick.

"Well, remember when we drove by the house after we lost out on that offer on the West Slope, and Walter wanted to rent a condo in the Pearl District?"

"I don't remember you ever giving up, Eloise." The broker took her sunglasses from the top of her head and began a severe polishing before glancing my way.

I stared out the window at a bird feeder, but not before she caught my eye.

"Well, we almost did!" Eloise said. "And then suddenly, there was my dream house. Right on the corner."

"That worked out wonderfully, didn't it?" Ellen continued to polish the sunglasses. "How are the kids?"

"But don't you remember what I said, Ellen?" Eloise darkened.

"Just drop it, Eloise."

"I said I'd kill for that house." Her eyes opened to great lengths before she reached across the table and took Ellen's reluctant hands. "And Mr. Buckwood dropped dead a week later!"

She squeezed her agent's well-manicured hands tighter while the woman pulled back. "I'm afraid I made a deal with the devil."

Ellen gave a solid yank and freed herself. "That's just ridiculous. You did no such thing."

Eloise attempted a sunny smile, but her eyes betrayed the sting. She nibbled on a cookie and said, "It is quite a coincidence, though. Don't you think?"

Ellen. I knew that name, and now I had a face to go with it.

◆◆◆

The walk back to Amy's gave me another mile toward my goal of five for the day but didn't get me there. Back at the house, I smoked a joint on the deck and thought of Ellen and her client. Trees bent and moaned with the breeze around the deck. I made a sad lunch with too many vegetables and wolfed it down. Gazing across the woods made me curious. I hit the trail next to Amy's property, hoping to find my way across the park.

The path dove into the ravine quickly. At the bottom, only specks of sunlight reached the ground. A stream babbled softly over rocks. I'd disappeared into a verdant wonderland in only a few hundred steps. The trail followed along the stream and up the hill along small waterfalls, where I eventually came up from the woods and stepped onto a yellow-lined road.

The Wilson accident happened six months earlier. I looked for skid marks or broken glass, but there was none. I walked the skinny shoulder, searching for disturbances in the shrubs on both sides of the road, but only found mounds of ivy and a few beer cans. On the way back, I peered along the route's vertical edge. A wide swath of sapling and brush lay flattened, and a tree with a scar of missing bark marked the spot. I climbed down the slope, skidding and grabbing at branches until I landed with a thud on the tree trunk.

Glass and metal still littered the ground. Someone had burned the image of a stag's head on the scar. I ran my finger up the antlers, amazed by the beauty of the image, curious about who had put it there, and uncomfortable with my rough intrusion on someone's sacred spot. I stomped through ivy and fern to get back down the trail because getting back up the hill to the road was impossible. When I finally returned to Amy's, I'd walked four miles for the day and needed another shower. Amy arrived home early to a clean, tired houseguest.

"Guess who I sat next to at the Maplewood?" I could barely wait to tell her.

She poured me a glass of wine, but I waved it away. "Nope. I didn't meet my goal," I said.

She shoved it in my hand. "You're on vacation."

"That's true. Kind of." I took the glass.

"We can walk to dinner so you can meet your goal."

I showed her a scrape on my elbow, proving the difficulty of my day. "Can we order in?"

Her face sagged with disappointment. "My friend's band plays at the Star on Monday nights. I was hoping to go."

"I promise to go next Monday," I said. "I'm so tired and sore. Look." I held up my shin to show her another scrape.

Amy resigned herself to staying in. She tossed me a large envelope full of menus.

"Guess who I sat next to at the Maplewood?" I asked again.

"Pick someplace to order from first, please."

"Guess," I said.

"Uh, Gloria Steinem." She put her hand on her hip, the first sign of her impatience with me.

"Come on. I'll give you a hint. She's a killer agent."

Amy raised her eyebrows and pinched her lips. "What did you do?"

"I didn't do anything. You told me to go to the café—I went. It's not my fault your wicked agent sat beside me, trying to stop her client from discussing another dead client."

Amy didn't care for my "detective antics," as she called them. It went back to when we were kids, and I saw a strange man looking out her window from inside her house on our way home from school. We ran to the neighbor's house to call the police. I know what I saw, but they only found Amy's mother passed out drunk on her bed when they arrived. Alone. Amy gave me the same look now as she'd given me then.

"Did Ellen see you?" she asked.

"Yes. But Ellen doesn't know me, remember?"

This fact calmed her down.

"Why are you so afraid of Ellen? Do you think she will sell your house while you're out of town or something?" I asked. "Or maybe kill you?"

"I have to live here after you leave, Lee. Please don't get me into trouble."

"Don't you want to know what I heard?"

"No," said Amy. "I do not."

We ordered sushi and spent the evening discussing everything but my marriage and real estate.

CHAPTER 5

◆◆◆

A HAWK LANDED in the canopy of the maple tree growing outside the guest bedroom window. Its claws perched on a branch, and its keen head turned back and forth, scanning for prey. I moved ever so slowly, and it flew away.

It took all of my energy to get out of bed. "I'm low today," I said over breakfast.

I hadn't mentioned my sadness, but for about the twentieth time since I'd arrived, Amy observed it, took a deep breath, and released it with purpose. "Do you think not talking about it is helping you?" She pushed an egg around a pan with her fork.

"I don't have the words yet. When I get the words, I'll share them with you." I downed my coffee before taking my plate to the kitchen and lied about my big plans for the day. When she left for work, I crawled back into bed and waited for the hawk to return until I fell asleep.

◆◆◆

The first time I saw Justin, he stood beside a food cart pod entrance at a bus stop, wearing a clean, matching Nike sweatsuit and new sneakers. He carried a small backpack. I'd just come down the hill on a trail from Amy's. When I walked by, I saw his lips move, so I removed a headphone from one ear. "Sorry?" I asked.

"Do you have two-fifty for the bus?" he asked. I looked him over, probably for too long. He was tall and had delicate features. There wasn't a whisker in sight, and his clothes hung loosely. Something in how he shoved his hands in his pockets hurt my heart, so I stopped looking.

"Are you hungry?" I asked. "I'll buy you lunch first."

"Sure," he said, following me through the entrance gate to the food trucks. "Thank you."

"What do you feel like eating?" Carts of every ethnicity and flavor corralled around, deciding difficult.

"Whatever you want." He continued to dig into his pockets.

"I'm going to sit at that table over there. Can you get us food? I'm a vegetarian, and please don't bring back drinks in plastic. I really hate plastic."

He laughed. "Cool."

"Is that enough?" I handed him one more twenty. "Here—get whatever you want."

I watched him walk away, mentally willing him from the macaroni and cheese stand. He must have sensed it because he went straight for the burrito truck.

My phone showed notifications of seven voicemails and five texts from Jack. "Your voicemail is full. Call me back," the last one read. Amy texted. She wanted tacos for dinner. I'd never lose any more weight at this rate.

He returned with two giant burritos. He pulled two cans of beer out of his pockets, dropped one before me, and released a pile of wrinkled bills and coins on the table.

I pushed the money back toward him. "Sit, please," I said. He hesitated and then decided to join me.

"I'm Lee Harding." I held out my hand.

"Justin Hendrix." He gave me a quick, solid shake.

I leaned in. "Are you old enough to buy beer?"

"Dude didn't even card me, which is good cause my wallet got lifted at the shelter last night. I always lose shit at the shelters."

"That sucks." I bit into my burrito and tasted pineapple—so wrong.

"I wouldn't have had to go there if the city hadn't cleared my camp." His knee rattled under the table, and his hand shook when he lifted his beer.

"Oh, that sucks," I said. The poor kid was a bag of bones. "What are you going to do now?"

"I'll try to sleep away from people—go as far into the woods as possible.'

"Sounds scary." I chewed slowly, wishing he'd gone to the mac and cheese truck.

"I've had coyotes stalk me, but people scare me the most, especially the dudes. It's tough to be a chimp, right?"

I didn't know what he meant. Between bites, I asked, "What did you do? When the coyote stalked you?"

"I tried to get a picture of it." He proceeded to eat his burrito in thirty-nine seconds. "Impossible in the dark," he said with a full mouth.

I opened the blanket of tortilla and picked out kale and pineapple. "So why do you think we're chimps?" I asked.

"The most aggressive male wins the best camp spot and the mate, just like chimps," he said.

"I believe you," I said, thinking about the smelly bears my kids turned into at a certain age, the hormones, and the anger. I'd kept them in constant activities to keep them tired. "Not to change the subject, but they put some gross shit in burritos here. Unnecessary things."

"They gotta keep it weird, I guess," Justin said.

I made a face echoing my lack of support for weird burritos. "So, where did you pick up your chimp theory?"

"I read some Darwin. Survival of the Spee-cies!" He made a heavy metal song out of the title.

I laughed. "I've never read it. Does it say we're all chimps?"

"Seriously? Human males are fighting each other for the future of their genetic line. That's what it's about." He pulled a nicely bound copy of Darwin's book from his bag. "That's why I prefer coyotes to humans." He passed a leather-bound book from his pack.

I paged through color plates of birds and animals I didn't recognize.

"There are too many chimps in the camps," he said.

I thought of the testosterone-filled seed-spreader I called my husband. "I get it."

Justin's face lit up, and I smiled.

"What?" he asked.

"What else do you have in there?" I passed the book back.

"Nothing." He put it in his bag. "It never leaves my side," he said. "I paid some junkie twenty bucks to steal it from Powell's."

"So, you stole it?" I asked.

"No, he stole it. I bought it from him."

"Not nice." I rerolled my burrito, satisfied with the exclusions lying on the plate.

"That book is the only thing that's kept me alive out here," he said. "I've read it six times."

"Where is your mother?" I asked.

"My Mom? She OD'd a year ago."

"I'm so sorry," I said.

"I found her." He tightly packed the dark memory into the ball he'd made from a foil wrapper.

"I lost my mom when I was young and my dad from cancer two years earlier. I'm the one that found my mom," I said.

"They made me sit in our apartment with her alone forever until the coroner took her. I was eighteen, so I got nothing but an eviction after that," Justin said.

A flash of my twelve-year-old self, crawling into bed with my mother and begging her to wake up, fluttered through my mind.

"How long have you been on the street?" I asked.

"Almost a year. I got my tent, all my blankets, and everything I had left of my mom's, taken on the anniversary of her death. That was two days ago."

I felt like an asshole, moping around while my kids ate healthy meals and sailed boats across a lake for thousands of dollars a week.

"What do you need?" I ask.

"Lunch was just what I needed. Thank you."

My parents left a publishing legacy for us three girls when they died. My sister Lacy was old enough to care for my middle sister, Alice, and me, so we didn't have to leave our family home. None of us pick our birthplace. It's all luck, and my kids hit the jackpot while Justin lost the life lottery in the womb. I had an idea and perked up immediately. "Listen, Justin, my life has been a breeze, so I'm happy to pay it forward. So, take me seriously, okay? What do you need the most? Name three things, and they are yours."

"You straight up?" he asked.

"I'm not some pervert or anything if that's what you mean—and I'm not trying to save you either. I'm a mom like your mom, and I want to help. What do you need?" I'd put it on Jack's credit card if he asked for a car.

"You're nothing like my mom, trust me." He hid a private joke with a laugh. "In this order: a hot shower, a bed, and a charger for my phone." He noticed my grin and raised an eyebrow. "What?"

"I thought you'd have asked for a car or a house. I can buy you a car." The more I thought about it, the more I wanted to put a car on Jack's credit card. My eldest, Jack Jr., was almost eighteen, and he would have asked for an apartment in Manhattan or a beach house in California.

My little one, Max, is only sixteen and had recently asked me to rent him a house on a golf course for the summer. He'd pulled up a listing online and argued it was cheaper than camp. We called him our little attorney. Privilege hit me like a brick.

"I don't drive," Justin said. "I just want a hot shower."

"Come on," I gathered the garbage from the table. "You can shower and recharge. We'll figure out the rest later."

CHAPTER 6

◆◆◆

I SNATCHED JUSTIN'S clothes while he showered and threw them in the washing machine on sanitize. If he brought bedbugs in, Amy would never speak to me again. I'd felt so good about bringing him home until we got there, and then I realized what a ridiculous and dangerous thing I'd done.

I smoked a joint on the patio and waited for him to come out of the bathroom, which made me paranoid. I thought Justin might be a psychopath, so I hid every sharp object from the kitchen under a chair cushion. He came out wearing a pair of my sweats and a robe I'd left for him.

"You hungry?" I asked, micro-cleaning the kitchen to compensate for bringing a stranger into my friend's house without permission—not just any stranger, possibly one of her patients. I winced at the thought. He'd be gone before she got home, I told myself.

"I could eat," Justin said. His backpack sat on the stool next to him. "Where are my clothes?"

"I threw them in the wash," I said. "Sorry. I have sons your age, so don't worry about me seeing your underwear."

He shrugged. "Thanks."

"Do you know Amy Doherty?" I asked. "From City Harm Reduction?"

He looked to his left and gave it an honest thought. "Nope. Why?"

"Just wondering," I said. "My friend Amy is the Director there."

"I might know her. Super-hot? Black hair?"

"No, Amy has red hair," I said.

"Nope," he said.

I didn't want him to be uncomfortable, so I didn't tell him it wasn't my house. Instead, I warmed up some leftovers. He finished two servings before his shoulders and eyes drooped.

"Go lay down on the bed. When you wake up, we'll find a place for you to stay long-term, and your phone will be fully charged."

He listened. "I'm cream-crackered," he said, plopping on the bed face down.

I had no idea what that meant, but it sounded gross. When I shut the door a few moments later, Justin was already drooling on one of Amy's pillows. I polished the kitchen some more and searched for monthly rentals online.

Two hours later, I folded Justin's clothes, noted sizes, and ordered three new sets of everything to be sent to Amy's. I made stacks on the chair by the bed and then tried to wake him.

"Justin," I sang. "Time to get up. Time for the fourth wish—the bonus wish!"

He didn't move. I watched his back rise and fall, and when the front door slammed.

"Hello!" Amy bellowed. "Leeeee."

I shut the bedroom door behind me and met her in the hall. "What are you doing here?" I asked.

"Good to see you too," Amy said, kissing me through the air. "I came home to play with you."

"You didn't have to do that," I said, wiping my brow. "Go. Go back to work. I'm fine." I poured a shot of bourbon and downed it.

Amy looked at me sideways for a second. "I'm already here, and I'm not going back."

"Well, let's go out for a walk then." I grabbed my purse from the bench by the door to my room. "I'm starving. Maybe we can walk to dinner." I took her by the arm.

"Jesus, Lee. Can I pee first?"

Fearing she'd use the downstairs bathroom, which Justin had showered in, I ran ahead. "I've got to go, too." I slammed the door and locked it, stuffing Justin's towel under the sink with the extra toothbrush I'd given him and wiping down the counters.

When I heard Amy walking around upstairs, I crept back into the bedroom room where Justin lay in a kind of coma. I lifted his arm and let it drop like a weight.

"Let's go, Miss Rushy-Rush," Amy yelled from the door.

"Do not leave this room!" I whispered. "Please," and left a half-dressed stranger in Amy's house alone.

I lit a joint to pair with the shot of bourbon I'd downed earlier and puffed it from the front yard. A couple of hits, and soon, I could breathe again. Across the road, Amy's neighbor clipped at something in her overgrown yard.

"Hey, Astral." Amy waved.

A bohemian goddess with waist-long dreadlocks and a big, toothy smile waved back. She put her clippers down and greeted us over a rotting picket fence. The garden bloomed around spinning rainbows and hanging chimes.

"Hey, Amy," she said. "Hey, Amy's friend."

"This is my oldest pal, Lee. She's here for a..." Amy paused until I nudged her. "Visit?"

Astral smiled without looking up, fussing with an overgrown vine without impact. I tried to hide the joint.

"Lee lives in New Jersey. They arrest you for weed there."

"You can't buy a sweater on a Sunday in my county," I complained. "Old Dutch laws."

"That sounds crazy." She focused on me like her eyes were magic magnifying glasses. "I can see your aura, Lee. I'd love to read your colors sometime."

I kicked a rock instead of looking at Amy. "Thank you," I said. My mother wrote books on skepticism, leaving me believing very little about the spiritual world.

Amy made excuses for us with Astral, and we left for a trail into the woods. When we were far away, Amy said, "If stars could talk, they would be Astral."

I nodded in agreement, but only an image of Justin rummaging through Amy's jewelry drawer came to mind. I lit another joint to forget. My feet throbbed as the cityscape appeared through a silhouette of Douglas firs. Amy called us a car after a few miles of listening to me complain. The driver picked us up in the woods, and I had no idea how he found us. We drove over a busy bridge to the southeast side of town, eventually arriving at the Roadside Attraction. We showed a man in a phone booth IDs and walked through a sort of Hobbit shanty patio, with tables in nooks and a swing by a fire.

Inside, a woman with half blonde, half black hair made us drinks while I admired the shrunken head dangling just over a black and white photo of Martha Gellhorn and ate too many free Thin Mints from a bowl on the bar.

"Gellhorn is my favorite. The woman who refused to be tamed," I said.

"Are you still hung up on Hemingway?" Amy asked, looking past my shoulder at a man on the patio. "I thought I dated a guy out there, but it's not him," she said.

"If by hung up you mean, would I still fuck him, the answer is yes. I think he was probably interesting and well-hung."

"I don't think so," Amy said. "I'd bet money he was impotent and boring—that's what all the elephant slaying was about, fake machismo."

"Martha Gellhorn does not strike me as a woman who would stick around for that, so I'm guessing the only reason she stayed as long as she did was that he was hung," I said.

I repeatedly texted Justin, hoping the sound would wake him.

My response disappointed Amy, who loved to debate the penis size of literary figures. She slapped my phone down on the table. "Where are you tonight, Lee?"

"Amy!"

The phone faced up, and she grabbed it before I could. "And who is Justin?" Her eyes opened wide when she saw how many times I'd texted him. "Oh, my god. You're obsessed."

"No!" I grabbed my phone and stuffed it in my purse. "It's not like that. He's a friend." I took a breath and looked away.

"Is this why you came out here? Are you having an affair?"

I sat up straight and sighed. "Amy, can we just get fucked up tonight like in the old days and not worry about anything. I'm so tired of worrying about everything." I leaned forward so she could see the bags under my eyes. "So tired."

Amy hated drama, so we let it go, but the drinking dragged us down by eight o'clock, and we were too tired to see the band.

"Who can stay up until ten to see a show on a work night anyway?" Amy asked.

I paid up, and we left. "Us, a few years ago," I said.

"Before we got old as fuck," she said.

I stopped on the street. "I'm not old as fuck," I said. The alcohol mixed with the exhaustion, and I started to cry. "I'm not," I managed to say through my crack-up.

Amy almost laughed until she saw what a mess I was. Before she could comfort me, our ride came. I wiped my eyes and hopped in the car. "I'll tell you everything when we get home, okay?" I said, holding onto Amy's hand in the dark car. The dam broke, but I tried to cry silently.

Amy stuffed a wad of tissue in my hand. I took a deep breath. The driver glanced through the rearview mirror.

"I'm sorry," I said. "I hope I'm not embarrassing you."

"Trust me, Mam. A few tears won't stain anything. Let it loose," the driver said.

I gave him a big tip even though he called me Mam.

Inside, Amy took me by the shoulders and looked into my red eyes, shaking me a little like whatever she thought possessed me would drop to the floor.

"This is yours and Jack's business," she said. "We'll talk when you're ready."

"I feel stupid, Amy. I feel like a real idiot. He's at it again. Fool me once; shame on him, right?" I started to cry again. "I have never been my husband's number one."

"I'll fucking kill him." She wrapped her arms around me tightly.

"Honestly, I'm not sure I even care," I said. "I'm tired of trying to make my marriage make sense when it doesn't."

Amy pulled away. "Lee, when your parents died, you wanted a family, and you and Jack have that...had it. Whatever. Maybe it is just time for a new chapter."

"I only know one thing, Amy," I closed my eyes and leaned on her. "I never should have had that last drink."

"Are you going to puke?" she asked.

"No! I need to go to bed." I wanted to cry again when I thought of Justin in my room.

"Okay. I'm going up. I've got early appointments in the morning." She clunked up the stairs and turned around on the first landing. "I'm glad you're here."

Three drinks failed to kill my guilt. Once I heard Amy's footsteps from above, I dashed for the guest room, half expecting to see the bed empty, half expecting to find him dead—but there Justin lay—in the same spot I'd left him—his chest rose and fell with each breath. I pulled a pillow from under one of his arms and headed to the couch.

CHAPTER 7

◆◆◆

AMY'S PIPES BANGED and rattled when she started the upstairs shower, announcing the morning and jolting me from the sofa. I quickly folded my blanket over the arm of the chair I'd taken it from and peeked in on Justin. The room smelled like boy-breath. I opened the windows and checked for signs of life. Once I found his pulse, I whispered, "Stay!"

Amy liked to read the news with her coffee, so I snuck outside to the quiet morning to steal the paper. Trees circled the house like ghosts in the mist. I found the newspaper on the walkway and tossed it under a bush, looking around to ensure no one spotted me. Across the street in Astral's yard, a civil war-type apparition in long johns watched. A cigarette tip glowed through the fog.

I tiptoed to the cold walkway and locked the door behind me. Amy came downstairs and found coffee waiting, followed by omelets and toast. I pulled out a chair and made her sit.

"Wow, Lee. Cheese omelets. I'm so glad you can still make them."

"I can make Eggs in a Hole too. I'm saving that for our last day, though."

She took a bite and smiled, weary of my sudden domestic prowess. "The garlic powder brings me back to the old kitchen on Taylor. Perfect hangover food."

I knew she was sincere when she stacked pieces of omelet on her toast and devoured it. Growing up in Amy's house, if you didn't eat fast, you didn't eat.

"That sucks about your paper." I tried not to rock in my chair. "I guess your newspaper boy is sick today."

"I guess."

"Well, at least you'll get to work early, and then you can come home sooner!"

She looked at her phone. "Wow. I am getting in early. Jesus. It's only seven."

"Well, you'll beat all the traffic." I cleared her plate and coffee mug before she chewed her last bite.

"What's your plan today?" she asked.

"I'm taking the Forty-four bus as you suggested, and I'll hop on and off on the Northeast side a bit. Maybe check out a hotel bar or two for happy hour. Can we meet downtown later?"

Amy tried to load the dishwasher, but I shooed her out.

"Go to work. Go." I handed her the lunch I'd packed. "So we can play sooner."

"All right," she said. "Going. Sheesh." But instead of leaving, she went back up the stairs.

Just then, Justin stumbled out of the guest room and zombie-walked to the bathroom, closing the door behind him. He produced a record-breaking stream—I swear it didn't end until Amy took her last step down. I dashed to usher her out the front door and down the walkway before she heard a flush.

My poor friend wore the same puzzled look she had since my arrival. "You get stranger and stranger each day you're here, Lee."

"Why, thank you." Bowing, I caught a glimpse of the newspaper under a fern frond and scooped it up. "Here you go. Something to read on the bus."

"Let's drink less tonight," Amy shouted backward as she walked the gravel road.

The mist began to settle, losing to a blue sky. I took a deep breath of piney air before returning to the house. Snores rumbled from the open doorway of the guest room.

"Justin, get up." I shook him. "Justin. You must get up." I nudged him with my knee. "Come on. Up."

He moved a little, mumbling, "Okay," and fell asleep.

"Justin! Get up!" I yelled. "Come on, get up." I pulled on his arm.

"Okay. Okay." He pulled his arm back, sat up, and looked around. "What time is it?" He searched for his phone, saw his clothes on the chair, glanced down at his lap at my fuchsia sweats, stared at me, and scratched his head.

"The next day. I'll leave you to get dressed."

I shut the door and paced the living room.

He came out dressed—groggy and shy. "I lost a day?"

"You've been asleep since three o'clock yesterday."

"Man, I'm really sorry."

The last eighteen hours aged me, but I felt his shame and embarrassment a thousand times more. "I'm glad you got some good sleep, kid. I'm going to make you an omelet, and then we will find you a new apartment," I said.

"You jexing me?" He rubbed his eyes and obeyed, dropping into a chair at the counter.

"I am not jexing you. I don't think I am anyway," I said. "How do you feel about this neighborhood?"

He shrugged.

"There's a roommate situation over by the community college. Can you do roommates?"

"Are you for real?" he asked.

"I am very real," I said. "We'll get you a place to live and some documents, like a birth certificate and an ID. And I hope you don't mind, but I ordered you some clothes."

His knee rattled again, harder than ever.

"What's the matter?"

"I won't get picked for a roommate situation. No job. And I've got no credit, so my score is low."

"How can you have a low credit score with zero credit?"

He shrugged. "It's the American way. The more debt you're in, the better off you are."

"Well, that's skeptical," I said. "And true."

"We'll just get you an apartment of your own," I said.

"I can't afford the rent on an apartment."

"I can," I said. "My cheating husband is wealthy, Justin, and that makes me wealthy. Not Bill Gates wealthy, but trust me, there's enough, and I will spend some of it."

"Are you straight up?" He cracked on the last word, and his eyes pooled a little. "Are you some kind of fairy godmother?"

"I love that," I said. "Yes. I'm your fairy godmother."

We spent an hour planning our morning. Justin explained how the river divided Portland from east to west, and Burnside Street marked north from south. We settled our search on the Northwest neighborhoods, where historic brick apartments were affordable. Someone knocked on the door just as we were ready to leave.

"Shh," I whispered.

Justin froze in his chair.

I recognized the sharpest haircut in Portland when I opened the door, but a slight tilt of the head told me Ellen Robinson, real estate agent extraordinaire, didn't quite recognize me.

"Hello." Her voice dropped to bass range as she shoved an ice pail filled with red, white, and blue party paraphernalia into my arms. If she knew Amy, she'd know she hated plastic, didn't decorate her house for any occasion, and wouldn't be home at ten a.m. on a weekday.

"I'm Ellen Robinson, Amy's broker. Is she home?" She tried peeking through the open door, but I stepped out and shut it behind me.

"No. Amy's at work," I said.

Ellen wore a well-tailored dress in size zero and looked up at me in sky-high Stilettos. Her white Mercedes idled in the driveway. "I'm just popping by." She stuck a business card on the bucket before darting toward her car. "Please tell Amy I'm sorry I missed her."

I read her business card while she bolted down the gravel road, then texted Amy a photo captioned, "She really gets you."

Amy texted back. "Bring it over to Astral's kid, would you? Remove the tag first. They don't care for Ellen."

"Why not?" I asked.

"None of your business," she texted back.

I carefully eliminated any signs of a stranger from Amy's house before we packed up to head downtown. Justin waited outside while I ran Ellen's bucket up the walk and dropped it at the front door of Astral's house. I knocked softly and ran, but the door opened halfway back to the gate. I looked back to see a tiny, barefooted girl stepping out. She wore a paint-stained dress and squealed when she saw the bucket full of flags and toys.

"For me?" she said. "It's so beautiful."

"It's from Amy." I pointed toward my friend's house. "Do you know who I mean?"

"Of course!" She pulled out a clapper and swung it back and forth as she ran toward me.

"Thank you for bringing this to me," she said. "Would you like to come in for tea?"

"That's very sweet of you," I said. "You must be Pearl."

"I am. What's your name?"

"I'm Lee." I smiled at her dirty feet and perfect manners. "I met your mom yesterday. Tell her I said 'hello,' please."

"Astral is at Celestial Beads. Have you been to her store? It's in the village and smells like Myrrh. Do you like Myrrh?"

"I don't know," I said.

"I like your dress," she said. She held out her paint-smudged skirt.

"Thank you. It's the first time I'm wearing it." I said. "I like that your dress has paint on it. You must be making the most of your day."

She looked past the fence to where Justin smoked a cigarette under a tree. "Is that your boyfriend?" she asked.

"No," I said. "That's my friend Justin."

"Smoking is bad for him."

"I know. It smells gross, too." I shrivel my nose in support. We both waved at him. He put his cigarette out and gave us a tired smile.

"Do you want to say hello to Henry?" Pearl asked. "He's out back."

"Is Henry your dad?" I asked.

"Yes, but Astral doesn't like labels."

"Isn't a name a label?" I asked.

She thought for a moment before deciding. "I think a name is a name. But I'll ask Astral when she gets home."

"Oh, no need. It was a silly question," I said.

"Henry says there are no silly questions," she said.

"I see." I disagreed but kept my mouth shut. "See you later. We have to keep moving so we don't miss our bus."

Her smile turned to disappointment, but she didn't pout. "Come back again, Lee." She waved enthusiastically.

"I will," I said. "I promise."

Justin and I walked toward the main road. "If a rainbow fairy lived in the forest, it would be Pearl," I said when we were far enough away.

"What?" Justin asked.

"Never mind," I said.

The cigarette seemed to help calm him down, but Justin's foot still vibrated against the rubber flooring of the bus on the way down the hill. No one called back about the apartments where I'd inquired. I secretly started to panic. Justin still couldn't figure out what I was doing with him, but he didn't say so.

I decided to book a posh little boutique hotel I'd wanted to check out for their rooftop bar. I'd keep him there until I found him something more permanent. They had a restaurant with room service so he could take his meals in and a pool I could use. I was excited to use the emergency credit card to make this happen.

Justin bummed a cigarette off a woman at the bus stop with surprising confidence. "I have better luck with the ladies," he said. He'd developed a slight swagger since we arrived on the city streets.

A doorman greeted us at the hotel. We received two passkeys from a desk clerk, which I handed to Justin. On the way up, a young woman entered the elevator wearing a swimsuit and a sarong, looking like the perfect hula doll.

Justin looked her up and down and said, "Hello."

"Hi," she said shyly.

"You staying here too?" he asked.

"Um. Yes."

I rolled my eyes. She'd already hit the twelfth-floor button.

"How's the pool?" I asked.

"Nice." She looked at her feet, obviously a girl who didn't know the power of her beauty.

"How do you like Portland?" he asked.

"Great. Love it," said Hula Girl.

"What are you doing while you're here?" he asked.

"I won a grant from Portland Arts. They're making a short film from a screenplay I wrote."

"How exciting," I said. "Will it play at the festival?"

She smiled proudly. "Yes." She stepped onto her floor, but once out, she relaxed and smiled at Justin, giving a shy wave.

"Hey, I'm Justin Hendrix. What's your name?" The doors began to close.

"Don't harass women in their swimsuits," I whispered.

She spoke suddenly into the doors before they closed. "Shannon Pulani Acosta."

"Room 1612!" Justin yelled.

I shook my head. "Romantic."

He shrugged. "I had to move fast."

"Maybe you'll see her around again," I said. "If you're lucky."

I let him open the door to the suite. He turned around in the hall before he'd even seen the view. "There are a lot cheaper places than this," he whispered. "This is some fancy shit."

"What kind of fairy godmother puts you in a dive, Justin?" I smiled, hoping he'd relax. "You'll feel at home here in a couple of days."

"Maybe too at home." He dropped his bag when he saw the living room.

"Well, you just arrived and already gave away your room number."

"Did you see her? Do you think I stand a chance?"

I didn't, but anything was possible. I opened curtain after curtain, exposing river and mountain views from floor to ceiling and a suite decorated in velvet, stone, and glass.

"Settle in, and I'll meet you on the roof for lunch in an hour, okay? I have to run an errand first."

I didn't care if Justin trashed the room, but I felt he wouldn't. He didn't seem comfortable enough to use a hand towel. A few days of luxury could change a person fast, though—I had to find him an apartment.

Outside, the day had warmed to perfection. A gentle breeze traveled up the hill from the river. With Justin out of Amy's house, I could breathe again. I walked to the river's edge, where a fountain rested on the grassy park, and children danced in its waters. Mount Hood's icy peak rose into the blue sky directly behind the river. A few short blocks away, an officer directed me to the third floor of the Police Bureau, where I requested and received a copy of the Wilson accident report. I had to know more.

CHAPTER 8

❖❖❖

PEARL HELD A STICK with long, colorful ribbons and waved it around the grassy circle in her garden. Her father wore a sweat-stained Henley and leaned against a porch post, watching with a pint of beer in one hand and a blank stare across his face.

"Lee!" Pearl saw me halfway through her spin. She hopped out the gate and over the gravel like a grasshopper until she reached my side.

"How was your day?" I asked. Fearing she'd invite me in, I pretended to be in a rush. She doubled her pace and kept up.

"I read Henry a Madeline book, and he chopped wood," she said. "Then Astral came home for lunch so Henry could go for a run."

"Who's your friend, Pearl?" Henry stood at the gate.

My mind flashed to the Civil War ghost in the garden from earlier morning. Henry was alive up close, with high, rosy cheekbones and a thick head of messy hair. According to his arms, he chopped a lot of wood. Henry was a man who could carry a girl over the threshold.

"This is Lee. She's Amy's best friend."

"I saw you out here this morning." He micro-smiled.

I wanted to run, but she took me by the hand.

"Now, can you have tea?" Her little face was a heart with big dark eyes that told you what she thought without a filter.

I bent down and touched the stitching on the pocket of her dress. "I would like that very much, Pearl, but I promised Amy I'd help her with something tonight. Can we do it another time?"

"Okay." She looked at her shoes.

"I love your pocket," I said.

"Astral sewed it on," she said. "She thinks everything should have pockets."

"I adore dresses and especially dresses with pockets," I said. "The rainbow stitching is cool."

"Maybe you could bring this dress when you come over, and Astral can sew a pocket for you."

"That sounds perfect," I said. "But I'm guessing Mom...Astral is pretty busy. How about she calls me at Amy's when she has time?" I looked at Henry for approval.

"I'll have to check with Astral. She's home tomorrow." He and Pearl walked to the gate.

I got to work at Amy's house, washing the boy out of the sheets and then relaxing on the bed once it was remade. Two pages into the police report, I fell asleep.

A bang on the door woke me up.

"I've been calling and calling." Amy turned on the light and opened the curtains. The late-day sun assaulted me on the bed. "Have you been in here all day?"

"No," I said, covering my eyes. "I toured the city and ate lunch on the roof of the Arcadian hotel."

"The Arcadian. Nice." Amy's eyes traveled down to the report lying next to me.

I folded the papers in half so she wouldn't see the police logo, but Amy didn't miss a thing. "What's that?" she asked.

"Nothing." I gripped the paperwork. "Give me a minute, would you?"

A wince flashed across Amy's face before she shut the door behind her.

I slid the report into a book and quickly stretched before meeting her in the kitchen. Amy sipped from a large glass of wine. "Sorry," I said. "I had an old fashioned at lunch, and it kicked my ass."

"You also smoked a month's worth of my weed in three days." The empty jar sat on the counter next to her. "What the fuck is going on with you, Lee?"

"What?" I said, not sure which thing she meant.

"What?" She laughed. "Well, for starters, your distraught husband called me today wanting to know why you were staying at the penthouse at the Arcadian instead of my house."

"He called you. What a fucking asshole," I said. "It's not the penthouse; it's a suite."

Amy's jaw tightened like it did before she blew up, but instead of letting her temper win, she took a breath and went into therapist mode. "If you have a suite at the Arcadian, why are you sleeping in my guest room?"

I took a glass from the cabinet and poured myself some water. I wanted wine, but Amy gripped the bottle and wore a don't-fucking-try-it face. I sat down next to her at the counter.

"I met a guy my first day here," I said.

"I knew it!" Amy said. "Justin, right? I knew it."

"Will you let me finish?" I asked.

"Okay. Okay," Amy said. "Go on."

"Don't look so smug, Amy. There's nothing sexy about it. Justin is a homeless kid I met at the food trucks."

She put her wine down. "Wait. What?"

"He'd just had his tent taken by the city, and I wanted to get him a place to stay until I could find him an apartment."

"Umm. Have you lost your mind?" Her eyes were almost as big as her gaping mouth.

"I am taking him on, Amy," I yelled. "I knew you would disagree, but I am not letting this kid sleep on the street one more night. The god damned coyotes are going to eat him."

"Whose kid are we talking about, Lee?"

"He's nobody's kid—that's the problem. His mom died, and he discovered her body—just like me," I said. "I could've been Justin."

Amy took a deep breath. "Oh, Lee. You can't believe every story you hear. He could be playing you."

"He's not. He's a good kid," I said. "If a puppy spoke human, it would be Justin."

"Puppies chew things up, Lee. They eat things they aren't supposed to."

"Is he playing me for food and shelter? Let him." I said.

"That's some shelter."

I smiled. "I used the emergency credit card."

We both laughed, and Amy brought me a wine glass, releasing the grip on the bottle after pouring. "You may not be able to fix him, Lee. Justin may have to do the fixing himself."

"What if he isn't broken?" I asked. "What if he just needs a little support to keep from being knocked over and trampled by life?" I heard myself and stopped. "Listen to me telling you. How many homeless kids do you know?"

She didn't answer because she didn't have time to count on most days.

"I know it doesn't make any sense," I said. "It's risky, and I could get burned and all of that. But I like Justin so much, and you'll like him too. I have some ideas about how to help him. Maybe you could think of my interference as saving you from one more patient?"

"How do you know he isn't already my patient?" she asked.

"He isn't. I searched his bags and found no evidence of drugs, just a serious obsession with Darwin and a rattle he can't get rid of," I said. "Also, I asked him if he knew you."

We sat quietly for a few moments. I pictured Justin strolling around the lonely suite by himself and felt sad.

"He's going to trash that hotel room," Amy said.

"Cheers to the emergency credit card!" A huge smile took over my face. "Jack is going to hate it so much."

"I'm glad you're back, Lee," she said. "Thanks for letting me in."

"Are you relieved?" I asked.

"No," she said.

"Maybe because you know finding housing is a bitch in this city?"

"No, that's not it," she said.

"Maybe because I have an appointment with Ellen Robinson to look at condos tomorrow?"

She didn't even flinch. "I figured something like that was coming," she said. "Are you buying a condo, Lee? Or are you investigating Ellen?"

I held up my glass and spun it for a moment, pretending to study the clarity of my wine. I could not lie to Amy again. "Both," I finally said.

"I figured."

"Do you want me to move out?" I asked.

"Moving out would imply you live here," she said, half-smiling. "Do you live here, Lee?"

"No, Amy. I still live in New Jersey—for now. But maybe a little condo will change my mind. Fish and guests, right?"

Amy rolled her eyes. "Whatever you need to tell yourself.

"Jack had no idea how expensive that internet affair would be."

"Is that what he's calling it?" I asked.

"He says they've never met," she said. "Does it matter?"

"He's met her. He's a liar," I said.

Amy's face turned scarlet. "I am such an idiot for believing him. I'm sorry."

"I don't see how it's different. I mean, are we Bill Clinton? There's more than one way to have sex." I sighed and got up, pacing the floor in my socks. "The weird thing is, I don't care that much," I said.

"I believe you. You haven't cared since he betrayed you the first time."

"I stuck it out after that, but you have no idea how many times I've wished I dove in with that cop. I've never connected with anyone like that. I resisted Erik for my marriage, and Jack cheated again anyway. I'm so stupid."

"No, you're not. You wanted to save your family. You did what you thought was the right thing."

"Wow. I never would have expected you to say so," I said.

I'd been ashamed for staying after the first time and imagined my sisters and friends thought me weak.

"Can we stay home and watch a movie tonight? Something funny that doesn't involve love?" I pulled my feet up on the sofa and covered myself with a blanket, happy to be with my oldest and most comfortable friend.

We cooked a frozen pizza and watched reruns of Seinfeld. I smoked enough weed to forget about my marriage troubles and the homeless kid I'd left in an expensive hotel suite, but not the possibly murderous real estate lady.

"Will you get us an appointment with Ellen Robinson tomorrow to see these places I sent you?" I asked via text message.

"Will do," Justin typed back.

CHAPTER 9

◆◆◆

ON THE CAMP'S homepage, I found a picture of Max holding a child over the dock by his feet. The kid wore a "Hi, Mom!" grin while his hair pointed straight into the water. Several boys photo-bombed the shot; one held rabbit ears over Max's head.

It always amazed me that the camp invited him back. The Camp Director drank too many mimosas at the annual fundraiser last year. He confessed they only gave Max children from large families because those were the only kids whose parents didn't complain about his unruly habits. My son's campers were famously late for meals and always happened to be the kids flipping the canoes outside of swim areas on hot days.

My oldest, Little Jack, worked the boat docks and taught paddling safety—the youngest to pass the rescue certification test in camp history. I found a photo of him surrounded by other paddlers on the lake. He appeared to be demonstrating a boat flip recovery, coming out of the water in a blurred splash. Like his father, Jack took everything he did to the highest level.

I read my texts from my husband, shaking off his blatant attempts to guilt me out of the hotel. Justin also texted the night before. "Ellen was busy tomorrow, so she sent me to someone else…Melissa."

"Too busy, huh?" I wrote back. "Let me see if I can get her. I'll call you in a few."

I picked out a pricy listing with too many bedrooms and a river view and called Ellen for an appointment. Magically, her day freed up. She agreed to pick me up at the hotel later that morning. "We're all lined up for noon. Looking forward to it!" Ellen followed her text with a smiley face.

"Can we add two more properties, please?" I typed the addresses and unit numbers. "My son will be with us today. I'll be buying him a condo while I'm here."

A long pause followed. "Sure. I'll line those up. You'll need a pre-approval letter to make an offer," Ellen texted. "Have you met with anyone regarding financing?"

"I'll be paying cash," I texted.

"We'll need proof of funds for offers," a new message said.

She hadn't asked me a thing about financing before the condos. "No problem, I'll screenshot a statement for you." I had my own money. Jack wouldn't even know about it. I phoned Justin, but he didn't answer. I called again before taking the trail into the woods behind Amy's house. The path dove quickly into the ravine, crossing a bridge over the creek before winding up to the other side. A crow cawed from above, causing another to answer from somewhere unseen.

Just before I reached the last switchback, I heard a more solid rustling—something larger this time—and peeked over the trail to see Henry pause, looking both ways before climbing over a fallen log hiding his path. He didn't notice me watching him wipe leaves from his shoulders and shake debris from his hair before he jogged up the trail. I hid behind a cedar. He ran past me, so close I could hear him breathe. Once he disappeared at the top of the hill, I took the rest of the trail to the fallen log. You wouldn't see the deer path along the other side unless you knew it was there. I wondered if it was a locals-only spot and decided to explore it later. Amos Patenaude waited for me on the other side of the ravine.

It took me several blocks to catch my breath once I climbed the steep hill from the park. I walked along the road opposite the accident site and followed the narrow shoulder until it straightened into a country road. I found the Patenaude mailbox and hiked up the driveway. An older man sat on a porch swing in front of a large, forested yard.

"Hello," I said. "I'm Lee Harding. Are you Mr. Patenaude?"

He used a stick to rise from his chair and held a hand out to greet me. "The fella who called didn't tell me a beautiful lady would be stoppin' by. Insurance inspectors are usually ugly bastards." He chuckled at his joke, steadying himself with his stick.

Amos wore Levi's held up with a leather belt and slip-on shoes that might double for slippers.

I felt guilty for lying to him and considered coming clean.

He shuffled past me for a few yards before turning back. "You want to know what I found, right?" he asked. "Come on then, and I'll tell ya." He stopped on the driveway to swat a pinecone before glancing back at the house. His mustard-colored bungalow sagged on one side and needed a paint job.

"My father and his brother built it with their own hands," the old man said. "My son, he wants nothing to do with it. When I go, it goes." He batted two cones across the road.

"It's a beautiful home. I love the old leaded windows," I said. "Do you have grandkids?"

Amos didn't acknowledge me because he was deaf or maybe the kind of person who chose not to hear you. He continued shuffling to the next pinecone before pausing at a pullout.

"I've walked in the park every day for as long as I can remember—rain or shine. I heard the skid, the crash, and the cries on the day of the accident. I'll never forget the cries," he said. "Not the first accident since I've lived here—these roads can be slick—but usually, it's up on the bend there, where they turn too fast." Amos scratched his head. "I still don't know how it happened where it did."

"Maybe a deer jumped out," I said.

"There ain't no deer in this park." Amos batted two pinecones from the trailhead, then walked down the hill until we were below the accident site. "When I got to the car, I could see it was Charlotte Wilson taking her last breaths. I knew that girl anywhere. 'Charlotte,' I said. 'Everyone was wondering where you've been.'" Amos stopped, put one hand on his hip, and rested on his stick with the other. "There's never been a darker day in these woods."

"And Lawrence Wilson?" I asked.

"He was hanging over a tree limb but alive." He shook the memory out of his head.

"Lawrence Wilson is alive?" I whispered.

Amos Patenaude stared at me for a second and then kept talking. "I'd been coming up to the trail here when it happened, so it took me less than a minute to get to them, see." He pointed up the hill.

"Did you see anyone else? Any cars driving away or pulled over?"

"I think it was just me. I climbed back down the hill, but Charlotte wasn't getting out of that. She whispered something to me—wanted me to pass along a private message—then died there, right there." Pools gathered in his eyes. "I knew that girl since she was born. I'm glad she had someone familiar to look at during her last breath. I hope I was a comfort."

"How very difficult that must have been, Mr. Patenaude. I didn't know you knew Charlotte. What did she say?"

He shook his head. "I'll tell you what I told the last person who asked," he said. "That message was delivered, and once it was delivered, it was forgotten."

"I can appreciate that, but what if it provided a motive for someone to murder her?" I asked.

He stared into the woods. "I hear she was buying that house back. It was Charlotte's mother's place, but that rotten father of hers lost it to booze. Whatever happened in that house made that little girl's eyes sad early on. I wouldn't think she'd ever want to return here, but I understood after."

"Understood what?"

Amos stared at me sideways. "You're not from the insurance company, are you?"

I couldn't lie to him again. "No, Mr. Patenaude, I'm not."

"What the hell are you doing with me then?" he asked.

"I'm a friend of the woman who bought Charlotte's house," I said. "When she told me the story, I had to look into it. The timing doesn't sit right with me."

"So, you're just nosey?" He leaned in on his stick and waited for my answer.

"Yes—kind of. My husband says I'll talk to a light post."

His head tilted slightly while he watched me fumble.

"I don't believe in coincidences," I said.

He nodded in agreement. "So, you think your friend killed her? To get the house?"

"No," I said. "She's not the murdering kind. Did you notice any glass or debris on the road, Mr. Patenaude?"

"No. Just whoever called the emergency."

"What color car?" I asked.

"Black, I guess. Dark and big." His voice trailed off.

"Who was it?" I asked. "Maybe they witnessed the accident."

"Nah, Nah," he said, his tone indicating a loss of patience with my questions. "The police would have known."

"Not if they thought it an accident," I said. "What do you think happened?"

"Well, they sure didn't take a sharp left down to nowhere on purpose, did they?"

"Who carved the elk?" I asked.

"I'm not talking about that," he said. "It's none of my business."

We stood on the trail, staring into the ghost of the car wrapped around the tree, the occupants suffering, the tree groaning from the weight. I couldn't think of anything else to say. We parted ways, he in his eternal campaign against pinecones, me down to the creek again and then up the steep trail back to Amy's. A chill passed through the trail. My senses alerted me to a presence. Maybe all the talk of Charlotte's death spooked me, but I pulled a canister of pepper spray out of my pocket and held it in my palm anyway.

◆◆◆

Justin didn't return any of my calls or texts. I knocked on his door for some time before panicking. *He's dead in the room. Overdosed.* I rushed down to the lobby for a key.

"Breathe, Lee," I whispered, placing the key on the electronic reader and opening the door. "Justin," I yelled. No answer. I walked through the living room, which appeared unused from the day before. Justin's phone was lying in the charger on a glass side table. The kitchen was spotless except for a glass of water next to the sink.

I called his name again before entering the bedroom. His beloved Darwin book sat proudly on the nightstand, and clothes were laid out neatly on the bed. The water ran from the shower in the adjoined bathroom. Realizing my mistake, I tip-toed backward quickly. Just before I hit the hallway, Justin's voice bellowed from the shower. "Ooh, ooh, sweet child of mine." I ran the rest of the way to the door, caught the elevator, and had a cup of coffee in the lobby, thanking the universe I hadn't called 911.

Moments later, I received a text from Justin. "I'm ready when you are."

I met him upstairs and paged through his completed reports. "Great job, Justin," I said.

"I don't mean to be nosey, but what are you up to?" he asked. "Just when I think I have it figured out, I get confused again."

"What did you find out about her?" I asked.

"Mrs. Jennifer Jorgenson?" he asked.

"She's married? What. A. Cunt," I said.

"Ha!" Justin rocked in his chair.

"Sorry," I said. "Go on."

"Mrs. Jorgenson, from here on, referred to as 'The Cunt.'" He chuckled but read on, "is a research analyst at Woodman Bridges and Company. According to her online profile, she's worked there for a year and researches retail companies out of the London office. Do you know what that means?"

"I do," I said. "My husband is a partner at Woodman Bridges and Company, and we met there when I was just out of college. How old is she?"

"Twenty-nine. Her maiden name is Marshall. She married Alex Jorgenson two years ago. No children found." He looked up. "I have a photo here. Want to see it?"

I thought about it for a moment. "No." I already knew what she looked like. Young. That's his type. "Let's get the story for today straight. You're my son, and we're looking for a condo for you and a house for me so I can be closer to you and your Aunt Amy. Got it?"

"Got it," he said. "Be some rich kid for the day. I can dig it." He played a little riff on the air guitar.

We walked to the elevator bank. "Do you play?" I asked.

"Used to. My guitar got stolen when I zonked out on Xanax."

"Is that your drug of choice?" I don't know why I asked—I'd heard the phrase somewhere.

Justin stopped short. "What makes you think I have one?"

"I'm sorry, Justin. I just assumed."

"You know what they say?" he asked.

"Never assume?" I asked.

"No. All homeless people aren't drug addicts. Oh, wait. They never say that."

"So, you don't use drugs. Didn't you just finish saying you've bonked out on Xanax?" I asked.

"Ha!" If a laugh had fingers, it would've pointed one at me. "Zonked," he sighed. "Ever pass out from alcohol?"

More than once, especially in my youth. "Yes," I said.

"Does that make you an addict?"

"Well, I probably am, if we're being honest."

Ellen waited for us in the lobby. "Any friend of Amy's is a friend of mine," she said, shaking my hand as if we'd never met.

"I didn't consider whether we'd fit in your car, Ellen." I lied. It's all I'd been thinking about, but I couldn't see a white two-seater ramming the Wilsons off the road. She had to have another vehicle.

"I brought Monster," she said. "She's parked out front." Ellen should have needed a footstool to get into the giant SUV. Still, she hopped up on her four-inch spikes and drove like a complete madwoman up the crooked streets of Northwest Portland, talking endlessly of the hot market and sometimes using both hands to explain her strategy for how we were going to win offers when they should have been on the wheel.

"I let people borrow Monster to get their houses ready for sale or move things, so let me know if you need her once we find something." Ellen patted the truck on the dash, and it responded with an extra bounce. By the time we arrived at the first house, I was pale and nauseous and practically fell out of Monster. If Ellen didn't murder the Wilsons, she'd scared at least a few of her clients to death.

The house we toured spilled across the hilltop in a U-shape, and large windows exposed each room to the city, river, and two volcanoes. The main bedroom had its original burgundy shag carpet and the same color fixtures in the bathroom.

"There's hardwood under here," Ellen said, pulling the carpet up in one corner. "The original owner just passed, but not in the house."

"How do you know that tidbit, Ellen?" I asked.

"Because it's my listing," she said.

I knew she was the listing agent when I booked it, but I wanted to see if she would say so since there was no signage.

"Have you ever sold a haunted house?" Justin asked.

Ellen thought about it. "Once, possibly—a Victorian with a ghost woman and ghost cat. Supposedly documented."

"Did you see them?" I asked.

"Oh, lord no. I don't believe in ghosts." Her tone implied insult.

"Maybe that's why I've never seen one."

"What about you, Lee?" Justin asked.

"You call your mother by her first name?" Ellen asked.

"We don't believe in labels," I said.

She watched us more closely after that.

The ceilings were high with warm wood paneling, stained in places where water seeped in, but the sprawling ranch had bedrooms for my kids and an apartment on the lower floor for Justin. Jack's stuffy design sensibility would never work there, and the thought of doing it without him excited me. Justin and I wandered the house and then met at a railing to admire the endless views. "Do you like this house?" I asked.

"For some people, sure," Justin said.

"What do you mean?" I asked. "You don't like it?"

"It's far away from everything. And when the roads get icy here, you can't leave the house."

That sounded nice to me, but I was forty-something, not nineteen.

"What do you think of Ellen?" I asked.

"She's cool. I like her."

"Me too." I surprised myself. "I like a woman who knows her shit. Here is the thing, Justin—and be cool when I tell you this because she's watching us from the upstairs window, okay--I'm pretty sure she murdered at least two people, maybe three."

He leaned in, hand over his mouth to hide from Ellen, and whispered, "Lee, are you FBI? Cause that would be cool and not cool simultaneously, you know?"

◆◆◆

The second house was a dud. Built in the nineteen-nineties, it shoved an overdramatic entryway in your face as soon as you walked in the door. Ellen continued to try to make me vomit in her car. I'd snuck an edible at the last house, so my ride back down did not include nausea. Poor Justin held his head out the back window like a dog to survive the trip.

"What part of town do you live in, Ellen?" I asked as we took a sharp turn on two wheels.

"I live in Lake Oswego," she said. "Just a town over."

"Ooh. Is there really a lake?" I asked. "I'm a paddler."

"Yes, but it's private," she said.

"Really? Is it small?"

"No. But our houses are built on it. You wouldn't want strangers in your backyard barbecue, would you?"

"What about the other people in the town? Can they access it?"

"There's a beach, some can. Residents only, of course."

"Sounds a bit exclusive to me, Ellen." We stopped, and I tied my shoe in front of the car to see if I could find hints of body damage on Monster, but all I noticed were bugs in the grill.

The neighborhood with the condos included two parallel streets occupied by coffee shops, breweries, and an independent movie theater. Old Victorians turned apartment houses and grand brick buildings with names like "The Ambassador" and "The Tudor Arms" ruled the neighborhood.

The lobby of the building we'd chosen had a great big fireplace with Art Deco tile and a beautiful worn carpet that looked like it had been there since opening day. The elevator terrified and charmed us with a manual door and inability to stop precisely at its designated floor.

Inside a ground-floor unit, Justin lifted the Murphy bed up and down twice and sighed "Cool" several times. The kitchen was for takeout only—no dishwasher, only a tiny oven, and a dining counter for one, but the original claw foot tub sat like a queen on the old hexagonal tiles. There was nothing not to love.

Justin wandered around, opening every door and drawer.

"Do they allow pets? I asked.

"Yes," Ellen said.

Justin played with the built-in ironing board and listened to our conversation.

"And ground floor units can be used for business?" I asked.

"Yes," she answered. "Professional offices only. There are no retail stores, restaurants, or medical doctors, but they allow therapists. There is one a few doors down."

"Do you like it, Justin?" I asked.

"Who wouldn't?" he asked.

"Then we'll take it," I said. "What do I need to do, write a check?"

"Don't you want to see the other one first?" she asked. "It has a remodeled kitchen."

"That's up to Justin," I said.

"Does it have a Murphy bed?" he asked.

Ellen shuffled through some paperwork before answering. "No."

Justin looked down at his feet.

"This is the one for us," I said. "Make it happen, Ellen."

CHAPTER 10

◆◆◆

ELLEN CHATTERED ABOUT strategy and process on the short ride home. I half expected her SUV to jack up on all fours and drive over traffic. Justin hadn't said a word on the way home, and after Ellen drove off, things got awkward between us.

"Do you mind if I come up and do some computer work?" I asked.

"It's your room." He stuffed his hands in his pockets, which I'd learned meant he was uncomfortable.

"No, it's your room, Justin," I said. "Can I come up?"

"Of course."

I sat at the desk as soon as we got in. I had to figure out how to access my money without asking my husband.

"So, you're going to buy that place?" he asked.

"Of course I am. Even if I financed it, it would be cheaper than paying rent."

"You're moving here?" he asked.

"No," I said. "You are moving in. I told you I would get you a place to live. Don't you believe me?"

"I don't know," he said, jumping from his seat. He paced like a coyote, looking for an escape. "I've had people take me home in the past, and it always gets weird. Fast."

"It's about to get really weird, Justin. Because I have a job offer for you, too."

He braced himself like something terrible was coming and rattled harder.

"Justin, I don't know what I am doing in this life. I'm a show house until you open the closets, and all the shit falls out and hits you in the head. But there's one thing I have an instinct for: people. I'm sure about you and about buying this place."

Grief pooled in his big eyes. I wanted to hug him but patted his shoulder instead. "Fairy God Mothers don't abandon their posts," I said. "I'll ask Ellen to type up a lease for us, okay?" He nodded, but his face sagged from grief. "So that you know you have a place to live legally. Renter's rights and all that," I said.

He took a double breath and wiped a single tear from his face. "Sorry."

"For what?" I handed him a small pack of tissues from my purse. I needed to figure out the money. It was out there somewhere in the internet land, and waiting on hold, pressing buttons, resetting passwords, and feeling sad were all things made more tolerable by cannabis. "Would you go get some snacks for us?" I handed him a twenty.

"Sure. I still have your change from this morning," he said.

I stuck the money in the desk drawer and closed myself on the patio. The street bustled with cars and tourists like a tiny simulation below me. Someone hunched over a shopping cart full of belongings, and I watched them inch up the sidewalk like someone with nowhere to be. Jack would say I bought a condo for a stranger to punish him, but it was my money, and Justin needed a place to sleep.

He returned with a bag of candy and tossed it on the desk. "Smell's good in here," he said.

I felt very guilty for smoking around him. "I have to call seventeen numbers and go through ten other menus before I reach a human," I said. "It's making me nuts."

Justin chuckled before he stopped short. "Hey Lee, what about that job you talked about?"

"The job is interesting and legal, and I need you to trust me. But first, the audition." I handed him a list from my purse and watched him read it. "Any questions?"

"I'm thinking of inviting that real estate agent I know to come here. Is that okay? I want to impress her," he said. "On the other hand, she may think I'm pulling a con game with this place."

"How do you know her?" I asked.

"Alison? She's my friend's older sister. Her mom let me sleep on the couch for a while. That's the last time I saw her."

"Take her to dinner upstairs before you ask her to help us and charge it to the room," I said. "Once you get the names of every client Ellen's worked with in the last two years, dig deep into each one, okay? Sales price, taxes, previous owners. I'm very interested in all the previous owner's whereabouts. Search their names with the word 'obituary' and see how many are departed."

"Got it."

"And get a new birth certificate while you're digging," I said. "I left money in the drawer for the first list, which you kicked ass on, thank you."

Amy knocked on the door, and Justin surprised me by volunteering to answer it.

"Justin! Nice to meet you," Amy said. She took his hand warmly before letting go.

"Thank you," he said. "Nice to meet you, too."

"Tell me what kind of trouble she's leading you into. When she told me she had a new friend, I worried immediately about your safety," she said.

"Shut up, Amy." I smacked her on the arm.

Justin laughed. "She does have me doing some pretty weird stuff," he said. "Nothing that will land me in prison. Yet."

"Oh, my god. Will you two shut up?"

"Did she tell you she has a bad habit of attracting murderers?" Amy asked.

"One of them drove us around today, trying to kill us with fear," I said.

Amy laughed a loud, honest laugh. "You got in the car with Ellen?" she asked. "Everyone knows you meet her at the houses."

"Now she tells us," I said.

Amy plopped herself next to him on the sofa. "Lee tells me you belong to the orphan club, like us?"

"Well, I'm not really an orphan because I don't know who my dad is," he said.

"Well, my mom is only dead to me, so I am not technically an orphan either," she said.

People who have suffered can bond over the dark stuff. The two of them swapped tales between laughter while I read and e-signed the contract on the condo. When I received an email from Ellen with an executed contract, I stood up to high-five them. "It's official!"

"I have some things for your new place, Justin," Amy said. "You can go shopping in my garage. My grandma's entire household is in there." She watched my expression turn to a frown and laughed. "What?"

"Nothing," I said. "That's super nice."

"She's not going to let you come over, Justin. I can already see it. She has a design scheme set up for you already." Amy leaned in to tell him a secret like I couldn't hear her. "She hates my decorating." Her décor choices left me fantasizing about remodels, but I didn't admit it. "It's Justin's apartment."
She cracked a smile. "We'll see."
When we were alone, Amy whispered, "If legs were instruments, Justin's would be tambourines."
"Right. What do you think is causing that?" I asked.
"Anxiety. The kid is riddled with it. Or maybe he's detoxing."
"I don't think he's addicted to anything," I said.
"Uh-huh." Amy rolled her eyes. "Regardless, I get it, and I like him too. What's not to like?"

Later, we discovered Justin had never seen one of the world's best movies, Superbad. After ordering in, we spent the evening laughing hysterically. When it came time to say good night, Amy squeezed Justin like he was one of her own.

Justin stiffed slightly, but Amy broke him in with her powerful grip. He pretended to bug his eyes out over her shoulder.

"The best thing about fairy godmothers is you can have more than one," I said.

We left him on the sixteenth floor with a list of things to do. In a week, I'd have my money and take the title on the condo. Everything moved so quickly that I'd hardly thought about Jack.

On the way home, Amy tried to make us take public transport. I ordered a car, figuring it would beat the bus. Jack called again, and when I declined the call, he phoned Amy. She turned her phone off.

I turned mine off, too. "He's probably just going to gloat about how he's showing up to parent's weekend, and I'm not," I said. "He wouldn't even know about it if I hadn't told him."

"That right there is why I never got married," Amy said. "And a reason why I never will. Every woman I know ends up the free house manager, yet somehow being a servant never makes it on the resume."

"But who am I without him? I've come to terms with who I am without the kids. I went back to school; I have my volunteer work. But I've been part of a couple for so long. How do I uncouple?"

"I don't know if I buy that, Lee. Every time I see you, you're on your own."

I'd started taking vacations without Jack when the kids first began going to camp, and I soon found out it was much more relaxing without him. By the time the kids were ten, it was a two-week vacation alone, then two with Jack because that's the most days he'd miss from work. As the kids got older, my solo trips got longer. I didn't miss my husband that month. Sometimes, the awkwardness of returning made me wish I'd stayed gone. I'm not sure he cared, either. I thought of all the sex he could have without anyone there to catch him and wondered how many affairs he had while I'd been gone all those times.

The car I ordered blocked the bus Amy had promised would arrive on time. She gave me a look that should have struck me dead but didn't complain as the driver took the curvy back roads to her house without stopping.

"I know this street," I said. We were on Garret's Ferry, where the Wilsons went over the road.

Flashing lights lit up the road ahead of us, and the car rolled to a stop. A police officer directed traffic while each vehicle rolled by slowly to watch firefighters dousing the blazing skeleton of Amos Patenaude's house. A coroner's van waited in the line of emergency vehicles.

CHAPTER 11

◆◆◆

SATURDAY MORNING BROUGHT a life hangover so big I could hardly stand up. It hung around my shoulders and dragged me down like my soul was tied to a weight. "It's fucking perfect out. Again," I growled.
Amy handed me a cup of coffee. "Did you get any sleep last night?"
"No," I said. "Is that crow staring at me? Fuck him."
"Lee, honey, I'm worried about you," Amy said. "And I speak as a friend, not a therapist. I mean, you bought a condo yesterday."
"It was cheaper than renting, Amy! You, of all people, should understand that."
"There are resources for kids like Justin. I could have helped."
"You have enough to do. It's a drop compared to how much money I have. I don't even know how much money I have. That's how much there is."
We sat quietly for a moment, listening to the rhythm of the forest. The tops of the trees swayed and rustled in the breeze.
"You poor thing." Laughter propelled her words so she could barely finish. "That must be tough."
"It is," I said, trying not to smile. "I'm an asshole."
"You're a human with a lot going on," she said.
"I read somewhere that grateful people are happier. I need to be more grateful," I said.
"You ready to tell me who Amos Tapenade is?" she asked.

"Amos Patenaude was a witness to the Wilson crash. At ninety-four years old, he still walked through the park, rain or shine, every day. He was first on the scene after the accident," I said. "By the way, did you know Charlotte grew up in this house?"

"No, I bought the house from the Olson family. They only owned it four years before divorcing," Amy said. "She wanted to repurchase her family home. Just, wow."

"Yep. And before Charlotte died, she gave Amos a message for someone—her last words. He said he never told a soul except for that person. Now he's dead on the same day I came around asking," I said.

"Do you mean the old guy who always swats cones off the path with his walking stick?"

"That was him," I said.

We sat in silence for Amos for a moment.

"I could never live in our old San Francisco house. I don't even drive by when I'm in town—it hurts too much," I said.

"Ha! You couldn't pay me to live in our house again. My mother is probably breathing vodka into the floorboards as we speak," Amy said. "Many people in this neighborhood still live in their childhood homes—Henry grew up in the house he and Astral live in."

"He must have known Charlotte then," I said. "Oh, by the way, I owe Pearl a tea party at some point in the weekend."

"Oh no," Amy said. "You are not dragging me into that damned patchouli patch. I've done my tea party more than once, and last time, Astral had just received her certification in bell ringing and made me sit there while she banged a triangle around my head."

"Why don't they get that kid some friends?" I asked. "Pearl is a tiny little adult—she needs other children."

"You know how I feel about children," Amy said. "I didn't even acknowledge yours until they were teens."

"That's not true. Remember when Max was seven, and you told him organized religion was for the weak? Lady Esther loved that."

"And was I right?" she asked. "And your mother-in-law can suck it."

I laughed so hard I almost spit my coffee out, but then a few lines of an online article caught my attention as I scrolled the news. "Look what they're saying about the fire on the village page," I said, showing Amy my phone. "They've already called suspicious."

"Ellen did it." She mocked me.

"Maybe she did. I'd guess she can smell death on a person faster than the Grim Reaper," I said.

"Lady Di said something about her kids when she was dying," Amy said.

"That's sad," I said. "Charlotte and her husband didn't have kids."

"Are you stalking dead Charlotte?" Amy asked.

"I have been a little. The woman was tragically beautiful. Want to see a photo?" I went to show Amy, but she looked away. "I don't want anything to do with this."

"Fine. Snot." I said. "Let's go to my home inspection and pretend nobody died last night."

"Leave this one to the police, Lee. Please," she begged, putting her hands together in prayer.

"Oh, I'll leave it with the police, all right. I'll have a file this big by next week." I told her a fisherman's tale with my hands. "I have an assistant now."

"Oh god, what are you doing to that poor kid." She slapped her forehead.

"I've got plans for him." I rubbed my hands together like an evil lord. "First, let's see if he delivers."

◆◆◆

The home inspection revealed little. Amy cheerfully distracted Ellen with questions about the market while I followed the inspector around. The almost hundred-year-old condo turned out to be in excellent shape. Like a true professional, Ellen carried a tape measure in her purse and sent me a referral for a decorator.

"I knew it," Amy said. "It's Justin's condo, but she's decorating it."

"Shut it, Amy."

Ellen looked up mid-text—her glasses hanging from the tip of her nose—to listen.

"This apartment will also be a professional office," I explained. "Do you think I should let a nineteen-year-old design the look?"

"You'd better run it by the board," Ellen said.

"I will. I promise," I said. "It's going to be a dog-friendly office."

"Again, approval." This time, Ellen texted and spoke at the same time.

We took the narrow hallway to the street after the inspection. "Amy, did you tell Ellen about your neighbor? She might know him."

Amy shot me a rabid glare.

"Which neighbor?" Ellen asked.

"The old man that walks the park daily," Amy said.

"Park?" Ellen pointed to her strappy sandaled feet, indicating she did not do parks.

"His name was Amos Patenaude. He lived on—what's the street where that couple died, Amy?" I sat too far away for her to swat me. "Anyway, someone burned his house, killing him in the process."

Ellen halted. "Terrible news. Where, Amy?"

"Garrets Ferry," Amy growled.

"Garrets Ferry? The Wilsons? I'm surprised you know about that, Lee." Ellen said. "Look at you. You're a local already."

"Amy told me all about it," I said, pushing the door open into the sunshine and trotting a few steps ahead so my friend couldn't hurt me.

"Well, you know what they say, 'One man's tragedy...'"

"Don't finish that sentence, please, Ellen." Amy shook her head.

"Well, there's five acres of land on the Patenaude lot. If you want to improve the housing crisis, let's build more houses," she said.

"I'd be thrilled if a subdivision of affordable housing went in there. But we both know it will be expensive homes on large lots or expansive homes on small lots—whatever brings the most profit," Amy said.

"Probably the larger homes on smaller lots," Ellen said. "I mean, who wants to take care of a yard?"

"You're shameless, Ellen," Amy said.

Ellen smiled. "No one hires me for my sparkling personality. I make things happen."

"That you do," I said.

❖❖❖

Amy and Justin waited for a table on the rooftop. I paced on the hotel balcony, smoked a joint, and watched Jack's name flash on my phone. Finally, I picked up.

"Hi, Jack," I said.

"Hi?" he asked. "Hi?"

"Don't yell at me, or I'll hang up." A long pause filled the air. I took a drag off my joint. "I told you I was taking some time." I exhaled and watched the smoke rise. "Why do you keep calling?"

He spoke between gritted teeth. "I haven't heard from you for five days. Is that what you meant by time? Because it was a long fucking five days. I didn't know if you were dead or alive. Did you forget you're the mother of two boys who need you?"

He constantly talked about how they were men, not boys. "I spoke to my sons yesterday, thank you. Did they call you?"

Silence.

It still hurt me to hurt him. I took another puff. "They asked about you. What do you want?"

"Oh. Are we being direct? Let's go straight to the text you misread and blame me for your fling in the penthouse of a pricey hotel. On my credit card! You knew I'd see it!"

"And...."

"And what? Do you mean the few hundred thousand dollars you withdrew without talking to me? Can you imagine if I'd done that? I guess you're moving to Portland?" He choked on the last words and took a deep breath. "Isn't he married?"

"Our entire marriage, you've told me my inheritance was mine. Remember?" I asked. "You've been fucking that woman since she started working with you, so don't try to gaslight me, and what are you talking about? Justin's not married."

"Who. The-fuck. Is Justin? Is that the spineless wimp that hung up this morning when I called the penthouse I'm paying for?" he yelled. "Is that who fucking Justin is?"

"It's not a penthouse. It's a suite!" I yelled. "Speaking of married...Jennifer is indeed married. Does her husband know you talk about shoving your face between his wife's legs? Does he know you've fuck her every time you were in London for the last year?"

Silence.

"Finally, you shut the fuck up." I listened to his breath turn to a quiver.

"I fucked up, Lee. I fucked up so badly, honey. I don't want to lose our family over this stupid thing. Just come home. We'll work it out."

"Fuck you." Fuck you. Fuck you. Fuck you, I repeated in my head.

"We can go to counseling," he said. "I let it go when you did whatever you did in San Francisco. We can get past it."

"I did nothing. It was one kiss. And you owed me. It wasn't a repayment I ever asked for," I said.

"It was way more than a kiss to you, Lee. Do you think things didn't change after that? You changed."

I thought back. He was probably right. Jack never felt the way Erik did about me. I'd never felt that kind of intense attraction toward my husband. "Why do you think Justin is married?"

"Who the hell is Justin, Lee?"

"Why do you think he's married?" I asked.

"I wasn't talking about Justin, Lee. I didn't even know there was a Justin." He stopped talking and took a deep breath. "I can't believe I'm going to be the one to tell you this, but it's the cop, Healey."

"Erik?" Just saying his name to my husband felt adulterous. "What about him?"

He grumbled a bit before he finally spoke. "It doesn't matter."

"You thought I went to San Francisco to pursue a married man?" I asked. "I'm not you, Jack." He knew Erik's first and last name and about his marriage to the DA in the sexy shoes in San Francisco. I wasn't the only one who'd Internet-stalked the dreamy detective.

"Do you expect me to believe you don't know he's there, Lee? Come on," he said. "If I can Google it, you can."

"Here, as in where?" I asked, not quite believing him.

"Jesus. You really don't know," he said. "He left San Francisco. He's head murder cop in Portland."

I heard myself gasp.

"Let's see how long it takes you to get yourself wrapped up in another murder," he laughed sarcastically.

"Don't say murder cop," I said. "It's so douchey." I hung up.

CHAPTER 12

◆◆◆

MONDAYS WERE FOR tea parties, according to my new friend Pearl. While Justin completed his research on Ellen, I went to Astral and Henry's cottage. Inside, a banner of ribbons hung from the ceiling and crossed the living room walls like a bunch of fairies threw up rainbows. Beaded poufs and pillows of every color littered the furniture and sat in stacks on the floor.

"You can sit here, Lee," Pearl said.

I obeyed, sitting on a square cushion on the ancient carpet, which smelled like patchouli oil and feet.

"We're so glad you came, Lee," Astral sang. "Pearl loves new friends."

Pearl delivered a teacup painted with African violets and a saucer with roses before returning to the kitchen.

Astral sat on the floor, surrounded by a group of clay bowls of various sizes.

After an awkward pause, I said, "Thanks for having me."

She smiled, pulled a long dreadlock loose from her shoulder, then raised a padded stick to tap on a disk. A soft hum filled the room.

Pearl ran back from the kitchen, her tea spilling over the cup as she tiptoed onto the carpet and sat beside me.

"One minute of magic," Astral hummed. "To center us."

It felt like a long minute at first, but as the soft tones filled the air, I closed my eyes and breathed deeply. As the vibrations dissipated and eventually slowed to a stop, my blender of troublesome thoughts somehow faded. But Astral didn't let up, and soon, the situation felt humorous. I feared I'd giggle, so I opened my eyes.

Astral looked like a Hindu goddess, her core drawn upright in perfect posture and hair wrapped around her colorful garments. While I wondered what her parents were like, she opened her hawk eyes and peered straight into me.

"Welcome." She bowed her eyes and lifted them with a smile.

"Astral is a sound healer," Pearl said.

"Oh. Cool." I smiled as if I spoke their language. Astral's sensitivity to humanity felt intrusive. "Sound therapy restructures the human system molecularly at a cellular level," she

explained. "Your Soundcloud will bring you peace and love through healing."

I took a sip of tea and nodded again.

"Henry doesn't believe it either," Pearl said.

Discomfort flashed across Astral's face, but she chased it off with a smile.

"I'm a skeptic of most things spiritual," I said.

"What's a skeptic?" Pearl looked toward me, but her mother answered before I could speak.

"A skeptic is someone who doubts the unexplainable," Astral said. "Would you say that's correct?"

"We skeptics require a lot of proof before believing a concept." I wanted to discuss her claim that bell ringing caused human molecular changes. Was there a peer-reviewed study on that? But Pearl watched me closely, and I was a guest, and really, what was the point?

"Some things aren't about science. Like the existence of a spirit greater than ours. Do you have a higher power?" Astral asked.

"My higher power is nature. It can take me any time; therefore, it's higher than me." I only had a higher power because everyone said I should. Having an answer usually shuts people up.

Astral stared through me again, watching me shift uncomfortably in my seat. "You're a trip," she said.

"Thanks," I said. "Tell me about yourself, Astral." This question had ignited ten thousand conversations—only a rare bird could resist talking about themselves.

She tilted her head sideways a bit. "Tell you about me..." she repeated, buying herself time.

"Well, I'm from Michigan originally. I came to Portland after Reggae on the River. I teach workshops there each year."

"Oh, is that how you met Henry?" I asked.

"I met him while couch surfing at a friend's house in Southeast. Never went back to Michigan again."

"Awe. Love at first sight? How nice," I said. "Amy says Henry grew up in this house."

"Henry's parents moved to Idaho and now rent it to us. Henry is an only child, so he thinks of it as his."

I looked around. A beam sagged through the plaster down the center of the living room ceiling, but the fieldstone fireplace was a dream. "Lovely," I said. "Henry must have known Charlotte then—the woman who grew up in Amy's house."

Astral stared at me, wide-eyed.

"What is it?" I asked.

"You're aura. Is it black?"

I played along. "Well, my husband told another woman he wants to...." I looked at Pearl, who hadn't taken her eyes off me. "He's been seeing another woman."

"Without permission?" Astral asked.

I blinked hard twice and took a moment to think about it. "I don't know what I would have said if he'd asked." I pictured a scene where I threw something sharp at my husband. "Probably best he didn't. Anyway, I had no idea that could turn an aura black. I would have thought it would be blood red, but black makes sense."

Astral sighed as if I had too much to learn in one afternoon and reached for a business card. I expected her to tell me she had a certificate in aura cleansing. So far, I'd never seen Henry do anything but run, smoke, and chop wood, so if bell ringing paid, who was I to judge? I chugged the rest of my tea and made excuses to leave.

❖❖❖

Henry jogged out of the woods just as I opened Amy's door to leave. I stepped back inside, watching through the crack as he bent to catch his breath. Until then, I had forgotten about seeing him in the park the day Amos died. When he disappeared through his garden gate, I descended to the bottom of the ravine, searching for a disturbance in the brush where Henry had come out before. I crawled over the fallen log, pushed through shrubs and branches, and followed a deer path to a faded Private Property sign.

A creek snaked and spilled through the soft ground, making low, fern-sided canyons before sliding over a flat rock plateau and dropping into a small pool. Sunshine beamed through the foliage, turning the grotto-like space into a sanctuary. I removed my shoes, soaked my feet in the cold water, and smoked a joint to the babble.

Past the No Trespassing sign, a long dead apple tree's remaining branches reached for the heavens in twisted agony. On the blackened trunk, an intricate image of a stag had been burned into the tree trunk. I ran my finger over the scar, tracing the image identical to the one at the crash site.

Beyond the dead tree, a forest of pine and cedar encircled a sun-drenched meadow. Blackberry bush threatened to swallow a stone shed. A worn path in the grass led directly to the rotting door, where a rusted latch held a lock. Neglected, not abandoned, it might have been a public utility shed or cannabis grow room. The silence enchanted and scared me at the same time.

My head was heavy with questions on the way home. Was Amos murdered because of me? Did someone see me talking to Amos at the crash site? What did the stag mean? And why did I want to turn around and go back to that meadow?

CHAPTER 13

◆◆◆

DESPITE THE EXPLOSION of discarded clothing on the bed, Amy's guest room closet still bulged with most of what I owned. I'd wanted to leave the dramatic effect of an empty closet when Jack got home. He probably didn't open my closet, and I had a room full of clothes I was sick of, didn't fit, or were too formal for Portland's casual fashion scene. The new dress I'd bought the day before seemed like too much now. I took a deep breath and sighed.

"Same old Lee," Amy said from the doorway. She held a cup of coffee in each hand and set one down on a table by the door. "I'd come in, but there's nowhere to sit. It looks just like your room growing up."

I picked up a pile of clothes from the corner of the bed and threw them on the floor so Amy could sit. "I can't decide. What do you wear when you run into the guy you kissed once, three years ago, but still think about?" I held up a structured mini dress and boots. "Power Girl?"

"No," Amy said. "But super cute if you want to get laid."

I had to think about it. "Not what I'm going for." I held up a sunflower-colored peasant shirt. "Too perky?"

"Yes. Save it for wine tasting."

"Ooh. When?" I asked.

"Before someone kills you for meddling," she said.

"Soon, then. Good."

A rare smile appeared on Amy's freckled face. I saw her ten-year-old self again—the one that left when her father did. I wanted to hug her, but she hated hugs.

"What about this? Elegant in Eileen Fisher?"

"No. Too baggy," Amy said.

I threw the beloved dress onto the growing pile.

"This one!" I held a long cotton summer wrap with a great fit around the waist and a swirly, long skirt. I put it on and pulled my hair back in a low bun.

"That one!" Amy said. "Romantic." She put her coffee down and picked up a pair of sneakers, dropping them at my feet. She bent for a leopard print sandal and looked for the other.

"It's like a game of concentration," I said, swooping for the other shoe. "I know exactly where everything is."

"Give it to me." She held out her hand.

"You're so fucking bossy. Between you and my sisters, I swear." I gave her the shoe.

"You look great. Don't fuck it up." She started toward the kitchen with my shoes. "By the way, we're out of weed again," she said.

I knew she was going into therapist mode again because when I put the sneakers on and went out to the kitchen, she'd placed both hands on the counter as if she needed to brace herself for what came next.

"Want to try not refilling the jar of weed? Or maybe only filling it halfway?" she asked. A deep sigh followed.

"Wow," I said. "Did you practice that in the mirror first?"

She laughed because it was true.

"Amy, I saw a text where my husband told another woman he missed nuzzling in her pubic region."

"Gross!" Amy said.

"Yes, it is. My eyes still hurt. I can smoke as much weed as I want right now. I can buy three jars of weed, which I'm going to because it's so much cheaper here, and it's kind of like shampoo, you know? I need to change it up sometimes."

"Okay." She waved her hands in the air as if to give up. "Just a suggestion."

"What about wine?" I asked. "Let's cut back. It's fattening, and I hear it isn't as good for your heart as they tried to tell us."

"I get it. I get it." She prepared her lunch, not looking up. "Get me something couch-locky, please."

"Alice told me she found my parent's weed stash after they died," I said. Alice is the second oldest Harding girl, the middle child. I sat on the sofa and straightened the skirt of my dress so it wouldn't wrinkle. "She said it was all dried up and shitty."

"Wasn't all weed shitty back then?" Amy asked. "My mom thought weed was for stinking hippies—like your parents."

I was back in time for a moment, laughing with my best friend over our parents and only worrying about what to wear.

❖❖❖

Justin's eyes doubled back when I appeared at his door dressed like a modern Grace Kelly. Before the news of Erik in Portland, I'd been living in baggy clothes and pulling my hair back into a knot before I even brushed it. That day, Amy insisted I leave it down.

"If you'd dressed like this when we went house shopping, Ellen would have believed you when you said you had cash," Justin said.

"Do you have a date or something?"

"Do I look like I have a date? Oh god. I'm overdressed." I sat on the couch and looked at my full skirt.

"More of a lunch date than an evening date," Justin said after a pause.

I took a breath. "Sorry. I'm not much of an adult today."

The suite was more lived-in than when I'd been there last. Dishes piled up in the small kitchen area, and Justin refused to let in housekeeping. He'd moved the computer to the dining room and spread paperwork across the table chaotically.

"I'm almost finished," he said. "I want you to have everything you need. You're going to love this."

With no sign of him slowing down, I walked to the kitchen and sorted the dishes.

"Please don't clean up after me, Lee. I promise to do it after this."

"I'll call housekeeping, Justin. You don't want them to be unemployed because of you." I said.

"Fine. Please, don't touch them." Justin hit one last key with some drama—the printer spit paper.

"Writing a book there, pal?" I asked.

"Alison gave me exactly eight hours to use her password for the local multiple listing service before she changed it. It took me two hours to figure out how the software worked. I'm learning a lot about real estate," he said.

He wore a Ramones T-shirt I hadn't seen before with the jeans I bought him. I made a mental note to order a couple more pairs (longer because his socks showed on his giraffe-length legs) and some t-shirts more in line with the person I was beginning to know—a kid who liked punk and needed a guitar. There was a poetic delicacy to his sharp features. His pale, thin face had filled out a bit since I met him, and his big eyes shined with the excitement of his task. I'd begun to care deeply about the boy, and for a moment, it scared me. There was barely enough of me for my family lately, and I'd added one more.

"What?" he asked.

"I'm thinking about something Amy told me—how humans need meaningful work to be happy."

He smiled shyly.

"I'm talking about myself, of course," I added. "I needed this project of ours badly."

"Is that what you're calling this? Our project?" he asked. "Are you ever going to tell me what it is?"

"Right after you show me your information."

"You ready to know what I found on Evil Ellen?" he asked.

"Evil Ellen," I repeated. "That bad?"

Justin handed me a stapled bundle of paper.

"It's huge." I flipped through. "What does it say?"

"To sum it up, thirty-five percent of Ellen's clients bought a dead person's house or listed it through an estate."

I jumped up from the couch. "Thirty-five percent! How many houses did she sell?"

"She averages thirty-eight houses a year and fourteen deaths yearly," he said.

I paced back and forth across the room, skimming the report. Justin included a map with the locations of all properties involved in deaths and the listings from each one, including taxes, names, faces when he had them, and any press on the situation.

"This is fantastic work, Justin," I said. "Awesome work."

"It was hella fun." He walked into the spotless kitchen. "I hope you don't mind, but my friend and his sister came over last night--the hot sister I told you about--I think she's into me."

"It's your place for five more days, dude, so enjoy it," I said.

"Something else happened today." He took an envelope from the desk and handed it to me. Inside, I found a copy of Justin's birth certificate. James Justin Hendrix. His birthday was a month ago—newly nineteen and on his own in the world. My heart ached. I scanned the documents for his parents' names, wondering how they felt when he was born. Anna Carpenter, his mother. James Hendrix, father.

"Do you want to find him?" I asked.

"Jimmy Hendrix? I'm pretty sure he's not my father."

"Really?" I asked.

He laughed at my naiveté.

"Well, at least she named you after someone cool. Congratulations on being official. When the copy comes, you can get an ID, right?"

"Yeah, I need a bill in my name, though. Something to prove residency."

"Easy. We'll put the electric bill in your name at the condo." I put the report in my bag and checked the time.

"I can't believe this is happening," he said. "It doesn't feel real." His eyes pooled up, but he took a big breath to tamp down his emotions.

I bumped him with my shoulder. "I'm so grateful we met."

He shoved his hands deep into his pockets and nudged me back, barely able to whisper, "Thank you."

"Thank you for the report." I straightened the skirt. "You coming to the station with me?"

"Sure," he said, grabbing his passkey and following me out the door. It was past noon. I waved at Sandy, the front desk clerk who'd initially checked us in.

"Oh, Mrs. Harding!" Sandy yelled. "I have something for you. May we speak privately?" Both of us glanced toward Justin.

"Anything you have to say to me, you can say in front of my son," I remembered that I'd called him my nephew when we'd checked.

"Okay." Sandy disappeared behind a door, returning quickly with what I recognized immediately as a Tiffany bag.

"Mrs. Harding..."

I interrupted. "Please call me Lee or Ms. Harding if you need to. My husband chose not to take my name when we married."

Sandy let a chuckle slip out but went right back to business. I eyeballed the box.

"Great. Sorry. You two are so cool—and Justin, everyone in the hotel is super impressed by how well you tip—but your message box is full. Jack calls us at all hours, so the entire staff knows him now. We all know him quite well." Sandy leaned forward and whispered, even though we were the only guests in the lobby. "The night clerk is concerned for Jack's welfare because of the drinking."

I rolled my eyes. "Jack loves himself far too much for self-harm. I promise. My apologies to the staff," I said. "I'll ask him to stop."

Sandy showed great restraint, not even glancing at Justin. "Well, your...Jack insisted I hand this to you in person. It came by special delivery."

I stuck the package in my handbag unopened. "I'll speak to my husband about calling here. Thank you for making me aware of the situation."

Outside, the sun had beat the cool Portland morning into submission. Mount Hood rose from the end of the avenue, her glacial peak sporting a perfect ring toss-shaped cloud. I sighed.

"You never get used to it," Justin said. "It's different every day."

CHAPTER 14

◆◆◆

DETECTIVE ERIK HEALY walked briskly down the hall. Each footstep bumped my heart rate and rattled my confidence. His hair was longer than the last time I'd seen him—his steely looks softened by more silver around the ears and a short, neatly trimmed beard. He'd adapted slightly to the casual northwest climate by shedding a well-tailored suit for carefully creased chinos, a sports jacket, and a fitted shirt without a tie.

The closer he got, the more I wanted to run. By the time he came through the door to the lobby, I'd created an escape plan—run down ten flights of stairs and run to Alaska—but I couldn't move my feet.

"Lee." He said my name like I was the wife of an old friend he'd met at parties once or twice. I wanted a hug, at least, but he held out a hand to shake. "Good to see you again." He glanced at Justin and gave him the same polite welcome. "I'm Detective Healy. I know your mom from San Francisco."

"Justin is my Godson," I said. At least he'd remembered I had boys.

"Oh. Good to meet you, Justin." Seeing me must have hurt his eyes because he avoided eye contact. "What brings you here?"

"I'm visiting a friend," I said.

His chilliness stung. I didn't expect him to pick me up and spin me around in slow motion or anything, but there was none of the initial intensity between us.

"I meant, what are you doing in the station?"

Maybe he'd just been a fantasy. I tried to hide my disappointment while handing him the report. "Have you heard about the fire on Garret's Ferry?"

He thought for a moment. "I did. How do you know about it?"

"I may have been the last person to see Amos Patenaude," I said.

"His killer would have been the last person to see him."

"So, it was murder?" I asked.

He shook his head. I wasn't sure if he was angry at me or himself for spilling the information. He tapped Justin's report. "What does this have to do with it?"

"It's a long story and starts with the death of Charlotte Wilson," I said.

Erik crossed his arms. "Who?"

"It's all in the report Justin made for you," I said.

He flipped through the file, stopping occasionally to read it. "What are you into?"

"What am I into?" I asked. "It's nice to see you again, too." I held out my hand. "Just give it back."

"We can make it an official interview," he said.

My eyes threw daggers at his stone-cold eyes, but he didn't blink. After a heavy sigh, I decided not to push him. "My best friend Amy bought the house where Charlotte Wilson grew up, and since I've been there, I've noticed some interesting connections between Charlotte's death and Amos's. I spoke to Mr. Patenaude about Charlotte, and then he was dead. Murdered, I guess, according to you. It's all in Justin's report."

I tried to tell him with my eyes that I'd dreamt of seeing him for the last three years, but he slapped the report against his hand. "I'll take a look."

"Let's go, Justin." I tried to pull the door open. Justin came to my rescue and pushed it. I practically jogged to the elevator bank.

"Dissed," Justin said.

"At least you waited for the doors to close," I said. "I'm just glad I wore sneakers today. I feel like a fool."

"Seriously though, there was some—tension—going—on." He sang the last part.

"Always the frontman." I rolled my eyes but smiled and bumped him with my shoulder. "He's hot, right?"

"A warm heart like yours needs a cool-down king like that," he said.

"You're nuts, kid." My arm wrapped in his when the elevator doors opened to the lobby. A guy with a baby-sized beer belly and a bushy, unkempt beard looked up from his phone to watch us, quickly looking down again when he caught my eye.

"Don't look. I saw that guy in the hotel lobby this morning," Justin whispered.

But I looked. "He's gone." I kept my arm around Justin's for the entire walk back to the hotel. "My husband is behind this. I'm sure of it. Go with it, please?" I asked.

"You're going to get me killed, aren't you?" He whispered back into my ear, holding me close like I was his girl.

Sandy looked more confused than ever when we walked through the lobby. We gave up the charade in the elevator. I left the parking garage and found a bus stop. I sat alone, smoking a joint while I waited for the ride back to Amy's house. I thought about flying home and forgetting anything happened—the Wilsons, Amos, and even Justin. Why should I care if my husband has sex with some married English woman? I didn't even like Jack anymore. She could have him. I could protect my kids by pretending for a few more years and quietly divorcing Jack when they left for college. It was the right thing to do.

Led Zeppelin's Kashmir looped while I dreamed of which island I could fly away to. The driver let me out at the bottom of the road, and I dragged myself toward Amy's house, feeling tired and unwanted.

"Lee!" Pearl bounced out from her gate like a feral fairy and scared the life out of me. "Look what Astral made me!" She waved a wand dripping with colorful ribbons around in circular motions while she tiptoed lightly over the gravel on her bare feet.

"Where's your dad?" I asked.

My question seemed to weigh her down. She stopped spinning her wand. "Chopping wood again."

"He chops a lot of wood," I said.

She took my hand and walked down the driveway toward the back of the house. "Astral says he's afflicted," she whispered.

"Addicted or afflicted?" I asked.

"Afflicted." Pearl let go of my hand and ran.

Thoughts about my problems came to a screeching halt when I stepped into the backyard. Walls of firewood enclosed the garden and threatened to take it over completely. There was enough wood to provide fuel for an entire village. A shirtless Henry—his muscles rippled and shining—continued to batter the wood. Across his chest was a tattooed stag's head, done in a hand very similar to the ones carved into the trees in the ravine. The sound of splitting wood hid my gasp, not that he noticed anything— the man was indeed afflicted. I backed up slowly and made my way back to the street. Pearl had disappeared.

◆◆◆

I spent some time pacing Amy's floors. When she finally walked in the door, I exploded. "Henrys afflicted!" I spouted. "And tattooed! He's the stag!"

"Do you mind if I put my stuff down first?" She dropped a pile of folders and a computer bag on the counter.

"He's cutting the entire forest down. You should see it," I said. "He's afflicted!"

Amy took a deep breath and sighed. "Afflicted by what, Lee?"

"I don't know. Guilt? Obsession? Fury? It's hard to tell. But the tattoo!" I paced some more. "Did I tell you about the stags in the forest? He's the stag. I don't know what it means, but it's him. He carved one on the tree where the Wilsons died. And there's another one by the weird shed in the meadow."

"Stags in the forest? What the hell have you been doing? I asked you not to fuck with my neighborhood, Lee. Come on!" she cried. "I still have to live here when you fly off to who knows where."

"I'm not fucking with him. Pearl ambushed me. She dragged me down there when I walked up the street. You had to see the man. He swung his ax like a possessed woodsman. He never even knew I was there. And poor Pearl—she's afraid to go in her backyard. She told me he's afflicted—the poor wood nymph—the tiny fairy girl. It was a cry for help, Amy." I threw myself down on the couch and lit a joint. "Do you have any bourbon? I could use some bourbon."

"No, I don't. You drank it all two days ago. Gin or rum?"

"Gin, please." I walked to the cabinet where she kept the liquor and poured myself a tall glass over ice. "Want some?" I held up the nearly empty bottle.

"I'll stick to wine, thanks." She took the joint from me. "How did it go with the detective today?"

94

I opened the bottle. "Terrible." I poured too much gin, but there wasn't enough left for another drink, so I emptied the bottle into the glass. "He barely remembered me."

Amy watched with raised eyebrows. "I doubt that."

"Well, he wasn't as excited to see me as I was to see him." I sliced two limes and squeezed them into the glass. "I turned him into a fantasy. No one can live up to that." I topped my drink with club soda. "Deck?"

"To your office." She motioned for me to lead the way.

"He's a cold mother fucker." I settled onto my favorite swinging bench. "I forgot how cold he was."

"He's a cop. What do you expect?"

"They aren't all cold. My friend from the lake is a doll. He's a widower. Maybe I should set you two up."

"Fuck you," Amy said. "You go out with him."

"I don't want anyone," I said.

"Why would you want me to, then? You suck as a friend," Amy said. "But I promise that detective didn't forget about you, Lee. You're unforgettable."

"Awe. You're too good to me. Oh, shit." I stood up. "Wait right here. I forgot I have something for you." I found my purse on the sofa, pulled the Tiffany bag out, and threw it to her. "A thank you gift for putting up with me. It's from Jack."

She laughed and pulled out the box. "I've never actually owned anything from Tiffany," she said. "I love the box, though, and it's big." She shook it, and something thumped around, but she didn't unwrap it.

"Open it." I stood over her like a hawk until she untied the ribbon, worried she wouldn't like what lay inside. She finally opened the lid. A gold Elsa Peretti Bone Cuff sat comfortably inside. We both sighed.

"I would have filed for divorce today if there'd been one single diamond," I said. "At least he remembered I think they're stupid."
"It's gorgeous. You should keep it." Amy held the box toward me.
"No way." I pushed her arm back. "Return it if you don't like it."
"What's not to like?" She put it on and held up her arm.
"Just like a bird." I watched my friend enter eighteen-karat-gold bliss. "Who'd have known you'd be attracted to the glimmer?"
"Jack." Amy smiled, but I detected something else in her eyes. My friend kept something from me. She looked down so I wouldn't see whatever it was.

CHAPTER 15

◆◆◆

THE EARTH CELEBRATED the sunny afternoon with a cool breeze, rattling the branches above and causing another psychedelic light show on the deck. I smoked a bowl from my new bong—a complicated thing etched with flowers—and waited for Justin to arrive. The water pipe was the first I'd owned since I'd met Jack two decades ago. After several large puffs, I set the bong down and peered over the deck into the forest below. A man in running clothes stared back at me. I immediately recognized his fuzzy beard from the hotel the day before.

Startled at first, I stepped back and froze. I heard movement in the bushes and peered over again. There he stood, looking up at me. "What the fuck, motherfucker!" He ran down the hill.

Amy kept a bowl full of pepper spray by the front door. I grabbed a pink canister and darted out of the house in flip-flops. The rubber shoes made a rhythmic slapping noise, giving me away for miles as I ran the trail. Unless he'd looped back, the man probably made it halfway to Garret's Ferry Road when I arrived at the bottom of the ravine. I hid in the brush in case he was also hiding somewhere.

A few minutes later, I heard footsteps. Too afraid to peek out, I held my breath. An owl hooted from the other side of the ravine, and a crow posed on a nearby branch. The footsteps stopped.

I jumped from behind the tree, keeping the fallen log between myself and whatever was on the trail. "Fuck you, mother fucker!" I held out the pepper spray with two hands to steady the shaking.

"Hey! That shit hurts, man." Justin put a hand to his face. "Don't point it unless you plan to spray."

"Oh no! Justin." I dropped my arms. "I'm so sorry." I took his hand. "Quick. Get over here."

He climbed the fallen log, and I pulled him off the deer path out of sight. We waited against the velvety bark of a cedar tree—so still, the squirrels forgot we were there.

The quiet finally gave me enough comfort to whisper. "The pregnant guy from yesterday is down here."

Justin's eyes grew. "Fuzzy Jowls?" He spoke too loudly.

"Yes. Smelly beard. Shh!" I mouthed. "Someone's coming."

We froze, talking only through the fear in our eyes as the rhythmic beat of a jogger's steps pounded the earth. One quick hoist over the log, and the pounding continued. Their footsteps came so fast that we didn't have time to scramble to the other side of the tree. Had Henry looked sideways as he ran by, he'd have seen the two of us standing there like idiots—but he hadn't. He wore the same intense face he'd had when cutting wood and hyper-focused on the trail ahead of him.

"Afflicted," I whispered.

"Most definitely," Justin agreed. "I guess we won't find out what's on the Stag Trail until he returns?"

"The Stag Trail," I said. "I like it." I looked at my phone. Service didn't reach the ravine, but my clock told me it was time to go. "We have an appointment at the house, kiddo. Are you excited?"

He shrugged. "Sure."

"Oh my god, you got too used to the hotel, didn't you?" We made our way up the hill.

"No." He spoke too quickly.

I laughed. "I knew that would happen. Who could blame you? I may move in there when you leave."

"Really? That would be cool cause I could use the pool and stuff."

"Sophisticated taste for a chimp," I said.

He nudged me in the arm, and I pressed back. We'd been communicating like this lately—our version of a hug. Right then, I felt someone behind us. Justin's eyes widened. He thought it, too.

I turned quickly and sprayed.

A tall, bearded man tried to wipe his eyes, but it only spread. He yelled in pain. "What the hell did you do that for?" He stumbled around, almost falling off the trail before he ripped his plaid shirt off and smothered his face in it. "Motherfucker, it hurts."

Watching him stumble around empowered me. "Why are you following us?" I yelled, pointing the empty canister toward him. But he moaned like a baby, and I started to feel sorry for him.

"Come on, dude," Justin said. "Let's get you to a hose." He helped guide the man up the trial to Amy's front yard.

"It hurts." He checked to see if his T-shirt was still around his stomach. "You didn't have to spray me."

"Fuck you!" I yelled. "You're lucky that's all I did. Why are you following me?"

He cried into his shirt until Justin led him to the hose bib in Amy's front yard. He sprayed his eyes and moaned in relief. I went into the house to get him a towel. When I came out, Justin was alone.

"What the hell?" I looked around. "Where is he?"

"He ran," Justin said. "Fast, too. I didn't think he had it in him."

"Faster than you? Come on! You're nineteen years old, and I'm pretty sure that guy lives on bacon and hops."

"He took off in a car." Justin pointed to the empty spot across from Astral and Henry's house, where blackberry bushes overgrew a gully and headed for the road.

"Well, if I see him again, I will kick him in the..." I growled. "Jack is going to pay."

"What does this have to do with Jack?" Justin followed me inside.

"I left this door open the entire time," I said. "With my luck, we'll find a coyote in here."

He plopped down on the sofa, making it scoot several inches back on the floor, and concentrated on his phone.

"Jack is having me followed. It has to be Jack." Anger poured from my mouth and nose like fire.

"Read your texts," Justin said.

I pulled the phone out of my back pocket. I read my text. "License plate HRM Four-five-five. Black Buick Regal." He'd also sent a photo of the car.

"You're a rock star," I said.

❖❖❖

Justin insisted on cooking dinner for Amy and me that night. We looked through magazines while our chef chopped and sautéed. Nas reminded us of whose world it was over the speakers. Amy lifted her arm, and I saw the cuff under her sleeve.

"Did you wear that to work today?" I asked.

"Yes," she said. "I'm allowed to show a little bling."

"Maybe you should save it for your days off." I typed into my phone and showed her the screen.

Her jaw dropped. "I could get a new roof with that kind of money."

"Take it back," I said. "I'll get you the receipt."

Justin continued chopping. "I would've looked up the price the first time I saw it."

"That's rude!" Amy screeched in a shrill voice, sounding just like her mother. I heard it, and so did she. We laughed, and Jack must have sensed my joy because seeing his name on my screen sucked it all away. "Hello, Jack."

"Hello, Wife. It's good to hear your voice," he said. "Did you like your gift?"

"I did like your gift." I winked at Amy. "Did you like mine? Or should I say, did your goon like my gift, Jack?" I walked into the bedroom and shut the door behind me.

"My what?" he asked. "What goon?"

"Did you even get a reference first? That guy is a total loser," I said. "Get your money back."

"Honey, I honestly don't know what you're talking about," he said. "Is someone following you?"

Silence.

"Lee? Is someone following you? Because I am telling you, it's not me. Who the fuck is following you?"

I took a deep breath, wondering the same thing. Did the bearded guy have something something to do with the Wilson accident?

"What'd you get yourself into?" he asked.

This angered me because it was true and because of the "things" he got into. "What did I get myself into?" I yelled. "Don't buy me any more gifts, Jack. Your face is connected to that married woman's pussy whenever I think of you, and there's no recovering."

Silence.

"Bye, Jack," I said.

"I made a mistake, Lee. I fucked up. Do you want a divorce? Are we breaking up our family over this?"

"Did you break our family up over this, Jack? And she's married too. A newlywed."

"It was nothing. It was just...." Jack stammered.

"Sex?" I started to cry because my feelings for him barely existed, and he did not matter anymore, and it hurt.

"What have I done?" He took a deep, quivery breath. "I fucked up so badly."

I gave him a moment, but his crying felt manipulative, so I hung up and returned to the living room to whine to Amy and Justin. But the room was silent when I plopped onto the sofa's corner seat. I looked at Justin, and his eyes were big.

"I was just telling her about the guy stalking us."

I thought Justin might have told Amy about the night I'd stowed him away in my room, which could have ended our friendship, so for a second, I was relieved. But Amy's face had turned crimson. An eruption began boiling the first time I'd implied her real estate agent was a serial killer. Heat boiled to the top, pushing everything I'd done to annoy her since I'd arrived to pour out of her mouth in flaming spurts. She was about to erupt.

I growled at Justin with my eyes.

He shrugged.

"I asked you not to mess with my fucking real estate lady. Is that asking too much, Lee? Don't mess with my fucking broker. She's like the mafia around here. She blinks, and your property value goes down. Plus, I like her. She's smart. And she dresses up. No one does that anymore." She hunched over me on the couch, and I leaned back, holding my drink for safety.

"How did that work out, Lee? You got one of my neighbors killed! That's how!"

"Ouch," I said.

"Would he be dead if you hadn't pretended to be an investigator? I think not! Now you've dragged your fucking drama into my peaceful woods. I mean, what the fuck, Lee? Are you trying to get me killed?" There she went. The top was off, and her fire spewed all over me.

I'd pretty much had enough by then.

Amy saw the change in my face and backed up a little, but she couldn't stop. "And now you're stalking Henry?"

I looked at Justin with blood in my eyes.

"I thought you told her already." He held his hands in the air, paralyzed by the tension in the room.

As she walked away, she yelled, "And you spilled bong water on my carpet!"

"I am so sorry I came here and disturbed your perfect little quiet life in the woods, Amy. Justin is moving into the new place tomorrow, so I'll move into the suite, okay? And I am fine, thanks for asking!"

"Oh, poor Lee. Your life sucks." She laughed before she stomped upstairs. When she didn't come for dinner, I apologized to Justin and called him a car.

CHAPTER 16

◆◆◆

I WORE MY favorite yellow pants and matching floral shirt when Mrs. Doherty got too drunk at Amy's tenth birthday party. She told my mother she was beautiful too many times in between shots of vodka in the kitchen. When we went to leave, Amy's mom hugged my mother until they both fell over—there was a loud slapping sound as they hit the floor. My mom got up and helped Mrs. Doherty, who seemed confused about where she was. Blood dripped from her elbow. The adults gasped in harmony, and Amy ran to her room. My mother iced the arm while other parents dragged their kids out of the house as fast as possible. I stayed with Amy in her room while she cried.

When my mother died, Amy wished it had been her mother instead.

◆◆◆

My best friend hadn't returned my calls in three days, but my sister Alice called to let me know the news was out.
"So you bought a condo." It wasn't a question.
"My husband is too big a coward to call you, so you must have talked to Amy."
"And you're living in a hotel. In Portland," Alice said. "Why aren't you in San Francisco with me and Lacy?"
"Here feels right at the moment," I said. "It feels like a place where I can learn to be myself. I don't even know who I am, Alice. Who am I?" I opened the sliding door to my patio and retrieved my bong. "I went from daughter to wife to mother. I need to figure this out alone. I thought I had Amy, but so much for that."
"You have Amy." It wasn't debatable. "Maybe somewhere deep inside, you knew Erik was up there? Just some subliminal thing you've forgotten about?"
"I swear, Alice. I had no idea."
"Tell me about Tyler," she said.
"Who?" I thought for a moment. "You mean Justin," I said. "He's an orphan, like us, only poor."
"Is he cute?" she asked.
"Is the nineteen-year-old homeless kid I've hired as my assistant cute?" I asked. "You'd love him. He's beautiful, a kind of free bird with nothing to lose—a frontman without a band. If he ever finds one, I might not see him again."
"Hmm."
"Hmm? He's one year older than Jack Jr., so don't be gross."
"I'm not suggesting anything."
"I'm fine, Alice. I'm fine even though I have never been enough for Jack. And I'm okay with the fact that the guy I thought of daily for the last three years is blocks away and doesn't care that I'm

105

here," I said. "Justin's place is almost done. Come up and see how great it looks. I let him pick stuff."

"Sure you did."

"I did. Ask him. You can ask him when you meet him. He's my godson now, so you must love him too."

"How are the boys going to like that?" she asked.

"My boys have huge hearts. They will make room for Justin."

"Yeah, right."

"Listen, I have to go. I have a meeting. Secret stuff."

"Big secret work that's going to get you killed?"

"Love you! Bye." I hung up and silenced my phone. If Alice heard the news, Lacy would know next. My oldest sister would try to fix everything, and some things can't be fixed. Avoiding all topics concerning my kids was best at the moment. They were the bull's eye of my pain around the possible end of my marriage. I wasn't ready to go there yet. I watched the busy cranes move around the booming city from the patio until Justin rang through the hotel phone.

"I've been trying to reach you."

"I was on the balcony."

"Oh man, don't spend too much time out there when you're like this."

"Like what?" I asked. "I'm fine."

He sighed. "Icy McDouchebag called."

"Icy Mc—Erik called? You? What did he say?"

"He's looking for you...something about the old man on Garret's Ferry. He wouldn't tell me anything else even though I told him I was your assistant."

"Did you give him my number?" I asked.

"Hell no. He was like, 'assistant what?' and I was like, 'assistant to Lee, that's what.' And he asked for your number, and I told him I'd have to check with you first."

"But you gave it to him, right?" I stood and touched my hair to see if I'd brushed it.

"No way. He's a smug motherfucker."

"What? Justin! What did you do?"

"Make him wait, Lee. He made you wait."

"Give me his number. It's not like I can't just call the station." I said it nicely this time. "Please give me the number, Justin."

"Okay. I'll bring it with me when I see you today. We're going to try to reach Lawrence Wilson, right?"

"Give me the number, Justin, or I will bury you in the woods."

"I'm excited about this. See you soon, Boss." He hung up.

◆◆◆

The downtown streets warmed under a blue sky. I wore my favorite white eyelet summer dress with big tiers to my ankles, paired it with a straw hat, and walked out of the hotel with a lift. A car took me to the Northwest, where I entered tall, wrought iron gates and wandered through a garden to get to the double doors of Justin's lobby.

He reluctantly posed for a photo, and I sent it to him via text, wondering who he'd share it with. We'd chosen wood tones for the house and mixed them with stone, bones, and other earthy things. We'd only had one disagreement about the black paint in his bedroom, but I could hear Amy call me a control freak and wanted to prove her wrong, so the walls were black.

Justin didn't know what a duvet was and kept telling me he needed a sleeping bag, but I wouldn't have it. The room looked amazing with the black and tan bedding he picked out, and it kept him from sleeping on the Murphy bed in the living room, which doubled as our office.

"I am psyched about today. Lawrence Wilson does some cool stuff. Have you seen Darkened Forest?" Justin said.

"I haven't. It's a TV show, right?"

"Yes. It used to kind of suck, but lately, it's twisted. There are all these amazing cursed tribes living in the park," he said. "I almost broke into that studio once. I wanna see how the magic is done."

"You're insane," I said, holding out my hand. "Erik's number, please."

He handed a tiny crinkled paper over.

I tucked it into my purse. "You were right. It can wait."

He smiled and bumped my shoulder with his as we left the building. "It never hurts to keep 'em waiting."

We walked a few blocks to the warehouse where The Darkened Forest was shot. The building took an entire block and had no visible markings except for numbers over the entrances.

"He wants you to call him, though," Justin said. "Especially after he ran the plate numbers from Beard Boy."

"Wait. What?" I asked. "You told him about that, too? Why?"

"Because trying to track down that information is hellish, and it took him three minutes."

"But now he knows," I said. "You're going to have to work on your secret-keeping."

"I don't get why it's a secret that someone is following you."

I didn't know either, so I let it go. The building was less than half a mile from Justin's apartment. We walked around the block, scanning the windows and entrances before going in.

"In Amy's case, it's because she doesn't like my 'Nancy Drew antics,' as she calls them. I got her into trouble once. Twice, maybe," I said.

"Who's Nancy Drew?" Justin asked.

"Oh, I am going to buy you every single Nancy Drew book for homework," I said. "She's only the world's first teenage sleuth, and I wanted to be her."

We found an open window on the second floor. Scarlet creeper covered the building's face, and I could see a way up for someone willing to climb it.

"Was she hot?" he asked.

"If you like girls in pencil skirts and fluffy sweaters. She drove a blue convertible and didn't have a mom like us."

"She sounds hot," he said. "I can get up there easily."

"Let's try asking first," I said.

We entered a modern lobby with high ceilings and giant Darkened Forest posters hung on white walls. A young woman with kohl-drawn eyes sat at a slab of polished wood. She wore a virginal plaid pinafore with fishnet stockings and giant black combat boots to match her lips and hair.

"Is Larry Wilson in?" I asked.

She looked us up and down, and I suddenly felt very uncool in my eyelet dress. "He doesn't like to be called Larry. Do you have an appointment?" Behind her, a mounted Sasquatch head sprung from the wall. Its eyes glowed, and something bloody hung from a fang.

"True. Only close friends and family call him that. I'm his late wife's cousin, and we're in town, so I thought I'd try to reach out. I'm Artemis. This is my son, Apollo."

"Cool." She nodded. "Lawrence doesn't come to the office much. No one's seen him in ages."

"Oh, so he doesn't work here anymore?" I asked. "How sad. He loved this show."

"He still works here but usually comes in the middle of the night. Or he'll drop something off and leave."

"How long have you worked here?" I asked. "Seems like a cool place."

"Three years now. Since before the show first aired."

"Oh, so you knew Lawrence a long time. Wow. Did you know Charlotte?"

"I met her once. You don't look alike at all," she said.

"Her mom and mine were best friends," I said. "They called each other soul sisters."

"Cool," she said.

I looked up at the Sasquatch, and it looked back.

"That's one of Lawrence's creations." She leaned in for a whisper. "I think it's watching us."

"You're brave to sit here all day," I said.

"You get used to it. Sometimes I forget it's there for, like, an hour."

"It seems dark for the show," I said.

"We lost Lawrence to the dark side after the accident and everything."

"Everything?" I asked.

"He was sick for a while after...you know," She pointed to her head, but the phone rang. Before answering, she said, "Try Lawrence at home."

"That's the thing," I said. "He moved after Charlotte died, and no one has seen or heard from him."

She typed a few words into her keyboard. "We still have their corporate housing address." She put her hand on the phone. "I've got to get this."

"I dig your boots," Justin said. "Maybe you could give me a private tour sometime?"

The woman smiled without looking at him. "Lawrence can arrange that for you."

"Dissed," I whispered outside.

"I wasn't even trying," Justin said. "No girl can resist me when I try." His jeans had filled out, and he had a slight swagger—a young man with game.

"I believe you," I said.

A smile flashed across his face, but a moment later, he growled, "Apollo?"

"What? It's a great name."

He rolled his eyes. "You have Wilson's new address."

"I do?" I pulled Justin's report from my bag and flipped through it until I found the listing sheet. The house had an extended front profile and a modern roofline. "Whoa. Nice Midcentury."

"He paid almost a million for it."

"Pricey. Maybe Lawrence got a nice insurance settlement?" I said. "Nice job, Justin. Way to think ahead."

"He makes bank working on the show," Justin said. "What's next?"

"Did you hear what she said? She didn't say injured or recovering; she said sick."

"Maybe he has cancer," he said.

"She was pointing at her head before the phone rang. How about you watch his house for a while and see if he goes in or out?" I asked.

"What are you going to do?" he asked.

"I've got some things to do at the hotel." Things to do included smoking weed and sitting at the hotel bar for happy hour. Depression made my arms and legs heavy. I'd be lucky if I returned to my room without turning into a puddle on the sidewalk.

"Well, at least you came out today."

I hated disappointing him. "I'm sorry, Justin. "I'm okay, I am. Tomorrow, let's hike the trail to the meadow, okay? Have breakfast at the hotel with me, and we'll go afterward."

Justin loved the French toast at the hotel and perked up temporarily. "When will you make up with Amy?" he asked.

"It's hard to make up with someone who won't take your calls," I said.

"Don't fornicate on the first date." He bumped my shoulder, put his headphones on, and strutted past me.

CHAPTER 17

◆◆◆

BARS USED TO be where people talked to strangers about their favorite local spots, exotic destinations, and unusual careers. When the cell phone came along, bars went from the most exciting place to the loneliest.

I sat on a stool, wishing someone interesting would sit beside me. Instead, on one side, a couple shared a screen and laughed at memes I couldn't see. On my other side, a guy argued with the bartender over his shaken bourbon. I wanted to cut in—nothing bugged me more than shaken bourbon—but I knew not to mess with the bartender. Instead, I repeatedly played with my napkin, folding it into neat squares until it broke apart. I'd never been so alone.

"Would you mind scooting down one?" a man asked. I didn't look up until the bourbon guy shifted over a seat, taking his foamy Manhattan with him.

"May I?" Erik stood before me, wearing a dark hat, glasses, and a polo shirt.

"I'm surprised you don't iron your jeans." I sipped my old-fashioned until it emptied. "How'd you find me?"

He sat down next to me. "Don't be mad at Justin. I told him I'd arrest him for an unpaid citation he had for urinating in public last year if he didn't give you up."

"And he caved? What a wuss." I signaled the bartender. "The kid can not keep a secret."

We ran out of small talk and sat there quietly for a moment like the strangers we were.

"Why would anyone cite a homeless kid for urinating in public?" I asked.

He shrugged. "I'm glad I don't work the streets anymore. It's a tough world out there." Our drinks arrived, and he took a civilized sip. "It's nice what you're doing for him. He told me."

"As I said, the boy can not keep a secret."

"Is that a secret, Lee? That you're a good person?"

"I just did what anyone would do if they could. The kid cast a spell on me with his authenticity. I get as much out of it as he does."

"Well, I asked a judge to dismiss the ticket, so I did my good deed also," he said.

I found that very sexy. "Thank you. I don't believe anyone in their right mind wants to use the bathroom on the street, and if they aren't in their right minds, they shouldn't be on the street."

"We agree on that," he said.

"Really?" I asked. "I expected you to be one of those 'rules are rules' guys."

"I'm a homicide detective, Lee. I care about solving murders."

"You're not called an Inspector anymore. God, I hated that," I said. "How do you like living in a legal state? I can smoke weed here and not get in trouble."

He laughed. "You've been smoking weed for decades without getting into trouble, and it's not like you ever called me Inspector. Not ever."

He smiled at the memory, and I grinned, too.

"I thought about calling you when the legalization laws passed. I wanted to know what you thought," I said.

"You thought about calling me." He repeated my words as if they puzzled him.

"I thought about calling you but didn't because I saw the engagement photo in the Chronicle, and it didn't feel right." He stared into his glass for a few seconds and then chuckled. "Yeah, that didn't work out."

"I didn't know," I said. "Sorry?"

"It was for the best."

"Well, my marriage is finished." It felt like both the truth and a lie.

His head tilted a little in surprise. "I'm sorry to hear that, Lee."

"Are you?" I waited for his answer, watching him stare at his beautiful hands. I wanted to touch him so badly—just one quick brush to see if the energy was still there.

He took his elbows off the bar and turned toward me. "It took me a long time to forget, Lee." He touched my cheek with his hand for the briefest moment.

I closed my eyes, but it was over before it started. "But?"

"I'm seeing someone. It's new, but it's a good thing," Erik said. "I have to let it play out."

"Of course you do," I said. "Good for you." Every muscle in my face sagged with disappointment. I put a big smile on, but my eyes gave me away, so I added sunglasses and asked the bartender to bring us another round of drinks. I made mine a club soda because more alcohol would give me away.

"Wait until I tell you about Amy's neighbors."

After discussing Henry, I asked for the tab, but Erik threw a card down, and the bartender took it.

"Thank you," I said.

"I haven't even told you why I'm here yet."

"I have an appointment with the pool," I said. "Tell me some other time." During the excruciating moments since he'd broken the news, I'd imagined his new girl to be a petite schoolteacher named Mary who still had her childhood piano (and kept it tuned) but was a tiger in bed. I fucking hated her.

"There was no smoke in Amos Patenaude's lungs. His death was ruled a homicide. You may be the last to have seen him alive." He grabbed my arm. "That puts you in danger. I'm not messing around here, and I don't have the means to post someone at the hotel. You need to look out for yourself."

Our eyes met. That's all it took. I stood up and inched between his legs as he sat on the barstool. "I never forgot, Erik."

He grabbed me by the arms but didn't push me away. "Don't play with me, Lee. You're the one who walked away."

"I had a family." I took a deep breath from his neck, letting the smell course through my blood.

"You still do." He let go of my wrists.

Buzzed from the drinks, I leaned in for more of him. "But I still love the smell of you," I whispered. "And I can take care of myself." I gathered up my things. "Good night."

The skirt of my dress draped naturally around my bare feet, and my hair was wild and loose in the rooftop breeze. Suddenly, I wanted to dance. Maybe later, I would go out—or perhaps I'd stay home and think of Erik's hands on my body and his breath on mine. Optimism floated in the warm summer air. I could do whatever I wanted for the first time in my life.

◆◆◆

The driver left me on Amy's street just before the end of the day. The cottage seemed to have fallen under a dark spell—a house people died over. The crow on the chimney read my thoughts and flew away.

I passed my friend's car in the driveway and knocked on the door, but no one answered. Three days earlier, I'd left my key behind in a dramatic gesture and now regretted it. I tried the knob but knew Amy kept it locked even when she was home. I sat on the steps momentarily, thinking she might appear, but eventually gave up.

I walked over to the trailhead and peered into the twilight woods. The drinks and weed gave me courage. My phone had a full charge, and I still had an hour before darkness fell. I'd use the hour to see how far I could get into the ravine. I set my alarm for thirty minutes—a turnaround time.

The birds settled into the dusk, and the ravine floor was quiet except for the hoot of an owl from far away. I had to lift my dress over my thighs to get over the felled tree blocking the trail. I followed the stream to the waterfall, climbing the smooth rock where the creek trickled into a grotto below.

I laid back on the smooth rock next to the water and watched the treetops move gently, their quiet rhythm lulling me to sleep for what felt like a second, but my alarm went off, warning me with a blast of Led Zeppelin's Kashmir that it was time to head back.

I'd just risen, still dusting debris from the back of my dress, when I heard something in the bushes by the trail. I reached into my bag and pulled out a canister of pepper spray and a set of kitty ear brass knuckles—I could remove two eyes at once with the pointy ears.

It was darker than I'd expected. The rustling stopped, but I could feel someone or something watching me. I dropped my bag and held out my fully armed hands. One held pepper spray, the other a pair of brass knuckles with sharp kitty-shaped ears that would take out both eyes with one punch.

"Come on out for round two, motherfucker," I yelled, but nothing moved. "If I come to you, it'll hurt twice as much."

A laugh rose from the bushes. "Jesus, Lee. Maybe you can take care of yourself after all." Erik stepped out toward the creek, his hands up. "Don't hurt me." He grinned like a laugh was stuck in his throat, and if he coughed it up, I'd know the truth about him—that he was not a (handsome) robot. "I don't mean to laugh at you," he said.

"That was a laugh?" The pepper spray went back into the handbag.

"You looked beautiful lying there, and I admit to watching for too long."

I couldn't help but smile. "Well, you're lucky I didn't take your eyes out." I clawed at him with my keychain before putting it away and sat back on the rock. "How did you find me?"

Erik climbed over the rocks until he was next to me.

"I've been looking all over for you." He kept his eye on the waterfall as it dropped below us into the shallow pool. "Why, on the night I warn you of danger, do you wander into the woods at dusk?" He sat down. "Are you trying to get killed?"

"How did you know where I was?" I asked. "You couldn't have followed me when I ducked out of the garage."

"If I found you, who else can?"

"You're evading the question. Are you tracking me?" I hoped he was, but it couldn't be. "Shouldn't you be home with Mary?" I asked.

"Who's Mary?"

"Mary. Whatever her name is. The schoolteacher." I sat with my legs crossed under the skirt of my dress so the mosquitos couldn't get me. I picked at a Doug fir cone.

Erik sat so close our shoulders touched. He watched me for some time before putting his hand on mine, gently taking the cone and forcing me to look at him. "Her name is Nellie, and she's a therapist."

"Nellie," I said. "A children's therapist?" I could feel the warmth of his breath now, so Nellie was toast.

He looked away instead of answering.

"I knew it." I fell back and watched day become night. The stars began reaching through the skies. "Look up."

He lay next to me, his arm hairs touching mine like magnets drawing us together. I stared up, conscious of every blissful breath I took.

"You're going to fuck this up for me, aren't you?" he whispered.

"God, I hope so." I opened my eyes, and he was still a dreamy shadow. My body pulsed while we watched each other for a moment—it was too much bliss. I touched him first, a light finger along his bicep.

He took a deep breath, trying hard to resist. By now, our bodies were millimeters away, our lips breathing each other in, and then finally, we kissed, slowly at first, until the hunger took over. He broke away, running his hand over my hair, cheek, and lips long enough for me to part them, and then worked down my neck. He stopped at my thin gold chain, which hung two tiny gold hearts with my kid's initials.

I woke up.

So did he.

My eyes pooled immediately. I hadn't felt anything in so long. I hadn't even realized how dead I'd been.

He wiped a tear from my cheek before rolling onto his back. "What are you going to do?"

"I don't know. My marriage is dead, and I'm mourning for my family." I sat up, wiped one more tear, took a deep breath, and forbade more to come. "Sorry."

He sat up, too. "It's a lot."

I looked at the sky one last time and wished I could be better at having affairs. A bright star shot across the sky, and I swatted at a mosquito on my arm.

"Let's get you back to the hotel before they devour you," he said.

"They're making me jealous."

The trail turned dark fast. Erik held his phone light out so I wouldn't trip over roots and rocks, even though I had my light. He'd parked his car across from Astral and Henry's house—in the same place the stalker guy parked earlier.

Erik pulled the car away from the blackberry bushes so I could get in. Amy's house sat dark and lonely, the front porch light the only one in the house turned on.

Silence dominated the ride back to the hotel. Erik turned the radio on, and a Chris Isaak song broke the air. We were strangers again. He parked by the hotel entrance, but not, to my delight, in the fifteen-minute loading zone. He turned the car off and took a deep sigh.

"You're coming up, aren't you?" I took my seat belt off and turned to him.

"I'm torn, Lee. I'd go home without question if I didn't think you were in danger. But you've got a lot to sort through. So do I."

That hurt. I hated Mary. "I don't want you to go home, Erik. I want you to come upstairs with me." I opened the door. "Coming?"

He shook his head but unbuckled his seat belt and followed. We held hands through the lobby. Sandy stood behind the counter, head tilted slightly, eyes widened. Was it judgment? Concern? No. It was Panic. Before I could ask what was wrong, I heard my name.

"Hello, Lee." I turned to see my husband rise from a velvet lobby chair. Portland wasn't the place for his tailored suit and shirt or his Master of the Universe attitude, but he looked right at home anyway.

Erik dropped my hand.

"What are you doing here?" I did not feel guilty about Erik and reached out to get the hand back, but he'd moved away.

"Well, I flew into town to find out if my wife was in danger, and when I couldn't find you, I panicked because Amy wasn't answering my calls either," he said. "I worried something had happened to you both."

"Well, I'm fine, as you can see," I said.

"I do see." He held out his hand. "Erik, good to see you again." The two had met briefly in a corridor three years ago, and now Jack acted like they were best buddies.

Erik shook his hand. "Look, I'm going to head out," he said.

"No. Jack is going." I turned to my husband. I wanted to punch him in his smug face. "Where are you staying, Jack?"

"I was going to get a room here, but the hotel has sold out. The whole city is sold out, apparently," he said.

Sandy, who pretended to be typing away in an otherwise empty lobby, looked up, adding an unenthusiastic, "Portland is happening now."

I let out a whiny growl. "Then call Amy."

"Amy blocked me a week ago." He said.

"Oh, Jesus." I paced. "Jesus, Jack!" I growled at him.

He seemed to find my predicament funny.

Erik stared at the exit.

"Even the airport hotels?" I pleaded with Sandy.

She shook her head.

"I'm sorry," I mouthed to Erik.

"You are lucky there's a sofa bed, or you'd be on a cot, pal," I said, walking past Jack. "Lose the smirk, or you can sleep in the lobby."

CHAPTER 18

◆◆◆

ERIK STILL LINGURED on my lips and skin the following day. Every flashback from the night before set me ablaze. Why hadn't we stayed by the grotto forever? I stared at the cityscape out my bedroom window, wondering where he was. Did he think of me? He hadn't answered my texts after his last "sort it out" message the night before.

Jack came in and announced room service had arrived, and I pretended to be asleep. I had to sit up when he set a cup of coffee on the nightstand. We'd been in a thousand hotel rooms together, and I couldn't remember him ever bringing me coffee in bed—that had been my job.

"Fuck," I mumbled. "Fucking fuck."

"Did you say something?" He re-entered with a covered plate of food and a rolled-up napkin in one hand and a mimosa in the other.

"What are you doing here?" I asked. "What the holy fuck are you doing here, Jack? I told you I needed some time."

"You did. And then you told me someone was following you. I know what happens next, Lee." He set the plate on the table, removed the metal cover, and handed me the mimosa.

"No, thank you. I don't drink anymore."

"Since when?" he asked.

"Since yesterday!" I snapped. "You're just trying to get me fat. Get out."

"Nice." He left the room like a sad puppy. "Do you want me to take the food away?"

"No! Shut the door." I tried to be nicer. "Please."

The food sat uneaten while I paced the room in a rage. A shower cooled me off, but the thought of the magic of the woods with Erik ignited me again. Jack opened the bathroom door.

"You have company," he shouted through the steam. "Justin."

I groaned. I'd forgotten about our date. I turned the water off and grabbed a towel to cover up. "Get out, Jack."

He left too slowly. "I can see why the cop is all over you."

"But did you see why I'm all over him?" I asked.

He winced and left. Erik was younger and hotter than my cocky husband, and money couldn't buy these things. He wasn't used to that.

When I entered the living room, Jack had made up the sofa bed, and Justin chowed down an omelet at the table. I stuffed my plate in my husband's hand, trying not to like him for giving Justin his meal.

"Eat this," I said. "I'd prefer the berries in the fridge."

Justin looked at us both between bites and said, "So I guess you two made up."

"Look at the sofa, Dude. What do you see?" I asked.

He got up and walked around the sleeper sofa. "I see a sheet hanging out, which wasn't there before. And the pillows are stacked on the chair." Justin looked at Jack. "Sorry, man. I should have observed before speaking."

Jack laughed. "Bravo, Justin." Jack saw my eyes light up in flames from the manipulation, but he came from a long line of polite people and would never acknowledge conflict in front of a stranger. Charming Justin meant getting information about me.

I washed berries and scrubbed counters Instead of smacking him in his perfect, smug nose.

Jack continued to show great interest in his new buddy, Justin. "Are you a Blazers fan, Justin?" he asked. "You look like you could score a few points. How tall are you?"

Justin loved to tell people he was six foot three.

"Let me guess. You prefer guitar." Jack wasn't clairvoyant; Justin wore a shirt with a guitar graphic.

"We're going to be late, Justin. Let's roll," I said.

"I do play guitar," Justin said. He wolfed down the last bite of the omelet as he stood up.

Jack rose, too.

"Don't get up," I said. "You're not coming."

It took a moment for my husband to digest the statement, but he backed off. "At least let me know where you two are going in case there's a problem, Lee."

"I don't need your help, Jack. Get a ticket home."

"I'm coming." He threw his cloth napkin on the counter to announce it finally. "I took a week off to be with you, Lee."

I stood in his way, anger seething between gritted teeth. "I don't need a week with you. I don't want a week with you. Got it?"

After a long stare down, he threw his hands up—a first in our marriage—and put on a false smile he used to save face.

This hurt my heart, so I threw him a small bone. "We're going to Lawrence Wilson's home. You'll likely find us chained to a wall in his basement if you don't hear from us by lunch," I said. "Be gone."

Justin shouted, "You can stay at my place if you want. I have a Murphy bed," as I pushed him toward the door.

"No!" I shouted.

"You're mean," Justin said. "I didn't know about this side of you."

"He's working you, Justin. Please don't fall for it. I did, and it cost me more than twenty years." I walked quickly to the elevator, half expecting Jack to chase us down the hall.

"I like him better than that cop. Which reminds me, he called again last night. Did he find you?"

"Yes." I pressed the button for the garage level and waved him in. The mention of Erik warmed my blood.

"Look at you," Justin said. "He found you, hmm. You went to Amy's, right? I knew you would." He almost squealed the last sentence.

"You'll make a good detective someday if you can learn to keep your mouth shut," I said.

"I know when to keep my mouth shut," he said. "Like when Jack gave me an omelet in exchange for information about the Robocop. I didn't tell."

Loyalty. I loved that and bumped his shoulder as we exited the elevator. A car waited for us at the curb, and we hopped in and disappeared—early morning explorers setting off on our next adventure.

"Have you heard from Amy?" I asked. "I hope she's okay."

"I texted her to tell her you went by," he said. "But she didn't answer." We both read from our phones while we sat in traffic.

"She doesn't care," I said. "She blocked me."

"Amy's right. We put her in danger," he said. "I can understand why she's mad."

"There's more to it with us. It goes way back. Somehow, for every bad thing that happened to me, a perfect thing also happened. With Amy, it was the opposite. Her mom would go to rehab and leave two days later. Amy would save for a car, and her mom would get drunk and crash it. Meanwhile, my parents were perfect because they were dead. I annoy her. My life annoys her."

"Or maybe she just doesn't want to be afraid in her own house or make enemies with her neighbors?" Justin lowered his voice. "You brought me—a total stranger—into her house, and I could have been a rapist. Or worse."

"Justin, what she doesn't know won't hurt her. Make sure it stays that way."

"Oh, she knows," he said.

I almost fell out of the car. "What are you talking about?"

"She knows."

I stared at him until he spoke.

"She told me she was relieved when she learned it was just me. She thought you'd come out here for a guy and was hurt you hadn't told her," he said.

"So she wasn't mad?"

"Oh, she was mega pissed at you." He fidgeted with his hands for a second. His rattle had begun to fade, and I feared it would return. "That's probably why she flipped out that night. I didn't tell her, I swear. She said she could smell that someone was in the house and that you acted super weird, and when she found out about me, she figured it out on her own."

"No worries, Justin." I bumped him. "Amy and I have been through worse, and we'll be fine. She fucked my boyfriend in high school, you know? And went to the prom with him. He'd dumped me first though, and Amy and I hadn't been close that year."

"That's a tough one. You or Amy? Damn. You're both hot."

I laughed. "Maybe Amy went away for the weekend." I tried calling her, but it rang to voicemail. A long, worried sigh escaped my lips. "What if the bearded guy got her?"

Justin shook his head. "Amy could take that guy."

I asked the driver to change course, and we went to Amy's house. Her car still sat in the driveway. "If she'd gone away, wouldn't she have taken her car?" I asked.

"We should go to Lawrence Wilson's house as planned. Amy's private. We shouldn't be snooping around," Justin said.

I was already out of the car, heading toward the guest room window, which I knew unlocked when jiggled. I climbed through. Amy had stripped the bedding like she was trying to forget I'd been there. "Amy," I called out.

Justin stood outside, shaking his head at me.

I pressed on regardless, opening the guest room door and peering into the great room, hoping I wouldn't find a dead Amy or a living one (because I'd be dead in that case). The lights were out on the first floor.

"Amy!" I called out again to a silent house. The sink was empty, and the dishes in the dishwasher were clean.

"Lee," Justin said. "I think we should go."

I ignored him, starting upstairs while calling Amy's name out along the way. Like a built-in alarm system, each stair creaked loudly. Her bedroom door was closed. I took a deep breath and swung it open. Daylight splashed on a neatly made bed.

Outside, a siren blared in the near distance. When I got downstairs, Justin stood in the yard with Astral, arguing about something.

"Lee, I didn't realize it was you. I'm so sorry."

We all watched the police car pull up.

"Amy's going to kill me," I mumbled.

"Justin told me you forgot your key," she said. "I'm so embarrassed. When I saw your friend standing near the window, I phoned the police."

The cops got out at a leisurely pace.

"All is good here, officers," I said. "Just a misunderstanding."

"Is this your house?" the short one asked.

"It's my friend's house, Amy Doherty. I'm staying with her."

He glanced at the open front door.

"I'm so sorry," Astral said. "Amy told me she caught some sketchy guy around the yard. She asked us to watch the house while she was away."

"I look sketchy?" Justin asked. A feigned hurt emanated from his face.

"No! I'm so sorry," she said. "It's just that, between the guy snooping around and the other guy in the car last night."

"What guy?" I asked. "What guy was here last night?"

"That one." She pointed at the road where a sedan barreled up to the house, creating a dust cloud on the gravel road. "He asked me if I'd seen you."

"He's a cop," I said. Erik walked toward us in what felt like slow motion. He wore aviators and perfectly fitted jeans. A sigh escaped from my lips.

Astral watched me closely. I wondered if she could see the scarlet lust wafting from my skin.

"His aura is mysterious," she said. "He's so cold I can't get a reading."

"I think he's hot," I said.

He read my lips and smiled.

I smiled back like a schoolgirl.

Justin rolled his eyes. "Amy will kill you when she finds out the police were at her house."

"She's already not speaking to me," I whispered. "What else can she do?"

Erik stopped a few feet from me, but it felt like miles.

"What are you doing here?" he asked. No hello. No hug. Just ice-cold, Erik.

"I haven't heard from Amy and thought she might be dead," I said.

Astral pretended Erik gave her the chills and shivered. "I'm going to head home. Again, so sorry."

He handed her his card. "Would you call me on my cell if you see anything else?"

"Sure." She folded the card in half and then unfolded it, the closest thing to nervous I'd seen her. "Is he dangerous?"

"No," I said. "I took that fucker down with pepper spray, and he cried like a baby."

Erik shook his head. "We don't know, Ms...."

"Astral."

"We don't know, Astral. That's why I need you to call me if you see him so I can find out who he is."

"I'll try to get a reading if I see him again. I didn't sense anything dark. There was something though...."

Erik made a conscious effort not to look at me. "Well, please don't approach him," he managed to say. "I'll have a patrol come through as often as possible."

I watched Astral enter her gate before asking, "Is she just like I described?"

A smile cracked through one side of his stone face. Our eyes met, but he looked away. "You two need a reminder that neither of you is a detective."

"What are you doing here, anyway?" I asked. "A homicide detective showing up on a burglary call?"

"I'm investigating a murder, remember? I asked the neighbors to call if they saw anything suspicious."

"On your weekend," I said. "Knowing I might be here..." I smiled my most charming smile, but he didn't budge. "Astral thinks your aura is too cold to read."

He smiled to prove he was human. "Yeah, well, Astral needs to smoke less of the herb."

"The herb," I repeated.

Justin exploded in laughter.

"All right. I'm out of the loop, okay? What are you kids calling it these days?"

"Ganja, pot, smoke, toke, skuna, droo, ott, kripi, ketra, kush, weed, MaryJane," Justin said. "I could go on all day."

"Cannabis, Erik." I interrupted. "Just call it cannabis."

"At least you didn't say marijuana, dude," Justin said. "I'm going to lock Amy's house up." An awkward silence filled the air when he left.

Erik looked at his watch. "Well, I have an appointment soon. Jack must be waiting for you."

"Hopefully, Jack is at the airport by now," I said.

"Somehow, I doubt he'll give up that easy."

"Maybe he'll be gone, and you could try visiting me tonight?" I asked.

"I meant what I said last night, Lee. Sort it out."

He didn't offer us a ride, so we started down the trail toward the Maplewood neighborhood to check out a house formerly owned by the deceased Craig Buckwood and now owned by Eloise and Mark Hanson. Eloise was the woman Ellen sat with the first time I met her, and like Amy, suggested something magical happened for her to get her home the way she did. I didn't have a plan, but I'd think of something.

On the way down the hill, I looked back at Amy's house. The upper level was all glass and deck, but the sloped lower side of the house had no windows. Once held together by a padlock, the plywood doors now swung freely. Amy didn't leave things open.

CHAPTER 19

◆◆◆

I FOUND A dead person once—an older woman from our canoe club in upstate New York. She was face-up, and blood surrounded her head like a crimson crown. I'd always thought I'd be afraid of finding a body—like it would rise and zombie-chase me. I'm a slow runner. Surprisingly, I'd remained calm.

Finding your best friend's body was another story. The open door swung in the breeze. I couldn't see through the dark hole into the underbelly of the house, and I couldn't move for fear I'd discover harm to my friend. Something happened on that hill—a culmination of my marital problems, my issues with Amy, and the general mess my life was in—I snapped like a tree limb.

"Oh my god!" I cried. "Oh my god, Amy!" I climbed and clawed up the steep hill, stepping through thigh-high forest shrubs, ferns, and ivy. I tugged on vines to climb the slope, crying, "Amy!"

"Lee, it's just a door. It doesn't mean anything." Justin could barely keep up with me as I slipped and pulled my way to the house.

Blinded by fear, I made it to the open doors, panting and crying, only to stop short. I couldn't face what I'd done to Amy. "I can't," I cried.

Justin turned his light on and went in. "So far, so good," he shouted out.

I braced myself, sure he'd find her any second.

"There's another door, he yelled out. When he came outside, his clothes were dusty, and he swatted at spider webs in his hair. "It hasn't been opened in a long time." When he saw me sitting in the dirt, crying, he stopped.

"Hey," he said. "She's not in there. It's okay."

"But it's not." I could no longer control my sobs. "It's not because Amy will never speak to me again, and she's right. What am I even doing?"

Justin sat down next to me. "She's going to get over it," he said. "She loves you. His soft shoulder bump felt like a hug.

"Your mom must have been lovely to make someone like you," I said, wiping my tears on my sleeves.

"She was cool," he said. "When she wasn't fucked up."

This made me cry harder. That's when we heard our names from above.

"Lee? Justin?" Amy peered over the deck. "What the fuck are you doing down there?"

❖❖❖

I squeezed Amy so hard that her feet came off the ground. "You're alive!" I cried. "You're alive!" I dropped her. "Where have you been?"

"Yes, I'm alive, you fucking idiot," she said. "I did a full moon hike up Mt. Hood with my backpacking group, remember? I asked you if you wanted to go when you first got here. I think you said something like, 'I'd rather eat worms.'"

"I remember now," I said.

Her moment of patience ended. She rested both hands on her hips and asked, "Why are you in my basement?"

"We were coming into the park, and I looked up and saw the doors swinging open," I said. "I knew you hadn't done it and thought...."

"I'm okay," she reminded me.

I searched the ground around the basement until I found the lock. "Someone cut it, look."

Amy peered into the darkness. "What would anyone want down here?"

"There's a door in there. It's hidden behind that chimney," Justin said. "It's boarded up, and someone used screws. If you have a screwdriver, I can get us in there."

"Great," Amy said. "There are probably bodies in there. Goodbye, property value."

"Or maybe it's a stash of bourbon from prohibition," I said.

"Or some old guy's workshop," Justin said.

"Only one way to find out," I said.

"You two are fucked up. Do you know that? She is fucking you up, Justin." Amy walked up the rough staircase carved into the hillside along her house and left Justin and me wondering if she'd return, but she soon reappeared, holding a bright pink box.

"Do you remember this, Lee? It was a housewarming gift from you when I bought the condo." She opened the box to reveal a rechargeable drill. "Best gift ever."

Justin pulled a tool from the box and went to work on removing the boards from the doorway. Amy and I watched in silence for a few moments.

My phone light shined on Justin, so I apologized in the dark. "I'm so sorry, Amy. I've been a selfish, thoughtless asshole."

"I'm sorry too," she said. "I should have more patience for you."

"No. You were right. I put you in danger. Look, now someone has entered your home. I'm leaving this alone," I said.

Amy laughed. "Before or after we find out what's in the room?"

I turned to her, putting my phone down. "Now, if you want. I mean it."

"Hey," Justin yelled. "Light, please."

"Sorry." I turned the light back toward the door. Justin had removed the top half of the slats.

Amy shook her head. "Forget it, Lee. Asking you not to pry into people's lives is like asking a dog not to sniff butts."

"I'm not sure how to take that," I said.

"What were you guys doing here, anyway?" she asked.

"I came to beg your forgiveness, but you weren't home. We were about to cross the park to get to a house near Maplewood. Do you want to come?

"Why?" she asked.

"Why what?" I asked.

"Why were you going to the house?" she asked.

"Because the woman who lives there thinks she's a witch," I said.

"Like you did when you got this house."

Amy shook her head. "Pass. You're going to get into trouble. Plus, I'm exhausted from the hike. We did ten miles up the summit of Mount Hood during the full moon. Incredible night."

Justin popped his head out from the dark basement. "Ready?"

I followed Amy in. "The inspector said we should open the room in case there was an oil tank or something, but Ellen told me I'd lose the house to another buyer if I made any trouble."

"Ellen," I whispered. "Always back to Ellen."

Justin opened the door and shined his light into a small room— It smelled like dirt. Posters covered the walls, and an old sofa sat in the corner.

"Looks like someone's hang-out." He picked up a Rolling Stone magazine with Johnny Depp dressed as Jack Sparrow. "July 2006."

I pulled on a chain hanging from the ceiling, and the room lit up. "It's a time capsule," I whispered. A Cold Play poster hung next to a Rage Against the Machine poster in perpetual conflict. Someone had drawn devil horns and a goatee on Chris Martin's face.

"It's like a millennial threw up here," I said.

Justin dusted off the play button on a cassette player and woke it up with the push of a button.

"Fade Into You," I said. "I love this song." An inch of dust-filled candles stood together on a side table. Rats had moved into the sofa long ago, making fluff-filled holes in the cushions. "A secret love nest?" I asked. "Did the last owners have kids?"

"No. And they didn't know when we asked them what was in here," Amy said.

"How could you buy a house without knowing?" I asked. "I would have pried that door open during inspections."

"I'm lucky I got the house at all. I wasn't going to make a fuss," Amy said. "I'm just glad there are no bones." She pointed her phone light in my face. "There are no bones, right?"

I shined my light toward the ceiling. A mesh fabric hung loosely from staples in the boards, shredded in most spots but whole where black paint held the familiar shape of a stag's head together. The image was more primitive than the other versions, with strokes like Japanese letters.

"I know who broke into your creepy basement." I made them wait for an answer. "Justin, do you know?"

He shook his head. "The afflicted one."

◆◆◆

"Just call him," I begged Amy. "Please. Tell Astral you need help with your plumbing. She won't be able to conjure anything up to fix that."

"I thought you said you were dropping this," Amy said, rolling her eyes. But she picked up her phone.

"You want to know why he was down there as bad I do."

"True." She dialed. "Hi, Astral."

Justin and I gathered around the counter where Amy sat.

"No, they did not tell me the police were here," she growled. "But that's not why I phoned. Do you think you could send Henry over for a minute? I need his advice about my deck. I think it may be falling off the house." She shook her head in agreement. "It is scary." She hung up the phone. "I am a terrible liar. Why did you make me lie?"

"What happened to the plumbing problem?" I asked.

"It sounded so cliché," Amy said. "Single woman has plumbing problems. Whatever. He's on his way."

"You should have told her there was a rat in your basement. Henry would be here already."

Someone knocked on the front door, and we all looked at each other wide-eyed before Amy got up to answer.

"I guess my deck falling off was code for get your ass over here," she said.

We followed her to the door, and when she opened it, Henry stood there like a dog in trouble.

"Come in." Amy held the door open.

Justin and I cleared the way for his entry and followed him and Amy into the great room. His clothes were dirty, and he smelled like a pine forest mixed with body odor.

Amy pulled out a kitchen stool and pointed for Henry to sit. He obeyed.

"Do you want a beer or a glass of water, Henry?" I asked. "I'm having a beer."

"Me too," Amy said. "Please."

"Sure. Thanks."

I poured three and slid one over to Henry.

"I'll have a beer," Justin said.

I poured water into a mug and brought it to him.

"I can go to war but can't have a beer." Justin ignored the water. "I can vote and pay taxes but can't have a beer."

"Have mine, dude." Henry gave him his mug.

Amy and I both released surprised, nervous laughs.

"Whatever," I said. "You're an orphan. When you are in charge of yourself, you're an adult."

"So you'll buy up for me?" Justin asked.

"No," I answered quickly. "Henry, are you aware there's a room under Amy's house?"

Henry's eyes shifted back and forth. He squirmed in his seat and then sipped his beer. "I'm aware." He pulled a rusted old lock out of his pocket, unlocking it before handing it to Amy with the key. "It's old, but it works. I can run to the hardware store if you prefer a new lock. This one has been lying around my shed forever. It only has one key."

"Why not when the house was vacant?" I asked.

"Once she died...I don't know. I guess I was feeling nostalgic."

"Why was it boarded up like that?" I poured him a new beer and sat down.

Henry took a long sip. "Charlotte's dad was an abusive drunk, and he tortured and beat Charlotte's mom until she killed herself. We set up the room, knowing her father never went down there, even dragging an old couch down when her pop was at Renner's getting shit-faced. For a while, we had all the time we wanted together. But a few months later, he found us." He took a swig of his beer.

"He beat the shit out of us both—kicked me until my ribs cracked.

"What did you do?" I asked.

"We ran into the park. That drunk fuck hadn't been down in the ravine in years," he said. "We stayed for months in the hut. I brought tools from my parent's house to get it into shape. Some of our friends initially brought us food and supplies, but the novelty wore off after a while, and then it just sucked. No running water or bathroom. It got cold. One day, I left to get supplies like I'd done a dozen times. I came back, and she was gone. I hadn't heard from Charlotte for four years. I thought he killed her, so I busted into the house. She'd taken some of her things, including the emergency cash her mother kept in a coffee can."

"Wow," I said. "Where'd she go?"

"She took a bus to LA and stayed with her Mom's aunt, who swore never to tell a soul she was there. I couldn't live across the street from her father after that. My dad worried I'd kill the bastard. I moved to a commune off of Hawthorne. That's where I met Astral." He stared at his feet.

We all sat quietly, imagining what it must have been like for them.

"I just wanted to see if there was anything left of us," he said.

"And was there?" I asked.

"No," he answered. "We good?" He stood up and set the padlock and key on the counter.

"We're good," Amy said.

"I'd appreciate it if you didn't mention this to Astral. She doesn't like me to talk about Charlotte."

"Has your wife ever met Charlotte?" I asked.

"Astral and I aren't married," he said. "But no, they never met."

"Why don't you look at my deck while you're here?" Amy asked. "I hear it's falling off." He grinned.

It was the closest thing to a smile I'd seen on his miserable face. When he left, I followed him to the door. "What was Charlotte like?" I asked.

He thought for a moment. "She was an injured fawn, alone in the forest without a mother."

CHAPTER 20

◆◆◆

JACK OCCUPIED MY hotel room, so I returned to Amy's house. Things between Amy and I had warmed up, but I stepped carefully and tried to be a better guest. Justin's condo had me dreaming of a place of my own, and Portland's sunny, mosquito-free summer seduced me daily. I'd never had a place of my own.

I ate an edible and smoked some weed before getting into Ellen's little car so I wouldn't throw up on her leather interiors. "Is that mid-century on the hill still available?" I gripped the handle above my door as we wound up a road at twenty miles per hour over the speed limit. "I've had fantasies about restoring the place."

She laughed. "Not a chance, honey. That house sold for cash the same day I showed it to you. You'll have to move fast on anything you like. And as I told you with the condo, I don't believe in the theory of "meant to be." If you like something, we need to make it happen."

"Make it happen?" I asked. "What does that mean?"

We climbed a narrow road with a velvety fern wall on one side and a sheer drop into the ravine on another. I hoped she'd say something like, "Kill your competitors," and make my life easy.

"It means bid fast and high, cash if possible, and don't be a pain in the ass during inspections."

I thought about what the creepy room in Amy's house could have contained and decided I wouldn't take Ellen's advice at my home inspection.

"It feels like Southwest Portland is one ravine after another," I said. "Do they have names?"

"Most of them have trails below. Ask Amy for names. She's probably been in everyone."

I laughed. "I thought Amy went missing this week, but she was just full moon hiking on Mt. Hood."

"Missing. Why would Amy go missing?"

I gripped the handle over the window while she whirled up the curves. "Didn't you hear? Amos Patenaude was murdered."

She kept her eyes on the road. I wished I'd saved the conversation for lunch to see her eyes, but thankfully, she kept them on the road.

"I thought that fire was accidental." The wheels screeched around a hairpin turn, and she swerved to avoid hitting a man and his hound. "Why the hell would you walk your dog on this road?"

"It was arson," I said.

"How do you know so much about it?" she asked.

"I ran into Amos in the park on the day he died. I was the last one to see him alive. Well, except for the murderer," I added. "Did you know Amos?"

"I know the property. Amos's son called and asked me to price it not too long ago," she said. "Of course, I told him I would do no such thing until he was the owner."

"You know everyone," I said. "It was a sweet house."

"This may sound macabre, but the fire improved the lot. Builders don't like the red tape and costs of tearing an old house down."

"The man I met would never have allowed that," I said. "He had great pride in that house. His dad and uncle built it by hand."

"I always advise my homeowners to use a professional contractor."

"Are you going to list that property?" I feigned interest. "It's a nice piece of land. Maybe I could build something on it."

"You don't have time for that. Plus, there will be ten builders bidding it up. They'll put four houses there, at least."

"Are you going to list it?" I asked again.

"It will go into probate if there's no will, so no one is listing it soon. But I know Alex Patenaude, and he will sell to the highest bidder once he inherits—he lives in Texas and is an only child. Between you and me, there is no sentimentality on his part about who gets it."

Another dead seller added to Ellen's coffers. Was she some psychological wizard causing people to die for real estate dollars? I didn't see her walking around in a Channel suit pouring gasoline on Amos's house, but I could see her motivating others to do her work. Maybe the hairy guy worked for her.

"Do you have a builder for that property?" I asked.

She pulled into the driveway of a tiny cottage and looked at me like I was a kid who told a dirty joke—unsure if she should scold me or laugh. "A builder? I have at least three."

The house looked small from the curb, but inside, it expanded into the treetops like a birdhouse. The living room and kitchen had views of the river and beyond, where the east side of town spilled out for miles across a flat valley, stopped short by Mt. Hood. The main floor was perfect for one person, and downstairs sported an entire apartment for the boys.

"I'll take it," I said.

Ellen smiled. "Don't you want to see the other five homes I picked for you?"

"No," I said. "I like this one."

"But you haven't even seen the Eastside yet," she said.

"I want to be close to Amy and Justin, and this will do," I said. "My own tree house. I love it."

I wanted the house, maybe more than anything in a long time, but the decision surprised me with a sting. Buying the cottage meant separation and likely divorce. "I'm going to have to get my husband up here," I said.

"Husband?" Ellen asked. "I had no idea you were married." She looked at my left hand.

"We're in the early stages of separation," I said. "I took my rings off after discovering I shared Jack with his co-worker in England."

Ellen made a face of disgust. "Men," she said. "Someone should tell them their seed is no longer in demand."

We shared our first laugh.

"Are you married?"

"Thirty years," she said. "Three kids. We've been to hell and back. I was a soccer mom until my husband's business failed. That's when I got my real estate license—the best thing that ever happened to me. We made it through a couple of affairs—one in retaliation for the other, and then we lost our son two years ago. We almost didn't survive that one."

"Oh my god," I said. "Ellen. I'm so sorry."

We stared at the city below us.

"Overdose. He started in high school," Ellen said. "Twenty bucks a pill. Oxy flows like candy through the streets of this country, you know?"

This sent a pulse of fear through my veins.

"He worked at the market part-time and had the money for whatever he wanted. I had no idea until I found him in my living room, unconscious. He survived ten rehabs and many hospitalizations, but we couldn't save him."

"I'm sorry, Ellen." I wiped a rogue tear or two. "I'm so sorry."

She gave me a quick pat on the back. "Cry for all the other moms. God knows how many more there will be."

She ushered me toward the house. "Let's call your husband!" She was hardcore Ellen by the time we got to the door. "Do you think he's available today? This house won't last."

◆◆◆

A do not disturb sign hung from the door handle. I knocked. Jack finally answered. "Why didn't you use your passkey?" His hair puffed out on two sides like a mad professor, and he wore pajamas.

"Were you asleep?" I asked.

"Just dozing." He ran his hands through his hair, which didn't help. "You want some coffee or a drink?"

Empty beer bottles and take-out containers littered the counter.

"Are you okay?" I asked.

"Am I okay?" He laughed a little. "Just exactly what is there to be okay about? You left me sitting here like an idiot three days ago, and I have no idea what's going on with you."

Suddenly aware of his mess, he said, "Look at you. You look great."

"Romance kills my appetite," I said. "You should have tried it."

He sat down on the couch, defeated. "You're ending our family over this?"

"Don't put this on me, Jack. Please." I sat down next to him. "At least take responsibility so we can be friends."

"I don't care if you fucked the cop. We're even. Let's start over."

"The cop isn't fucking me, Jack," I said. "Yet." I looked into his eyes, squinting to find the tiniest bit of something worth saving.

"Is that disappointment I see in your eyes? You want me to fuck him." I stood up. "You think it would get you off the hook."

He looked away. "If it saves us, then yes."

"At this moment, there is no us. There is no me and you." I rose from the sofa and paced back and forth across the room. "It's going to be a new era, Jack. If you want to stay married, you must do it my way. If I stay married to you, I'm doing it from Portland."

He stood up quickly. "What? What about the kids?"

"What about the kids?" I repeated. He knew the kids were all I thought about—the only reason I considered staying. "I've been a single mother for years. It's your turn. Put your kids first for once."

"You've been well provided for, Lee. Why do you think I work twelve-hour days? For us!" His shoulders sagged, and he appeared small to me for the first time in our relationship. "Max still has two more years of high school. You're going to destroy him!"

"You will destroy them if you blame this on me. Don't make me tell the kids their father is a cheat and a liar. I'll cover for you, but only up to a point.

"We'll tell the kids I got a job I couldn't refuse. It's not a lie. I can go back and forth, and they can come back and forth. Jack Jr. is going to college," I said. "They aren't babies. They can handle it."

"My wife is not living three thousand miles away," he said.

"But she is—unless you want a divorce. Then it will be your ex-wife who lives on the West Coast, and I won't have to ask you to help me buy a house."

He slumped further into the couch like a spoiled man-child.

"Open the email and sign the papers," I handed him his cell phone. "Before someone outbids me. And get dressed. I want to show you the new house, and we'll go to Happy Hour afterward to celebrate."

CHAPTER 21

◆◆◆

DARK CLOUDS FORMED in the valley, turning Portland's blue skies heavy in dark patches, one of which hung over Justin's building. He'd invited me to meet a candidate for a project we'd started calling One at a Time. We hadn't talked about the plan in front of Amy or Jack. Amy would tell me I was unqualified to help addicts. Jack would call it one of my "little projects."

Inside Justin's apartment, a tiny woman in torn fishnet tights, cut-off shorts, and a leather jacket lay face down on the new sofa. Black smudged makeup around her eyes added to a corpse-like appearance, but her body rose and fell with each breath.

"Do you think choosing a female is a good idea?" I asked.

"Well, Kelly kind of chose us," Justin said.

"Please get her on the bed," I said. "She's leaving drool marks on the fabric."

"She passed out waiting for you to get here," he said.

"I was having Miserable Hour with Jack on the east side when you called," I said. "You phoned just after I asked for an open marriage."

Justin laughed hysterically. "For realz?"

"For realz," I said. "It was already open; Jack just hadn't told me."

"About the female thing—she's super old, like thirty-eight or something." He shivered as if the idea made him cold. "Older than my mom would be. So, you don't have to worry about me and her."

Old like me, I thought. "We can lift her. She's probably less than a hundred pounds."

Justin pulled down the Murphy bed. The sheets were new and clean.

"What if she has bedbugs?" I mouthed.

Justin rolled his eyes. "I bet you thought the same about me."

"I made you shower first, remember?" I asked. Centipede-shaped track marks inched near the creases in Kelly's arms, but I didn't see bug bites anywhere.

"Is that why you stole my clothes?" Justin asked.

We counted and lifted on three, swinging her dead weight clumsily onto the bed, where she landed too near the edge but still hadn't moved.

"Keep her on her side in case she pukes," I said.

Justin rolled his eyes. "She's a meth addict. She just needs to sleep it off."

"She smells weird. Like you did at first." I covered her with a flat sheet and then a blanket.

"It's the chemicals coming out of her skin," Justin said.

A mixture of disappointment and fear dragged my face down. "I thought you didn't do drugs."

"Don't cry," he said. "I'm okay. I swear."

"Ellen told me her son died from an overdose. It's so sad."

"Sucks," he said.

"Are you okay?" My mind filled with images of needles, and Justin slumped on the floor of some crack house.

"When you live on the street, you have to stay up all night if you want to keep your stuff. And meth is practically free—sometimes it is free. When I met you, I wanted to come down somewhere safe more than anything, and maybe if I hadn't found anywhere, I probably would have used again because what did I have to look forward to, man? You want to feel good for a minute, you know?"

"Why aren't you addicted?" I asked.

"I don't want to be my mother," he said. "Or my father. Who knows what he's like?"

If he were my kid, I'd make him promise never to do it again or maybe force him into rehab. Justin was not my child. I didn't know what he was, but I tried not to punish him for his honesty by freaking out.

"It's free. Wow." I shook my head and took a deep breath.

His eyes pooled, so he walked over to his desk and shuffled things around. "After I lost my stuff again, I was ready to give up my conscious mind."

Kelly had tiny freckles on her nose, and I wondered if she had a mother who'd imagined big things for her. "So, what's her story?" I asked.

Justin grabbed his laptop off the counter and opened it. "You should know a few things about her first." He handed me the computer.

I scrolled through mug shots, the first of a pink-haired, baby-faced woman smiling at the camera. She'd lost a tooth by the last mug shot, and her skin was scarred and weathered, aging her decades in less than eight years.

"Five assault charges, Justin." I shook my head.

"Her parents cut her off." Justin closed the program on his computer, and Kelly's many faces disappeared. "She has two kids she's not allowed to see and an ex-husband who's remarried and won't talk to her."

"And you think we can help her how?" I asked.

"A safe bed and shower for starters." He walked to the refrigerator and pulled a pot out. "A meal." He opened the lid, and the smell of something meaty spilled out.

I sighed deeply. Justin was trying to save his mother.

"Did you think this would be easy?" He put the pot back in the refrigerator. "It's not going to be pretty."

"You were," I said.

"You lucked out, Lee. That's all." He heard himself. "That's not what I meant. I just...the timing was perfect. I wanted off the street."

"I know what you meant," I said. "I get it."

He sighed. "We don't know what we're doing, is all," he said.

"We're just going to help any way we can, right?" I asked.

"Yep. It's a start," Justin said. "You know who would be a great person to help her?"

"No. No way," I said. "Amy can't find out about this. She'd murder me and then yell at my corpse."

CHAPTER 22

♦♦♦

ELLEN WANTED ME to waive inspections on my cottage on the hill because another cash offer came in right after mine. I lost the house for refusing. She got so angry I thought she might fire me.
"I don't like to lose, Lee," she said. "It makes me feel like a loser. Do you want to lose?"
We spoke over the phone. "No, Ellen. I don't want to lose, " I said. "I also don't want to pay for a house that needs a new foundation and roof or is in the process of being eaten by termites, especially a house that hangs over a hill."
"You didn't love it enough to do what it takes. I have a few things I'd like to show you. Are you and Jack available today?"
If Ellen were anyone else, I would've fired her for even speaking Jack's name, but I needed to keep her close. Plus, Jack asked if he could come with us next time, so if shopping for homes made him more comfortable with the situation, great.
"Send me a list," I said.
"Already done, Dear," she said. "What time shall I pick you up? I'll bring Monster."
"I've got an address for you. Eight-five-six Alta Heights." I said. "Can you get us in?"
"Alta Heights," she said. "That's a bit higher than your price range."

"Jack is into it," I lied. "Let's just appease him—and Amy has loaned us her car," I said. "We'll see you there."

No chance I'd ever get in a car with her again.

I phoned Justin and put him on speaker while preparing to leave. "Good morning. How is Kelly?"

"Dead to the world," he said.

"Can you leave her there for a few hours? I need you to do something for me."

"Uh, I could, but what if she wakes up and steals all my shit?"

"It's a quick task. She'll be out for at least eight more hours if she sleeps like you that day."

"Okay," he sang, doubtful.

"Take a car to the two addresses I texted you and ask if they've worked on the Monster. Focus on the broken headlight. These are the only two shops in Ellen's town that work on foreign cars."

"Couldn't I just call them?" he asked.

"No," I said. "Go in person so you can see the look on their face when you ask. Tell them it was a hit and run—it was dark, and maybe the person didn't realize they'd clipped you. Say you want to contact them, so you don't have to go to the police."

"I don't feel so good about leaving Kelly here alone," he said.

"Wait until she wakes up and take her with you."

"You should meet her before you say things like that," he said. "I'll go now."

"Guess who's neighbor put their house up for sale?" I asked. "You'll never guess, so I'll give you a hint. Does Infinity Terrace ring a bell?"

"Infinity Terrace? That's Lawrence Wilson's house," Justin said. "Next door?"

"It's not exactly next door…."

"Watch out for those neighbors up there, man. They chased me right out."

"Maybe because you dropped cigarette butts all over their streets and stood in their bushes," I said.

"Nah. NIMBYs. They probably thought I'd set up a camp somewhere and wanted me gone," he said. "I never got a single look at Wilson. He must be some kind of phantom. You breaking in?"

"No," I said. "I'm not a criminal. Jeez, Justin. I'll poke around and maybe get a look at him. Maybe he's our bearded stalker..."

"Poke around. Right," Justin said.

❖❖❖

The house above Wilson's sprawled dramatically across a wedge of flat land rare for the west hills, where most homes clung precariously over the edge. Inside, Jack lived in a fantasy world of "we" and "us" as he opened each cabinet and door.

"We could make this an apartment for the kids," he said of space over the garage. "Our room," he declared, walking through the master. He asked Ellen questions suitable only for a serious buyer, even opening the refrigerator. While he poked around in a basement furnace room, I took the stairs to the backyard, peering down the hill at Lawrence Wilson's roof and garden.

I climbed over a rock wall and held on to tree trunks, working my way downhill in hopes of at least getting a peek at the mysterious man who lived there. I couldn't see anything, so I slipped down further and then too far before losing control. I dug in my heel but fell backward. Gravity took course, dragging me down the hill like a human sled. I grabbed and clung, but with nothing to hold on to, I only picked up speed as I slid toward the bottom and caught air over a small retaining wall, enabling me to land on my feet on the lawn. I'd recovered beautifully for a tenth of a second—Olympic medal-winning—but the impact hit. I went down with force, skidding a few yards on my face.

I heard gasps, and a dog licked my mouth. The fall took my wind, and I couldn't move momentarily.

A man shouted, "Tiger, come!"

I covered my mouth from Tiger, a shaggy mixed thing that disobeyed its owner, sticking his tongue in my mouth and then licking my cheek.

"Are you okay?" The man leaned over long enough to block the blaring sun from my face before standing again.

I closed my eyes and breathed deeply, then raised myself onto my rear end and wiggled my toes. Everything worked. I took a quick look and pulled my shirt down over my stomach, praising the closet gods that I hadn't worn a dress that day. Grass stains covered my knees, and my feet were bare. "I'm okay."

The thin man leaned on his walking stick. A benign face kid behind a pair of aviators. Homicide detective Erik Healy stood next to him. He frowned while reaching his hand out to help me up.

"I've got it." I did an awkward twist to get up, and a spike of pain shot through my right foot. Tiger sniffed the dirt on my knees. Erik gathered up my favorite daisy flip-flops—which had followed me down the hill—and dropped them at my feet.

"Thanks so much." I stepped into the shoes and dusted off my knees, trying to hide the stabbing pain radiating from my ankle.

The two men watched while I did a quick inventory of what hurt. "Excuse the intrusion. I was looking at the house above you with my real estate agent, and I guess I peered too far over the wall."

Erik crossed his arms and rolled his eyes.

"It's not every day someone drops into my garden." A tall man but frail man and leaned on a cane. "Are you sure you're okay? Can I do anything for you?"

I held out my dirt-caked hands. "If I could use your restroom to clean up, I'd be grateful," I said.

"Why not rinse off with the hose?" Erik said. "I'm sure your broker is looking for you."

I pictured Jack inspecting the fireplace and asking Ellen more questions than she could tolerate. He'd never done a thing around our house, and suddenly, he was a licensed contractor.

"Of course, you're not using the hose. Come in," Lawrence said.

I smiled at Erik as I passed. He squinted and feigned a smile before following us inside.

Except for the framed Tim Burton sketches in the bathroom, there was no hint of my host's profession as a creator of special effects—only clean lines and modern art. I couldn't picture him living in Amy's little charmer of a house.

"I'd better get back before my broker calls out a search party," I said. "I'm Lee Harding." I held out a clean hand.

"Lawrence Wilson. Do you like the house you were touring?" he asked.

"The wall is a little low." I tried to be funny, but both men stared at me. "It's the first place I've seen today. But yes, I like it. Maybe we'll be neighbors. I promise not to drop in again unannounced."

"How long have you lived in the neighborhood?"

"I just moved in a few months ago," he said. The meticulous room held little hints of who occupied the home. I admired the landscape over the fireplace and the midcentury furniture but imagined a garage full of unpacked boxes. Not a single framed photo.

"Beautiful home," I said. "Is it just you and Tiger here?"

"I'm a widower," Lawrence said. "And not quite moved in. Busy with work and all of that."

"I am sorry to hear that," I said. "You seem so young. Was it an accident?"

He stared at me momentarily, his sunglasses an emotional barrier. Finally, he spoke. "Something like that."

"I can give you a ride up the hill," Erik said. He walked toward the front door.

"I hope to see you around the neighborhood, Mrs. Harding." Wilson didn't exactly push me out the door as much as he willed it with his presence. Once I was on the front stoop, he closed the door halfway. "I assume you got what you needed, Detective?"

"Yes. Thanks for the time, Mr. Wilson." Once Erik heard the lock click from the inside, he turned to me. "What the hell are you doing here?" he asked. But when I clutched at my throbbing ankle, he shook his head and helped me to his car.

I answered my phone to Jack, shouting. "Where the hell are you?"

"I had a little accident. I'm okay," I said. "I fell down the hill behind the house."

"Oh my god! Are you okay?" Jack asked. "She fell over the cliff."

"Good Lord!" Ellen cried.

"I'm fine. I'll be there in a second." I hung up. Erik watched me, and I watched back. The fire surged immediately.

"Jack is with Ellen," I said. "Maybe just drop me at the bottom of the driveway."

We drove up the narrow hill in silence. He stopped in front of the For Sale sign.

"Don't go buying any houses to get close to Wilson. I can save you the time and money and tell you I don't think he killed Amos Patenaude."

"Why? Maybe he hired that goon to do it," I said. "Did you ask him about Charlotte's last words?"

"He'd never even heard of Amos Patenaude, and he was at work during the fire. Says he signed in and everything."

"Oh, well, that must be the truth then. Did you check Amos's phone records?" I asked.

He shook his head. "Lee...."

"I know, I know. You can't say." I opened the car door. "I better go."

"Are you sure you don't need a hand?" he asked.

"I'm fine," I lied. It hurt like hell to put weight on my foot. "For one quick second, I was proud of that landing."

Erik chuckled. "It looked like you fell out of the sky." He struggled to speak again. "And then the shoes came flying down..." He put his hand over his face like he was ashamed for laughing.

"Okay. Enough." I shut the door and hobbled over to his open window. "This house is too big for just one person," I said. "I'm looking for something cozier."

"Really?" he said. "Is your husband aware of this?"

"He is. We've sorted things out," I said. "And he leaves the day after tomorrow." I crossed my fingers. "Where do you live?"

"I live in Southeast," he said.

"Well, maybe you could show me around soon."

"Maybe." His smile cooled, but I knew it was in there somewhere.

I wanted to stare at him all day, but they waited. "Wish me luck," I said. "Jack is suddenly a home inspector, and Ellen encourages him." The limp prevented me from doing a sexy walk-off, so I waved, waiting until he drove away before hobbling up the driveway toward my confused husband, stopping only to answer a call from Justin.

"Monster lost a right front headlight six months ago. Ellen told the mechanic that one of her clients did it."

CHAPTER 23

◆◆◆

IN SOME FANTASY world of Jack's, we lived happily ever after in the sprawling home above Lawrence Wilson's. But a Victorian three-story reminded me of my childhood home in San Francisco, and I insisted on making an offer. The foot injury got me out of lunch with Jack and Ellen. They dropped me at Amy's, where I changed into a sundress and hobbled down the street toward the village.

The Multnomah neighborhood has more owls and coyotes than hipsters, and its heart lies on a winding street lined with funky shops, bars, and brew pubs. My foot had its own throbbing heartbeat when I sat at a bar, where a guy with a giant beard killed my pain with a Manhattan.

A cat lay in the bookshop window next to Celestial Beads, where a waft of incense I didn't recognize poured out when I opened the door. Inside, a rainbow of beaded chandeliers, swags of ribbon, and brightly colored artifacts from around the world hung from a crowded ceiling. Beads dripped from the walls in strips of color in every shape and shade, and jars cluttered a table holding even more treasures.

"Wow," I heard myself whisper.

Astral floated through in a tsunami of color. She wore a floor-length dress under a crocheted duster. Her dreadlocks were tied up high, and beaded earrings dropped from lobe to collarbone.

"Lee!" She put a strand of something down and rushed to the door to embrace me. "Welcome to Celestial!"

"It's amazing," I said.

She took my hand, and we wove through a narrow merchandise alley toward an open space in the back. "This is where I do my sound bowl treatments," she said. Worn Turkish rugs and sheepskins layered the floor, and golden bowls sat about the fluffy nest. A neon light hung on the wall above the space, spelling "tune in" softly in cursive.

"Cool." I didn't know what else to say.

"Want a reading?" she asked.

I wrinkled my nose. "Not really."

Astral knew how to see a person. Bowl therapy must be good for focus because she didn't take her eyes off me. Finally, she spoke. "I'm reading your fear. What can I do to help you?"

"I do need your help," I said. "And I am terrified."

Astral nodded with sad satisfaction.

"Can you help me assemble some authentic Portland care packages for my two sons? They will follow a difficult conversation I will have with them later today—thus the fear."

"I see." The idea took hold of her, and she began a purposeful search through her aisles.

"How old are they? Tell me about them?" She dug into the clutter, rehanging a woven poncho and then picking up some clay flutes.

"Jack Jr. likes to race kayaks and do maths. He's about to be a college freshman. Max is creative—he's good at putting things together but hates directions. The only thing interesting him these days are girls."

Astral picked items off the shelves and threw them in a basket while I wandered around the back of the store. A shaggy ribbon and gauze lion's head hung from a door in the back. Creamy satin ribbons, beads, and gauzy fabrics made up the mane.

"This is spectacular," I said. "The beadwork is gorgeous."

"I made it for Pearl, but since it scares her, we keep it here." She pulled her hand from a jar of tiny dice and led me to the counter. "This will do."

"I bought a house today," I said. "Well, the sellers accepted my offer. Inspections are tomorrow."

She dropped the dice evenly into little velvet pouches. "That's exciting. Where?"

"A little Victorian sweetie in Goose Hollow. I can walk to everything," I said. "I used Ellen Robinson. Do you know her?"

Astral wrinkled her nose.

"Not a fan?" I pulled two rain sticks from their stand and laid them on the counter with a growing pile that now included Mexican blankets, Day of the Dead dog figurines, and a strand of bells and bobs—nothing that even whispered "Portland." Astral read my mind.

"A local artist did the Tarot cards," Astral said. "And this triangle was forged by a friend in St. John's. The most incredible native woman made these leather and bead pouches from the Gorge. Do you think they'd want to make some jewelry?"

"Great idea. Yes." I hoped my growing bill would encourage her to open up. "Ellen has been making me insane, but we're too far in to fire her."

"I don't have anything against Ellen." She busied herself with the task while she spoke. "Well, except for her driving."

"Oh, God," I said. "Agreed."

"It's Ellen who holds the grudge. We were going to move earlier in the year. But then the situation changed, and we decided to stay. Ellen had loaned me her truck to move practically everything to storage." She looked up. "Do you know what she said to me in my house?"

I nodded to indicate I did not.

"'All the hippy-dippy stuff must go.'" She stopped shopping for a moment. "She said it just like that." Astral exhaled with purpose.

"She told me my new kitchen was dated," I said. "It's vintage, and I love it. I'm talking about nineteen fifties countertops with the little metal strip without burn marks or anything."

She nodded in understanding. "She only met with us twice. That's it. But when we told her we weren't moving, she freaked out. I told her I'd pay her for gas, but she wouldn't take a dime, then marched out of the house. She's a dark one—so pushy."

"Let's see; she constantly referred to my husband for his opinion even though she knew I was the customer, not him. She said the house I bought was 'tired' and 'she doesn't care for the neighborhood.' And she tried to get me to drop my home inspection contingency!"

Astral shook it off. "I don't like to spend time on negative energy. Let's focus on your boys."

"You're right," I said. "Plus, Ellen did get the agent to pull the house off the market before the open house this weekend, so I guess pushy worked for me this time."

The pile on the counter grew into a mound. I handed her Jack's emergency credit card and scribbled the address to camp on a notepad. "I'm surprised Henry even considered leaving his family home."

Astral handed me a receipt to sign. "All that neighborhood holds for Henry is the past," she said. "I wish we could get out. But Pearl loves it, and Amy's moving in changed the vibe to positive."

It must have been a great relief to her when Henry's first love didn't move in across the street. I wondered if I was the love of my husband's life and if he was mine. Neither was true, and both were true, and it was okay.

CHAPTER 24

◆◆◆

THE FOLLOWING DAY, my ankle swelled, and my stomach burned from the anxiety of the phone call we'd make to the boys later. Jack would fly back the next day, and I would take over the suite until we closed on the house the following week. Things were getting real. I got high to kill the pain.

Jack, Ellen, and I met at the new house for inspections. Jack followed the poor inspector around the entire time, asking questions and telling long stories the guy didn't have time to hear.

I strolled the rooms, dreaming up designs for each of the three bedrooms and measuring for a sofa. The house smelled like old wood. I loved the high ceilings on both floors, the vintage kitchen, and the tiny butler's pantry cabinets no one had ever painted.

I'd never lived alone before, and it was exciting to think of the house as all mine.

I found Ellen on her phone in the dining room, with paperwork sprawled across the table. She hung up when I sat down. "Big dreams?"

"Not that big. I love the lighting and the woodwork. I'll get the floors polished and do some painting."

"What about that ghastly kitchen?"

"I told you, Ellen, I love that kitchen."

She rolled her eyes. "When you have to use it, you'll change your mind," she said.

"I'm no gourmet," I said. "Oh, I meant to tell you—I ran into another of your clients this morning. Astral. You get around, girl."

"That sack of patchouli is no client of mine. Do you know she hit something with my truck and never fessed up? She claimed it was already damaged when I gave it to her." She shook her head. "Then I found out it's not even their house—it's in his parent's name. They tried to list it." She dropped her voice and let her glasses fall down her nose. "They aren't married, you know?"

"Seems like all he does is roll cigarettes and chop wood," I said. "Does he work?"

Ellen shrugged. "I feel sorry for that poor child. She has no sense of reality, and they homeschool her, so God only knows what she learns from her mother. Did you know Astral charges people to listen to her banging on bowls with a drumstick? Every time I walk through the park, she's there with her disciples, spread out on the lawn like Hari Krishna. She charges a fortune." Ellen pushed her glasses back up to her eyes and checked her phone.

"I'd imagine that house would be a tough sell with the walls of firewood out back."

"Firewood? I'm not sure what you mean," Ellen said.

"You haven't seen his fort of firewood?"

Ellen shook her head. "It wasn't there when I viewed the home. If I recall, the back was a patch of dry grass and weeds." She laughed a little and went back to her paperwork. "Must be a new hobby."

"I guess I'd better go see what they're up to downstairs," I said.

"You're husband's a doll. You sure you want to let him go?" She didn't look up from her phone. "At your age, there's a run on men with hair and jobs."

"Hair is overrated," I said.

I took the door to the basement, pretending the idea of someone snatching up my life when I left it didn't bother me.

◆◆◆

After the inspections, Jack and I walked a few short blocks down a steep hill mixed with apartment buildings and old Victorians to the Goose Hollow Inn.

"Oh my God, I have a house right by a place that makes veggie Reuben sandwiches," I squealed.

Jack didn't look up from his lunch.

"What's wrong?" I asked.

"I'm nervous about telling the kids their mother is moving to Portland," he snapped.

"Would you rather tell them the truth—that you've been fucking that English cunt?" I made a grossed-out face, but the Reuben was delicious, so I took a huge bite and chewed while my husband squirmed in his seat.

"It was a mistake," he growled.

"Tell me the truth. How many times have you been with other people since we married?" I peered straight into his eyes.

He looked down. "Don't go there, Lee."

His admission of guilt paralyzed me for a few seconds. When I could finally speak again, I said, "I go where I choose, Jack, as you know." He made me sick, but I didn't put the sandwich down. "I'm here now, for example."

"You go where you want, Lee. Maybe this is just the excuse you needed to go even further."

"Maybe." Damn, that sandwich was good. "Another good thing about Portland, besides its perfect summer and amazing people, is the amount of vegetarian food they offer. That must be hard when they all love bacon so much."

He didn't pretend everything was okay. I wished I could not feel for him, but he was so pathetic, and I loved him even when I didn't want to. He insisted on walking me downtown to the hotel. Diners chatted in packed rooms and spilled out onto the sidewalks, their joy almost offensive compared to our gloom.

Jack shoved me up against the wall when we got into the elevator. I feared he would try to kiss me in one last pathetic effort, but his face was hot and red, and he spoke between his teeth with a rage I'd never seen before. "Don't do this!"

I struggled to escape, but he held me until I pounded on his chest with my fist and cried. "You really fucked us, Jack. Why did you have to fuck us so badly?" I sobbed into his chest for the rest of the ride up.

We spoke to the kids from the hotel suite briefly later. It took two martinis to make the call. "Guess what Dad and I did today?" I faked chipper. "We bought a house in Portland!"

"We're moving?" Jack Jr. cried.

"No. Mom is starting a new project working with the homeless in Portland." I teared up, but Jack held it together. Eventually, they'd figure it out. I'd be the villain unless I told on their father, and I would never do.

Max asked if he could spend time in Portland when we weren't there.

"I'll be back and forth," I said. "You can spend next summer with me." I assured them their home would be in New Jersey until they both graduated college and then changed the subject.

"How are things going there?" I asked.

They told us about bedwetting kids and a boy who almost drowned. I told them to look for their care packages, and we hung up.

"That went better than expected," Jack said. Then he covered his face and cried. The only time I'd seen Jack cry was when his father died. I thought about a photo of my family, the boys in their funeral suites, looking like tiny versions of their father—the pillar about to crumble.

"They have no idea what's going on." The end of our family progressed, and it felt like someone stepped on my soul. "What am I doing?" I cried. "Did we lie to them?"

Jack held me until my sobs turned to exhaustion. "I'm so sorry," he whispered over and over.

Lonely and hurting, we comforted each other for the last time. Soon, the holding wasn't enough, and we clutched at something lost. Wrapped in the familiar and desperately sad, our union ended in a final act of love.

I pretended to be asleep in the morning when he whispered, "I'll never stop fighting for you," and slipped out of the bedroom.

We were free, and it felt like shit.

CHAPTER 25

◆◆◆

AFTER JACK LEFT, Portland felt like a one-night stand, but I didn't have time for regrets. Justin called with a rattled voice and begged me to come right away. I took a car to his condo and knocked on the door repeatedly.

"Use your key!" Justin yelled. A loud thump followed, with a crash soon after.

Inside the apartment, I found him sitting on top of Kelly, who lay on the couch, squirming and clenching to escape. Blood was smeared across her face and all over the sofa. Crimson hand prints clashed with the newly painted white walls. She kicked and squirmed underneath Justin, screaming through a throw pillow Justin held against her mouth.

"She's insane. I woke up to her sitting on me with a butcher knife in her hand," he yelled. His eyes were bugged with stress. "She thinks there's two of me, and she can tell us apart by our feet."

"Don't suffocate her," I said.

"The other one is in the mattress!" Kelly spoke with the voice of a centenarian smoker, face bright red from

"Are you hurt?" I asked.

"I'm not, but she is. The knife slipped out of her hand when she stabbed the bed; she won't let me look at it. Go look at my room," Justin said. "Go!"

I obeyed. It looked like an angel had been slaughtered. I walked through a flood of white feathers to see Justin's mattress torn apart and his days-old bedding destroyed. Scarlet drops spattered the bed and floor.

I ran back out and leaned over the furious woman. "Kelly, are you hurt?"

She spat, and I jumped back in time to get hit in the leg instead of the face. "Fuck you! Ring leader! Devil!" she yelled.

Justin muffled her scream again.

"I want to ask Justin to let you go. If he does, can you sit up? He's the only Justin here, and I know him. He's very nice."

She tried one last time to fight her way free before giving in with a dramatic collapse.

"I'm going to open the door, Kelly, so if you want to leave, you can." I opened the hall door and shouted, "See, you can go anytime." A woman froze in the hallway with her plastic garbage can in hand. I waved hello.

"Hide the knives," Justin shouted. "I'll hold her until then."

The neighbor retreated to her apartment. I heard the lock click.

"Calm down so we can let you go," I spoke in my elementary school volunteer voice, the one I used on my kid's hyper friends, and put the knives in a paper bag before throwing them atop the refrigerator.

I nodded to Justin, and he jumped off her as if she were a striking rattlesnake.

Kelly wiggled herself into a standing position and darted out the door. "Fuck you!" she yelled as she ran down the hall and out the doors.

Justin dusted bloody feathers from his shirt. "She's a demon." He touched the scratches on his face. "I'm going to take a shower."

I picked up the broken pieces of a large ceramic sea urchin and threw them in the garbage before stripping the sofa.

Justin took a very long shower. When he returned, the furniture was naked, and except for the occasional feather, all signs of violence were gone.

"Sorry about your room," I said. "I ordered new bedding."

"It's fine."

"I don't think so," I said.

Justin plopped himself down on the couch exactly as my kids did at home when upset, knocking it back several inches.

"That must have been scary," I said.

"You think? She tried to fucking kill me." His knee rattled. "I'm still shaking." He held out a trembling hand.

"You need a lock on your bedroom door," I said.

"I need to stay away from the meth heads." He leaned over and put his head in his hands for a few seconds. "They get psycho."

"Was Kelly psychotic when you met her?" I asked.

"A little. She told me about a large network of people after—they always think someone's after them."

"She thought there were two of you," I said.

"Yep. One in the mattress."

"Let's get brunch," I said.

"Nah. I gotta clean up all the blood on the bed."

"Done," I said. "Sleep on the Murphy bed until I pick some new stuff up later."

Justin grabbed the bag of knives from the top of the fridge with a single jump and sorted them into a drawer. "Next time, I put these away first."

"Next time? Maybe we should rethink our ideas about what's helpful," I said.

"I like the Genie in the Bottle model. Three wishes. Food, shower, sleep," he said. "Everyone needs those things."

"In Kelly's case, she probably needs antipsychotics, a shower, then sleep," I said. "I think you're right. We need Amy." I pulled out a check from my purse. "Look what Jack gave us—our first foundation donation. And guess what? If I make us legit, his company will match it.

He grabbed the check and held it to his face to be sure he hadn't imagined it. "Whoa! He must be seriously rich."

"Seriously guilty is more like it," I said. "It's my money too. I get half our money for bearing and keeping Jack's offspring alive. Also, I was his driver, manager, landscape designer, and decorator. And then there was the sex."

"Gross. Stop. I get your point," Justin covered his ears.

"Plus, I have my own money, and since it's an inheritance, I don't have to share it with him," I said. "We can hire Amy if we want."

"Amy will never work for you."

"True," I said. "We can hire an Amy-like person to help us."

My phone rang, and I answered. "Were your ears ringing? I was talking to Justin about you." I put the sound on the speaker.

"You didn't come home last night, whore," Amy said.

Justin yelled, "Ha!"

"Hi Justin," Amy sang from her side.

"Hello," Justin said.

"Get up," I said. "I'll tell you where I was if you have brunch with me."

"Give me an hour."

I hung up. "It's Sunday, Fun Day, Justin," I said. "Come have breakfast with us and shake off this thing with Kelly."

"You're afraid to tell Amy what happened without me there, aren't you?" he asked.

"Yes. I am. Amy's nicer to me when you're around." I bumped him with a shoulder. "Plus, she wants to talk to me about something. Please?"

◆◆◆

Justin almost fell asleep in his eggs, so I had his meal packed up and sent him home. Amy and I moved from a table to the bar at an Irish pub with beer-soaked floors in gritty downtown. We were on our second Bloody Mary when a group of twenty-somethings took the long table next to us. They wore last night's make-up and hadn't brushed their hair. I couldn't get my eye off of a tall, pony-tailed thing. His hair fell out in wisps, and his jeans were worn in all the right places. He saw me admire him and smiled. The girl beside him pawed at his T-shirt, letting me know he was hers. I wondered what he did to her last night and felt my blood rush.

"I completely missed my youth." I turned around to face Amy. "When my body was tight, I chased kids around the playground instead of fucking consumptive poets." I finished my drink in a long sip. "And I didn't get to show off my midriff. Do you see how flat that girl's stomach is?"

"You didn't miss much." Amy turned around to see what I found so fascinating. "I don't like a guy's butt to be smaller than mine."

"You're going to be single forever, then." I laughed and quickly leaned away so she couldn't hit me.

"Bitch." She slurped her glass and signaled to the bartender for another round.

Before he headed out the front door, I watched the pretty boy bum a cigarette from his pink-haired girl.

"I'm going to smoke." I held out a joint. "Join me?"

"No way," she said. "I'll fall asleep before the music starts."

"No sleeping today. Order me coffee, please." I tried not to limp on the way to the door. Once outside, I took a second to bask in the sunlight. When I opened my eyes, the pretty boy waved with a nod of his chin.

I lit my joint and said, "Hey," as I exhaled. "Want?" I held it out.

"Cool. Thanks." He took a deep drag and handed it back. "Smooth."

"I grew it myself." The lie spilled so quickly that I surprised myself.

"Nice." He took a deep hit.

"It's called Vah-Jay-Jay Kush." I passed the joint back with a straight face. "It's a blend of Vallecito Jasmine and Blue Jay Kush." I made all of it up right there.

"Right on." A laugh spilled out of his full red lips.

"What?" I looked him up and down with a slight smile. He wore work boots but hadn't bothered to lace them, and I imagined he smelled like wood and tar. He checked me out, too, and there was a quick moment when we thought the same thing. But last night's girl slinked out with her flat stomach and cotton candy hair, ruining my buzz. She puffed on my joint while I hobbled back inside.

I sat beside Amy and listened to the gruff bartender tell her a way-too-long story about his cat. I had to interrupt.

"Let's talk with British accents for the rest of the day, " I said, combining Australian and Tennessean accents.

Amy agreed, answering in the Queen's English.

"Blimey," I said in my best Eliza Doolittle. "You're too posh for me."

"You never want to get laid again, do you?" she asked.

"Not really," I said. "I need some time to get over the man I thought would be my partner for life."

Amy rolled her eyes. "How long do you think it will take for Jack to fuck someone else?"

"He's probably mile-highing a flight attendant right now." It felt better to be mad.

"Right, then," she said. "Too-ta-loo, Jack."

I took a breath of courage and changed the subject while she still felt bad for me. "Do you know a woman named Kelly? A tiny little thing? Thirty-eight and crazy as fuck?"

Amy's eyes went big. "Kelly Childers?"

"That's the one." I sipped my drink and watched the ponytail guy come back in with his pink shadow behind him. "That girl will never be able to give birth with those tiny hips."

"I like your Va-Jay-Jay," he shouted.

"Thanks, Lovey," I said in my best Cockney. "'Ope you enjoyed it." I turned quickly because the confusion on his face broke me. But the harder I tried to suppress it, the more the convulsive laughs came until the tears flowed—not a little—and I had to focus on breathing to speak again.

Amy handed me a package of tissues from her purse. "You're a mess today, Lee. Maybe alcohol isn't the best choice."

I took a moment to calm myself. When I could breathe again, I said, "Back to Kelly."

"Back to Kelly," Amy said. "She is indeed my patient, so I can't tell you anything about Kelly except that I do not recommend taking her on as your 'assistant.'" She made quotation marks with her fingers. "She's no Justin."

"Indeed, she is not," I said. "Justin let her sleep it off in the apartment, and she trashed the place."

"Oh no," she said.

"He found her in the park last night and felt bad for her." This wasn't the entire truth. I took a deep breath. "I told him to find someone. She wasn't what I expected."

"That's what your secret project has been?" she asked. "I thought you were going to make Justin your private investigator. Which isn't a bad idea, you know?"

"I wanted to help people," I said. "One person at a time."

"You are helping someone," she said. "Justin. Hasn't he been through enough? Let him go to college—or at least finish high school. Kelly Childers is a very sick person, and no Genie-in-a-bottle trick is going to help her."

"I think he picked her because of his mom. It breaks my heart," I said. "He wanted to save her."

Amy shook her head. "She needs long-term hospitalization. But every time she's feeling better, she checks herself out."

"She needs a guardian," I said. "Where are her parents?"

"Tired of trying to save her," she said. "Addicted children are soul-crushing. Many say goodbye rather than watch their children destroy themselves."

I shook my head. "I'd never....."

"Don't judge, Lee. Not on this," Amy said. "Watching an addict repeatedly dive headfirst into death is unbearable for loved ones. Many have to look away to survive."

On the way out, I asked Amy what she wanted to talk to me about, but she said, "Let's save it for another time."

❖❖❖

Justin didn't answer when I knocked, so I used my key to get in with the new bedding and mattress cover. I found him curled up in the fetal position on the stripped Murphy bed. I covered him with the new comforter and began another round of cleaning his room, sucking up stray feathers with the vacuum while wondering how many neighbors heard the excitement. I hoped the police wouldn't show up when they found a bloody, babbling Kelly on the street.

When Justin woke up, his room was back to normal except for a new pillow top to cover Kelly's slash marks on the mattress. He wasn't impressed by the quick turnover. He'd fallen into a low I hadn't seen before. "At least your double can get out of the mattress if he wants," I said.

"There are holes for him."

My joke fell flat. The kid could barely hold his head on his shoulders as he picked at leftovers I'd reheated for him. "Dude. I'm worried about you. Why don't you stay at the suite for a few days until I close on the house?"

"I like being here," he said. "It's starting to feel like home. You know how many times we had to move growing up?"

I busied myself in the kitchen, not sure what to say. Justin poked at his food while I sat with him. "I'm sorry about Kelly. We are going to have to rethink things."

"I need to get a job," he said. "And pay you rent."

"Jack and I agreed, no rent until you're out of school, training, or whatever. Until you're employed full-time," I said. "Get a part-time job, keep busy, and have money in your pocket. Or maybe you could volunteer with Amy and work for me. I will need help with the new house—especially the gardens."

He shook his head, struggling to talk. Tears flowed silently down his face and landed in his Eggs Benedict. Every bit of the mother in me wanted to hold him, but I also knew it wasn't what he wanted, so I dusted furniture until he wiped his face and invited me to walk to the market with him for milk.

CHAPTER 26

◆◆◆

SANDY WAVED LIKE an old friend as I limped through the lobby. The distance between the curb and the elevator felt like a mile—the elevator to my room, like two. The weekend tourists were gone, and the sixteenth floor felt abandoned.

Once in the suite, I lit a joint on the balcony, put my foot up, and called Erik.

"What are you doing?" he asked.

"Looking out over the river and wondering which house is yours," I said. "What are you doing?"

"Wondering where you're resting your head tonight and hoping you haven't gotten yourself into any more trouble."

"Romantic," I said. "At least you're thinking about me, I guess."

"You know what else I'm doing?" he asked. "Pouring over the phone records of a dead man so I can find his killer before he finds you again."

"That is romantic," I said. "Do you have Charlotte's phone records, too? Who did Amos call last?"

"I'm not going to tell you," Erik said. "You'll assume it's the killer and confront them. And no, I don't have Charlotte Wilson's phone records because I'd need probable cause for a warrant, and you're the only person who believes she was murdered."

"You believe me," I said.

"I believe you've poked at a rattlesnake den."

"The question is which snake did it. Come over here so we can figure it out. I'd feel much safer."

He laughed. "If you're saying that because you think you'll get information from me, you're wasting your time."

"It could be fun to try." I surprised myself.

He laughed, then sighed. "What are you trying to do to me, Lee?"

My body lit up thinking about the answer.

I heard his breath through the phone, slow and controlled.

"I'm going to limp down to the pool for a swim. Do you want to join me? They keep it heated to eighty-two, and I usually have the place to myself the last hour it's open."

"I have to finish some work that will take at least an hour. How about a nightcap later?"

"Room sixteen hundred. I'll see you in an hour and fifteen?"

"Perfect," he said.

My marriage existed as one long rolling hill of familiarity. Erik and I felt like uncontained wildfire—the heat was almost unbearable.

The hallways were quiet. Gone were the mother yelling from behind room sixteen-twelve, the young couples wearing over-curated vacation clothes, and the stacks of dirty dishes after room service. Lust and guilt clouded my mind.

The pool required a key to swipe through the doors. The day before, a five-year-old followed me around and spurted pool water from his mouth like a human water filter, so I was thrilled to find the pool empty.

City lights spread across the river through the windows and faded into the valley. I inhaled the view before setting a canister of pepper spray, phone, and room key down on the edge of the pool deck, covering them with my towel so they wouldn't get wet. A security camera hovered over the pool, and I wondered if anyone was watching. When I took the stairs into the water, Guster played on shuffle from my phone. With each step in, my pain lightened. I swam my problems off until I was too tired to lift myself up the ladder. I laid back and floated, thinking of the ceiling beams, the sound of the water, the feeling of my hair fanning like tentacles. I don't know how long I lay there, weightless, before a presence caused me to sit up.

A man in a trench coat, little round sunglasses, and a fedora had entered the pool room. At first, I smiled, thinking he might be a guest checking out the pool—but his unflinching, sinister expression told me otherwise. I understood completely when he grabbed the long pole with the net from the wall and walked it toward me. I swam toward my towel.

He followed.

I swam faster and underwater.

He followed casually with a stiff grin.

I retreated to the center, where he couldn't reach me, and I couldn't touch the bottom.

"What the fuck do you want?" I yelled. "They're watching you." I pointed to the camera, waving my arms and imagining some idiot waving back from a desk.

He didn't move.

"Sunglasses and a trench coat? A bit cliché." I tried not to sound out of breath while bobbing in the pool's center. My body stiffened from the threat, making it harder to float. It was ten minutes past closing time—maybe security would ask us to leave before I drowned. "You look like the Nazi in Indiana Jones," I shouted. But having to tread water made me weak. After a few long breaths, I began to relax, and once again, I could float to rest.

He sat down to wait. The smugness infuriated me. I drifted slowly toward the ladder. He watched from the chair, confident he'd be seconds behind if he wished.

"When I get out, I'm going to fuck you up," I said. His body convulsed from a silent chuckle. He knew security wasn't coming, leaving me with no out. Finally, he stood up and rapped the pole on the concrete pool decking hard enough to cause an echo through the room.

I swam underwater as fast as possible and shot diagonally across the pool. He had two sides to walk and miscalculated, assuming I'd aim for the ladder. Instead, I grabbed the towel, scattering my phone and the spray cartridge. He kicked the phone across the room while I jumped at the canister of pepper spray.

He raised the pole, net up, to strike hard, and I hit him in the mouth and nose with a steady stream of burn. As he shrieked, I shot toward the bottom of the pool, but he brought down the pole, grazing my head and landing on my shoulder.

I gripped my canister, praying there was enough left for a second assault, but when I came up on the other side of the pool—gasping for air and swaying from exhaustion—he was gone. I crawled up the steps, my ankle throbbing, and collapsed face down on the deck.

Erik and a security guard stood over me when I opened my eyes. I heard one of them shout, "Call an ambulance!"

"No!" I rolled over and breathed before sitting, checking my suit, and coming to a stand. "I'm fine." I held my shaking hands together.

"Is it too late for room service? I'm starving."

❖❖❖

Erik propped me on the sofa, poured me a bourbon, and iced my throbbing ankle. I took a large sip to calm the internal rattle of adrenaline. A bruise formed on my shoulder and grew its own pulse.

"At least it only grazed my head. The guy was so creepy. His face never moved. And he hid his voice—such a silent maniac."

Erik gently traced the red lump on my shoulder.

"Who is he?" I asked. "Does he work here? Is he staying here?"

"I don't know, but I'll find out," Erik said.

I believed him but wanted to find the guy first.

Room service arrived with a knock. He let them in and then watched me down a bowl of pasta, a salad, and a chocolate mousse.

"Astral borrowed Ellen's Monster and returned it with a broken headlight the same day of the accident," I said. "Charlotte Wilson was the love of Henry's life, and she was supposed to move across the street from Astral and her family. Can you imagine how our little hippie felt about that?" I asked. "That's motive right there."

"Can you see how there's a slight chain of custody problem with that evidence?" he asked.

"It's a start. Do you want to hear about how Henry broke into Amy's basement? Or how Charlotte's dad found the two of them fucking? Or what he did afterward?"

He took a sip of his drink before leaning in close. His breath was a warm winter fire. "I love it when you talk suspects to me," he whispered. "But someone just tried to kill you, so how about giving it a rest?"

"Henry is a suspect. I knew it."

He sat up and sighed.

"What about Ellen?" I asked. "Have you eliminated her? Because she could be lying about the truck—using Astral as a scapegoat. Astral told me a different story than Ellen, never mentioning car damage. And I still think Ellen did something shady to get that listing in Maplewood—the buyer thinks she willed it herself, the poor thing. Ellen isn't easily ruffled. She kind of scares me. Half of her clients are dead."

"Mostly from old age," he said.

"Charlotte Wilson was only twenty-three when she died," I said. "How old is Lawrence?"

"Nice try. We can't talk about Lawrence. Is that all of your suspects?" he asked. "You're forgetting someone."

"You're trying to distract me. He's got to be in his late thirties. What did you find out from him today?" I asked.

"I found out Wilson is a mess from losing his wife on top of his leg, which has many pieces of hardware in it," he said.

We didn't know each other well, but I understood he wanted me to leave it alone.

"What about Amos's son? But that wouldn't have anything to do with Charlotte. Unless. No. He's got a motive. Inheritance. Only child."

"His dad's estate is small change for him. And, as you said, there is no connection to the Wilsons. Plus, Patenaude has a solid alibi. He was in New York at the time of the fire." He sighed. "Are you going to make me say it?"

"Say what?" I asked.

"For a super sleuth, you sure do let personal feelings get in the way," he said.

Super Sleuth. I liked the title, but not where he went with the conversation. "If you're talking about who I think you are, stop now."

"She has a motive," Erik said.

"Amy? Whoever killed Amos is most likely trying to kill me. They probably think he told me Charlotte's last words. Amy would kill me herself if she wanted me dead, and she would never hire a bear in his third trimester to do it for her. Plus, I was with her the night Amos died."

"You don't know that the two are related," he said. "You're sure the guy who followed you tonight was the same?"

"Yes. I could tell by how the freak squealed when I sprayed him," I said. "Only it didn't look like him…I can't put my finger on it. His face was so creepy and still. He must have shaved—or maybe a mask. But it wasn't a mask."

"I'm just glad you weren't hurt." Eric took my hand and slowly kissed each fingertip, never taking his eyes off mine. Everything felt better. He worked his way up my arm, kissing the area around my welted shoulder.

I managed to say, "He should grow the beard back," before leaning forward for a long, slow kiss—the kind that starts a night's worth of fires.

Someone knocked on the suite door. I was content to ignore them, but Erik pulled back, sighed deeply, and said, "I want to get this guy before he hurts you."

"You'd better find him before I do." Whomever the guy was, he wouldn't have a third go at me. Amy supplied me with an arsenal of pocket-sized weapons on a ribbon necklace after the last attack. First, I'd spray—the guy hates spray. Next, I'd follow with the kitty-eared brass knuckles to poke his eyes out. A metal spike had slots for better finger grip, and I'd punch him. I wasn't sure how to use the whistle and alarm simultaneously, but I made a mental note to practice outside the next day.

"You scare me," Erik said.

"You know that phrase, fool me once, shame on you, fool me twice, shame on me? It's my new mantra. A gift from my husband." I smiled, but it faded when I thought of my family.

He touched my cheek, stroking downward, tracing my jawline until he reached my neck. I took a deep breath, so ready to dive into him. Someone knocked on the door again. Erik stood up. I grumbled and followed him to the door. Sandy and the security guy from the pool stood in the hall.

"How are you feeling, Lee? Is your hand okay?" Sandy never called me by my first name, so the concern was genuine.

"We haven't officially met. Tom Walters." The security guard reached his hand out to Erik.

"Any news?" Erik asked.

"We've learned someone stole a guest's wallet outside the hotel today. He focused on alerting the credit card companies and used his partner's card to get into the room instead of asking for a new key."

"This is Lee Harding." Erik waited for the guard to acknowledge me, then motioned for them to come in. Tom delivered a limp handshake.

"Did the cameras catch him leaving the building?" I asked.

"We found a trench coat on the patio that we think is his." The guard never looked me in the eye, addressing Erik instead. "I bagged and tagged it for you."

"A figure in a hoodie exited the garage shortly after you and I arrived at the pool," he said. "We think it was the perp."

I tried not to roll my eyes. Tom had a man crush, and who could blame him? Erik was as cool as an iceberg—calm and able to sink big ships.

"I'm so sorry. Please know there will be a full review of pool security, and we've changed the code to your room." Sandy handed me two new passkeys.

"We have eyes on the sixteenth floor." Tom pointed to his eyes and then to me.

"Great." Just what I needed—security smelling weed from outside my door.

CHAPTER 27

◆◆◆

THE HOTEL PHONE rang, startling me awake. I found myself on the sofa, leaning against Erik in a way that made my neck stiff.

"Good morning," he said.

Daylight crept through the curtains. I did a quick drool check. "I fell asleep?" I moaned, disappointed in myself. My hand traveled across his warm chest, waking his hands, too. The hotel phone continued to blast. We ignored it. My cell lit up and buzzed alternately.

"Somebody wants to talk to you," Erik said.

I groaned and chose the hotel phone first. "What?"

"Ms. Harding?" said a man. "This is security. Sorry to wake you, but there's a guest here to see you. Justin Hendrix. Can he come up?"

"Of course," I said. "Don't screen my guests, please."

"I'm just following orders, mam."

My cell phone stopped ringing. "Justin will be here in a minute." I groaned. "He's going to think we had sex."

Eric laughed. "Do you want me to hide or something?"

"No." I leaned into his chest and took a deep breath of him.

He put his hands in my hair and held on like I was precious. "I'm going to pick that coat up from downstairs and see if I can figure out what the hell is going on."

I sat up, missing his body instantly. "Dinner tonight?" he asked.

"A date?" I smiled. "Yes, please."

He kissed me gently before walking down the hall. "I don't suppose you'd consider staying in your room today?" He didn't wait for an answer before opening the door, where he and Justin greeted each other before he left.

Justin wore a huge grin when he saw me. "Two overnight guests in two days, Ms. Harding," he said. "I didn't think you had it in you."

"Do you notice I'm fully clothed?" I asked. "In sweats, at that."

"Whatever you need to tell yourself. I don't judge."

"Be nice to me. I almost got murdered last night," I said.

Justin's jaw dropped. "Really? Is that why I had to pass a security clearance to get here?"

I told him the story after we ordered room service.

"Did you bring your swimsuit?" I asked.

"No, man, I'm not up for it today." He dropped onto the sofa with a heavy thud.

"Are you going to a funeral?" I asked.

He looked down at his black shirt and jeans. "Fits my mood."

I ran into the room and came back in a black dress. "I bought this for fall, but I'll wear it today in solidarity." I twirled.

"You bought a dress for fall? You do realize it rains here from November to July. Or it used to—maybe December through May now."

"That's what raincoats and boots are for," I said. "Want to see my new boots?"

"Not really," Justin said. "That's pretty ballsy of that guy to come into the hotel like that."

I reminded myself to look for some additional friends once I settled in. I'd already missed NY Fashion Week and had to believe there was more to Portland than forest wear.

"Maybe you can sit with me while I swim today?" I asked. "I hate to admit it, but the freak shook me."

"Sure." He could barely shrug.

"You good?" I asked.

"Tired," he said. "Low."

I sat next to him. "Feel like talking about it?"

He looked as if he could drip off the couch. After a long breath, he said, "Seeing Kelly like that brought stuff back. Memories. I miss my mom, you know?" He struggled with his last words, but with a long inhale came anger. "Why did she have to be so fucked up?"

"We're all fucked up, Justin. It's just a matter of luck and magnitude."

◆◆◆

City Harm Reduction sat on a corner near a sad little Chinatown that was absent of Chinese people—a vacant-faced man lumbered by with a bulging shopping cart. The door was locked, and no one sat in reception. I rang a bell until a young woman in a Queen t-shirt, jeans, and high-tops ran down a staircase to answer.

"Do you have an appointment?" A petite woman who barely looked out of college yelled through the glass door.

"We're here to see Amy," I said.

"She's with a client, and you'll need an appointment." She spoke through the locked doors.

"I'm a friend, not a client," I said. "She's expecting us. I'll text her."

I sent a quick message to let Amy know we'd arrived. Seconds later, she came down the same stairs—a young mother and baby following closely behind. Amy handed her a bag of groceries on the way out.

"Sorry, Mara, this is my friend from San Francisco, Lee Harding. And her godson, Justin Hendrix."

"Mara Martinez." She held her hand out and gave mine a solid shake.

"Mara is our nurse practitioner." Amy took a head-to-toe look at me, then Justin. "What's with the clothes? You guys going to a funeral?"

"Solidarity," I said.

Amy shrugged.

"I know Justin," Mara said. "Hey, Dude. You look good."

"Thanks, Man. I have an apartment now." He stuffed his hands deep into his pockets.

"That's awesome. Should I take you off the waitlist?" Mara asked.

"Yes," Amy, Justin, and I spoke simultaneously.

"So you're short-staffed?" I asked. "Justin happens to need a job."

"Can you pass a drug test?" Mara asked.

"Sure." He spoke without hesitation. "I'm going to Portland Community College part-time in the fall, though, and I'd have to work around my schedule."

"Justin, that is wonderful news," Mara said. "We can work around school. What do you think, Amy?"

"I am a fan of Justin, so yes, please." Amy smiled and patted Justin on the back. "It's minimum wage."

"That's cool."

"You can work your way up to outreach. I think you'd be great on the street," Mara said.

"Sure," he shrugged.

"Come back tomorrow at eight am, okay, and we'll get things going." She gave him a fist bump before jotting up the stairs.

"Did I just get a job?" Justin asked. It had been Amy's idea, and she'd said that if Mara was okay with a former client working there, she'd be willing to hire him.

I bumped his shoulder and squealed, "Yes! Eight a.m. tomorrow, dude."

We walked to Kell's, an ancient pub with a giant fireplace and lonely stage. Amy listened to my story about the pool.

"It was the bearded guy from the park, but without the beard. He tried to drown me in exhaustion. That's the second time I sprayed that fucker." I held up two fingers.

Amy grabbed them. "Lee. Damn, it." She swatted my hand. "You're going to get yourself killed. Can't you stay out of trouble for five fucking minutes?"

"We must be getting close if someone wants to kill me," I said. "But who?"

"It's that bitch, Ellen," Amy said. "I never should have bought a house from her when I knew her moral compass had cracks. I'm selfish, and I just wanted a house."

"How is this your fault?" I laughed. "I used Ellen too—for selfish reasons. I don't think she'd have me killed before Friday."

"What's Friday?"

"Closing day on the new place." I laughed. "I don't see her missing a commission check. She and Jack are the only ones who know where it is, so if someone comes for me there, we know it's one of them."

"Jack." Amy laughed for a second but stopped. "Do you think?"

"No." After thinking about how much money it would save him, I said, "Maybe."

"No way," Justin chimed. "Jack still thinks he's going to win you back."

"What makes you think that?" I asked.

"He told me."

"Whatever," I said. "Oh, and you and Amy know where the house is. That makes four."

"Four suspects?" Amy asked. "Now we're suspects too, Justin."

Justin shrugged and said, "I got no motive," before taking a bite of his burger.

"Well, let's hope your uptight knight in shining armor gets the bad guy first," Amy said.

Justin laughed. "That guy is so uptight."

I rolled my eyes. "Erik won't tell me anything about his interview with Lawrence Wilson. I will crack that iceberg," I said. My mind drifted to last night—of ways to melt him—and I lit up like a furnace.

"Hello," Amy said. "Where did you go?"
"I was thinking about Lawrence Wilson."
Justin eyed my red face and said, "Right." He turned to Amy. "Erik slept over last night."
Amy gave me owl eyes.
I squinted at Justin. "What did I say about the big mouth?"
"I did meet the elusive one yesterday, though. That's where I got this." I held up my wrapped ankle. "Wilson is a mystery. You can't find anything but digital interviews with him; no photos are anywhere. I saw him, though. I met him."
"But did you?" Justin asked. "He is a special effects guy. How do you know it's not him stalking you?"
"Can we talk about something else besides the Wilsons? Please?" Amy asked.
The waiter came to take our order.
"Want a mimosa?" I asked.
"Do I want to go to work at the clinic after a drink?" Amy asked.
"No, I guess I don't either," I said. "It'll just make me need a nap, which I will take anyway. When Mara said Justin had to pass a drug test, did that include weed?"
"Yes. Because of people like you." Amy said.
"Very funny," I said. "What about alcohol? Do they test?"
She didn't let me finish before chiming, "No."
"No breathalyzer at work?" I couldn't stop myself.
"No," she smiled with gritted teeth. "I don't own the place. I work there." She changed the subject. "How are you holding up? Have you heard from Jack?"
"He's been sending me old photos all day," I said. "He doesn't realize they are reminders that I haven't been happy in a long time. The man is clueless."

I showed her a photo of Jack, the boys, and myself in boats on Lake Montego. Jack sat in his sprint racer, and I in my solo canoe. The kids were rowdy puppies, still sharing a two-seat scupper. Jack left us right after the photo was taken. I spent my day fishing the boys out of the middle of the lake each time they'd "accidentally" tip outside the swim zones to cool off.

"Jack is a kayak, and I am a canoe," I said. "It's always been a problem. It's why Jack shared his dick with that whore in England. I've never been racy enough. I bore him."

Amy laughed. "There are a lot of words I could use to describe you, Pal. Boring isn't one of them. You do walk too slow, though."

"You walk too fast."

"No, really," she said. The waiter arrived with more water.

I waited for Amy to stuff a bite of hummus and pita into her mouth before saying, "Erik implied you were a suspect last night."

She stopped chewing and mumbled, "I'm listening."

"Well, he claims your motive is the house; you wanted it so badly you killed for it."

Amy turned scarlet. She swallowed her food and dropped her wrap on her plate. "This is why I asked you to leave it."

Justin dropped his burger to watch.

"What are you talking about?" I asked.

Amy put her elbows on the table and rested her head in her hands. "Why couldn't you leave it alone? Now I'm a fucking suspect? I could lose my job."

"Only if you did it, Amy."

I was joking, but she didn't find it funny and made an excuse about a meeting before a quick exit.

CHAPTER 28

◆◆◆

FIR-COVERED HILLS and winding roads replaced the gridded streets of downtown on our way to the Maplewood neighborhood. Justin handed me a listing sheet for the house on the corner of Glen and Forest that Ellen and her client had discussed in the cafe the day I'd overheard them. The trip through Amy's neighborhood felt familiar, and the conversation I'd overheard in that cafe seemed a million years ago.

"Are we going to talk about the Amy thing? Or do you want to pretend it didn't happen?" Justin asked.

For the first time, I wondered if Amy would forgive me. Portland felt too small for exes.

"Pretend," I said. "I don't know what she's hiding, but I know she didn't kill anyone. The best way to help Amy is to prove who killed Charlotte."

"I'm down," Justin said.

The driver left us a block away from the residence, and we stopped on the corner to regroup.

"According to the tax records, the homeowner's name is Eloise Hanson," I said. "Who can blame her for thinking she has special powers? Eloise pointed to her dream house, and the next thing she knew, the man who owned it died. It's more than coincidental, don't you think?"

"Craig Buckwood would probably think so. He's the dead former owner. What are we going to do?" Justin asked.

"We're going to knock on the door," I said. "Remember, 'I'd kill for this place.' That's the line."

"As in die for it?" Justin rolled his eyes.

"Don't say die. Say, kill. Just like she told Ellen in the cafe," I said. "Got it?

"I don't know," he said. "Feels like a weird thing coming from me."

"Just trust me," I said. "But wait until she's about to shut the door on us before you say it, okay? It's insurance."

We passed an eclectic assortment of shingled cottages and stopped in front of a garden lush with roses, columbine, and iris. Ivy covered the chimney of the Tudor-style home and climbed its way around the windows. The front door had a rounded top with a tiny window for a peephole.

"Not a fan of the pink," Justin said.

"Forget the trim color. Look at the roofline. It's like gnomes live here."

"Or witches."

"I think they prefer Wiccans." I knocked.

Behind the door, a sweet falsetto sang, "Who is it?" Eloise Hansen opened her entry wearing a dress with a large floral skirt and sang, "Hello."

"Hi..." I feigned confusion. "I'm looking for Cousin Buck." I leaned back to examine the doorway. "I may have the wrong house. It's been a long time."

"We don't have any Bucks here, sorry." She squinted while remembering something. "Do you mean Mr. Buckwood?"

"Yes. Craig Buckwood. Sorry." I placed my hand on my chest. "We call him Cousin Buck. I'm Lola, and this is my son, Tiger."

Justin grumbled.

"Where is Cousin Buck?" An exaggerated look of concern spread across my lying face.

"Well, honey, I don't know any other way to say this except that he's moved on." Sincerity pooled in her big, round eyes. She took my hand. "As in passed through."

We stared blankly.

"Crossed the rainbow bridge," she added.

"Oh," I cried. "No one told us." I thought only pets crossed that bridge, but I didn't say so.

"That's terrible," she said. "From what I hear, his daughter Sheila had a big get-together before she left."

"We moved to Winnemucca ten years ago, so I wouldn't have expected her to invite me," I said. "Where did Sheila go? I haven't heard a thing from her."

Before she could answer, Justin spoke. "I'd kill for a house like this," he said, not even pretending to believe it.

Haunted by hearing her own dreaded words spoken back to her, Eloise waved her hand as if fanning herself would cure the shock. "What did you... Oh, please don't say that," she whispered.

"I didn't know Buck was sick." I tried to get her back on track. "Was it sudden?"

"It was very sudden, from what I know." She didn't take her eyes off Justin, stepping back into the doorway, her bright smile sagging a bit. "Are you looking for a house? Because I'm probably moving," she said.

"No, thank you. I just bought in Goose Hollow." A genuine smile spread across my face at the thought of it.

"Oh, good for you. I guess you can come home again." She wrung her hands nervously as if they needed washing.

"Let's go," Justin said.

"Tiger, don't be rude." I gave him my best evil eye, then smiled at Eloise. "You don't have Sheila's address, do you?"

"I can call her right now," Eloise hummed. She pulled her phone from a skirt pocket, eager to help.

"Oh, I am not ready to have 'that' conversation right now," I said. "I've been terribly out of touch. Please, let me send a condolence card first?"

◆◆◆

Sheila Buckwood's modern townhouse sat atop a grassy hill on a bend along the Willamette River. Picture windows faced the water where rows of small boats occupied slips on the docks. I adjusted the skirt of my dress and stood straight before knocking on the door of unit number nine. The transom looked straight through the living room to the river.

"Sheila has very different taste than her father," I said.

"What are you going to say?" Justin asked.

"I'm going to ask her if she killed her dad, of course."

Justin tilted his head while he stared, probably trying to figure out if I was insane. "Don't call me Tiger."

I knocked again.

"Hold your god damned horses," a woman grumbled behind the door. She frowned through the glass—scanning us up and down—before saying, "Get out of here. I'm an atheist."

I took great offense. "Do I look like a missionary in this dress?"

The plunging neckline convinced her to open the door. It was happy hour, and Sheila wore a cat sweatshirt and flannel pajama bottoms. "Sorry. I get a lot of weirdoes," she said.

Her smoker's voice intimidated me, and I had no idea what to say next.

"Well?" she asked.

"This is going to sound weird, okay? But bear with me. We are Wiccans. Do you know what that is?"

"I knew it." She tried to close the door, but I stuck my foot inside.

"I'm not trying to convert you, Sheila. I have a message to deliver, that's all."

She lightened up on the door before my toes turned purple. "A message from who?"

"Craig. Dad, as he calls himself," I said.

She squinted at me like my cranky freshman math teacher. "Who the hell are you? Some kind of charlatan?"

"I'm Esmeralda, and this is Edward. I'm a Licensed Wiccan Medium."

Her face turned scarlet.

"He forgives you," I repeated. "But he wishes you hadn't done it. He says it's destroying you." I leaned in. "He wants you to turn yourself in."

She muttered, "Move your foot or lose your toes," before slamming the door.

When we were far enough away, Justin growled in a tone familiar to me from motherhood.

"Edward?" he asked. "I'll pick the name next time. And tell me, how does this relate to Charlotte and Amos?"

"Who is the common denominator?" I asked.

"Ellen? How is she tied to Amos Tapenade?"

"Amos Patenaude lived on five acres of buildable land. How much will you bet Ellen sells it before it hits the market?"

"You think she burned a man alive to sell his house? She'd be more likely to run him over or bake him poison cookies?"

"You're right," I said. "She doesn't seem like the arson type. Too messy. But I can see her using minions to do her dirty work. I'll bet she convinced Sheila Buckman there was no other way?"

"Your kind of reaching," he said. "Are you going to tell Erik about Amy?"

"I have no idea what you are talking about," I said.

"Gotcha," he said.

❖❖❖

Erik canceled our date after I told him Sheila Buckman had killed her father. I tried not to beg, but I couldn't help it. I'd already shaved my legs and picked out a new dress for our night. "Come on, Erik. She hasn't even confessed yet. And you have no proof it was me."

Every second of his silence felt like an hour. He sighed a long, sad sigh. "Why did you tell me?"

"Because I don't like secrets," I said. "Plus, I thought you might want to know the woman is a murderer."

"Did she confess?"

"It was in her face." I knew it wasn't enough. "She didn't deny it. That's why I told her to confess to the police."

"What are you going to do if she commits suicide instead?"

I hadn't thought of that until later. "Justin said the same thing. I didn't plan it," I said. "I went with my instinct. There was something on Ellen's face that day in the cafe. She knew. I am telling you, she knew."

"Okay, tomorrow I'll arrest her because a witness saw something in her face."

"You're mad at me."

"I am," he said.

"I'm sorry I screwed up our first date," I said.

"Me too." He spoke gently and said goodnight.

Amy wouldn't speak to me either. My sleuthing inflamed her more than usual. Maybe she felt free of her past in Portland—my permanent residence could open up a time capsule of bad memories. Or perhaps she didn't want to live on the side of a wooded open space with a stalker *I'd* attracted.

Eloise phoned Ellen to report the strange visit. Ellen phoned me six times. When I didn't answer, she called Jack and told him I was walking around Portland pretending to be a witch. She recommended a local hospital for me. He used this as an excuse to text and call. I couldn't make Justin babysit me forever, so I didn't get my evening swim.

There wasn't enough weed left in Portland to get me high enough. I didn't own a cat sweatshirt but would have worn one that night. Instead, I sported a tank dress and wrapped myself in a sweater. I fell asleep shortly after episode one of Magnum PI began, the bowl from my long-gone ice cream still on my lap. I moved to the big empty bed in the middle of the night.

In two days, I'd close on my first solo house. I wondered if my agent could fire me before then and if I'd have any friends left to visit once I moved in.

CHAPTER 29

◆◆◆

DISCOVERING THE MURDER of Craig Buckwood didn't make me any friends. There was no way to prove Sheila Buckwood guilty because she'd thrown her father's ashes over the deck of the Spirit of Portland the same day she received them. The thought of forcing a confession from a murderer thrilled me. On the other hand, not seeing Erik during a lengthy trial would finish us before we started. He'd move on, probably with his little schoolteacher, and we'd miss our chance again.

I finished the first and second seasons of Magnum P.I. from bed, surrounded by room service trays. Everyone was always mad at Magnum, but he still got the hot girl at the show's end, which made me feel better.

"Can you fly that broomstick of yours home for the weekend?" Jack texted. "The boys come back Saturday."

"You know I close on the house tomorrow," I texted. "I haven't had time to order furniture. You're going to have to handle it alone."

"Nice," he responded.

"Remember how I picked the kids up from camp without you while you were on a business trip with Andrew last year? London? You were fucking her while I drove the four hours to camp alone. So, fuck you," I texted.

"You prefer it that way, Lee. Admit it," he said. "You don't have to listen to financial news or The Who. You can open the windows and drive the slow lane."

As accurate as it was, it still angered me. "All of the excuses to the kids and myself about how hard you worked. But in the end, you were just fucking around on us." I hung up and cried for a few minutes out of frustration more than sadness.

"I'm sorry," I texted Erik. "Bad improvisation. Honestly."

Silence. Cold silence.

"I'm heading to the park. I want to see what's in that shed," I texted, hoping he'd meet me.

By happy hour, restlessness took over. Heat settled into the valley, and the warm air mixed with wildfire season tinted the air pink. I touched the window, and the glass was hot. Warm days meant white cotton dresses. I slipped on my favorite eyelet shift and tied my sneakers before walking to Pearl Hardware to buy a pair of bolt cutters. My foot still hurt, but it was getting better. Jack lit up my phone, threatening the battery life, so I turned it off.

The bus to Amy's wound through the lifeless college campus and over the precarious bridges of Barbur Boulevard that clung to the edge of Portland's soft, verdant hills. Before arriving on the wooded streets near Amy's house, we turned into the Hillsdale neighborhood, passing a food cart pod on a high school lawn, three breweries, and a community garden.

The gravel road to Amy's was dusty, and the air was still from the heat. Somehow, I felt guilty going into those woods without a connection to Amy, but I couldn't stay away from the secret of it.

I walked by Astral and Henry's empty yard, passing Amy's cottage to reach the trailhead, where a few steps down the trail, the shade of the tree canopy cooled the air, and the world came alive again. Birds scattered about in the underbrush and screeched from above.

A squirrel chased another across the path. Tiny gnats glittered in the sun rays dappling the fern beds. Crossing the log to follow the deer path felt like a precious secret—an excellent place to walk the dog off-leash or smoke weed as a teen. My shoulder drooped from the weight of the bolt cutters. "Hoo, hoo, hoo-hoo. Hoo, hoo, hoo-hoo." My Barred owl call had resulted in a return greeting once before, but not this time. I smoked a joint and enjoyed the anonymity of the forest floor. Even in the shade, the warm air lingered—everything moved slower that day.

I paused at the stag carving, ignored the bullet ridden "No Trespassing" sign, and finally arrived in the meadow. The shed sat between a scraggly apple orchid and a collection of shaggy, cone-shaped cedars that dappled the edges of the field like a cartoon Christmas scene.

The worn path to the door proved someone still came to the little building. I snipped the lock off with less force than I expected and slipped the tool back into my shoulder bag. The door swung inward, and I got a giant whiff of mildew. My taser doubled as a flashlight. I stepped into the shack and moved the light around. Two chairs joined a small table next to a tub of clean dishes.

A large store of water sat nearby in a camping jug. A more feminine version of the stag—more organic, with twisted vines and flowers—hung on plywood over a saggy, made-up bed. On the bed lay a complete set of antlers—still attached to a piece of skull.

I lifted them toward the light by the door, startled at first by what I saw. The eye sockets were made of natural bone, as was the snout. Moss and vine dripped from the horn, creating a forest horror version of a stag. Scarlet paint dripped from both eyes and streamed down braided twine in natural drips.

"Admirable," said a voice from the doorway. "It certainly fooled me."

A man blocked the light in the doorway, and I jumped two feet in the air and let an involuntary shout escape my lungs before I recognized the voice.

"Lawrence?" I touched my chest to see if my heart was still inside. "What are you doing here?"

"You're like a drug-sniffing dog," He growled, stepping inside. His delicate features gave him a youthful look, and his dark, intense eyes flowed with rage. I realized how few people had seen him, and a shiver crawled up my neck.

"Thank you," I said. "I wondered what you really looked like. Handsome. No wonder Charlotte didn't mind the age gap."

The compliment didn't move him.

"How did you two meet?" I asked.

He chuckled, and I thought he'd say something snarky, but he just stared at the stag. I didn't know whether to push past him or try to calm the rage in his eyes.

"She was a waitress in Studio City. She could have been a model, but she hated the camera. It took three years for her to say yes to a date. She said no to agents, actors, and photographers. Her aunt was deeply religious, so we snuck off like kids in the night two months after we met. She would have done anything to escape that house. So, she married me."

"Where's your cane?" I held onto the flashlight but had set my bag down on the bed and couldn't reach it.

"Turns out I never really needed it," he said.

"I don't like that you're in the doorway," I said. "Please move away."

"Shut up." He rattled like a bomb. "Just shut up for a minute."

"Lawrence, you're scaring me."

"It was him all along," he screamed. His spittle sprayed in the light around his head from the doorway.

"You're scaring me, Lawrence," I said. "Just let me out, please." I leaned toward the bed to get my purse.

"Don't move! I'm done taking your shit," he yelled. "Spray me again, and I'll shoot you in the face." He clicked something I couldn't see but assumed was a gun, then swiped at my bag, tossing it out of reach.

"What do you mean it was him?" I switched the light off on my Taser and lowered my hands.

"HENRY. That obsessed little fucking child. He got to me. I let him get us."

"What are you talking about?" I asked.

"Henry did this to me!" He paused to wipe his face with his shirt sleeve. "He did this to me. He ruined everything. Henry," he sobbed.

"Please, Lawrence." I used my calmest voice—the one I used on my dogs when they ate something dangerous. "Be an adult and put the gun down. I want to know what happened to Charlotte, too. Let's figure this out."

"I've barely left my home in six months," he said. "He gaslit me the entire time."

"How, Lawrence? What did he do? Please, tell me." I whispered. "I want to help."

"None of this would have happened if she hadn't insisted on that fucking house of horrors. She never had a happy day there." His voice toggled with emotion before ramping up in anger again. "Why the hell did she insist we buy that damn house?"

I gripped the taser like the last chance it was.

"I will kill him. Do you hear me?" he yelled.

All I could think about was protecting Pearl.

"Henry is a real douche nozzle, Lawrence. I completely agree," I said.

"He's a fucking mama's boy who lives in his mommy's house," Lawrence said, his face streaming with tears.

"Why do you think he dresses like a Civil War veteran? So curated," I said.

"Charlotte told me about this place," he looked around in horror. "This shit shack he stuck her in."

I turned my flashlight on and looked around. "But why would he kill her? Or Amos Patenaude?"

"That!" he screamed, pointing at the stag horns. "The mask!" He lowered his face. "Oh my god. I'm so stupid. I'm so stupid. I killed her."

I thought he might lower his gun (to wipe his nose, at least), but he'd stopped caring. Then, suddenly, he was done. He wiped his face with his arm and laughed. "I can't believe I fell for it."

He couldn't leave. All I could think of was Pearl, and I knew he'd go straight to Henry. I had to keep him talking. "But why Amos? Why would Henry do that?" I asked. "Let the police find out why. Please, Lawrence."

He lowered his voice to a mad growl. "I killed Amos." He poked himself in the chest several times, frantic. "I killed him." He started to cry again. "I didn't mean to, but he wouldn't tell me what Charlotte said," he whispered. "He would not tell me, no matter how I begged. No matter what I did. And then he fucking died. Can you believe that? He fucking died on me."

I gripped the flashlight, wanting so badly to lunge at him, but the gun stared right at me. "Poor Amos," I cried. "What could he possibly know worth dying for?" The tears would not stop.

"I was heading to the crash site when I spotted you. I got close enough to hear you and Amos talking. I had to know what Charlotte told him. Don't you see?"

"It's my fault?" I cried. "I got him killed?"

He disappeared in his thoughts for a second and, in a low whisper, said, "All he had to do was tell me."

Part of me wanted to sink into the floor crying, but I thought of Pearl and what she would see if he left the ravine. *Keep him talking*, I told myself. "Did you carve the stag in the tree?"

"No!" he yelled. "It had to be Henry, that obsessed piece of shit. He can't even leave her alone when she's dead. Now he's going to tell me what I want to know."

"I don't know that anyone ever really knew Charlotte. Henry doesn't have the answers you're looking for. Henry compared Charlotte to an orphaned fawn, and Amos said she had sad eyes as a child. At least you got her to yourself while she was an adult. Charlotte wasn't happy a day here."

He shook his head, his face wrinkled with pain. "You don't understand," he cried. "I couldn't make her happy either. Why do you think we came back?"

"Did it work?" I asked. "Was she happy?"

He couldn't speak, so he shook his head.

"Poor Charlotte." Sometimes, sadness hung over me like a heavy, wet blanket. I understood the challenge of finding happiness. "Why follow me, though?"

"I wanted to ask what you knew," he growled. "But you sprayed me in the fucking face."

"Good intentions don't require a disguise, Lawrence. You'd already killed once by then."

He looked down at his feet, maybe in a moment of shame.

"My friend Justin thinks you're a genius. He's going to be so bummed when he finds out about this."

"What do I care?" he said. "I am finished giving a fuck." His body slumped with grief and resignation.

"Amos, me, Henry. That's three," I said. "I can see the headlines now, 'Psychotic Special Effects Guy Goes on Killing Spree.' I'm guessing they'll cancel the show. Three makes you a serial killer."

"He did this on purpose," he said. "You see that, right?"

I nodded in agreement. "I can get Henry to confess," I said. "Let me help you."

I may have reached him, but a call came from outside the cabin.

"Mr. Wilson, step outside, please."

I heard myself sigh before Lawrence turned around to face the meadow. He lifted the gun to his mouth and pulled the trigger. Through rays of sunlight, skull and brain matter flew from the back of his head like an exploding universe, whipping me in the face in a shower of horror.

His body collapsed into a corpse. The blast made my ears ring, and for a few seconds, everything vibrated. Sunlight filled the room in his absence. Blood coated my eyelashes and dripped from my brow, burning my eyes and blurring my vision. I couldn't move to wipe them.

I must have looked like Carrie standing in my white, blood-soaked dress. I heard Erik yell my name, and he was there, stepping around the shell of Lawrence Wilson and scooping me up and over the dead man. I remember the heat as we left the shack, the beating sun, and the overwhelming cold.

I dripped in crimson. A chunk of brain matter sat on the toe of my sneakers. Pieces of Lawrence dotted my lips, my dress stuck to like paste, and I trembled uncontrollably.

Erik set me down under the shade of a cedar tree. "I'm going to get some water, okay?"

I nodded, trembling. He returned with Henry's water jug and a blanket. Shivers overtook me.

"You're in shock." Erik helped me pull my dress over my head.

"Get it off me," I cried.

He held the water jug while I cleaned my hair, face, and arms. My feet were still stained in blood when the water ran out. He wrapped me in the blanket and held me tight, repeating, "I'm so sorry. This is my fault." He didn't let me go until I needed him to.

I barely remember walking up the hill or hosing myself off in Amy's yard. The police and ambulance arrived. A stream of first responders marched down the trail. I imagined them flattening the deer path and violating the quiet of the meadow where Lawrence Wilson lay alone.

Henry and Pearl came outside to see what had happened, as did the rest of the neighborhood. Pearl tugged on her dad when she spotted me, but he ignored her, distracted by the frantic scene. She shrugged and left the yard alone, running halfway across the road before he noticed.

"Pearl," he yelled. It was too late. She'd already reached me with a tiny head full of questions and a genuine look of concern.

"Are you hurt?" she asked.

I sat on the fender of the ambulance, my feet hanging out the door. "I'm okay, honey."

"Pearl!" Henry shouted again.

She ignored him. "Where are your clothes?" she asked.

My favorite white dress lay in the meadow, covered in blood. I never wanted to see it again. I mustered up a smile, unsure of what to say.

"What happened to you?" She took my cold hand with her little fingers, and for a moment, I felt better.

"I'm okay." I forced a smile. "There was an accident, but I'm okay."

"Is someone dead, like Charlotte?" she asked.

"How do you know about Charlotte, Pearl?" I asked.

Her father stood at the gate like a curse prevented his crossing, the street full of cops his River Hades. "Pearl!" he shouted again.

"Your dad is calling, honey. Look." I pointed at Henry.

She ignored him.

"Did you know Charlotte, Pearl?" I asked.

"Pearl!" Henry growled.

The words were inside her tiny body—I watched them rise. But her father called again, ferociously this time.

She shook her head of dark curls. "I'm not supposed to tell." She ran tiptoed across the street and through the gate to her father, where she took his hand. They walked to the front door together. Henry looked back at me, sending anger from across the street.

"I know what you did," I whispered. But I didn't know because Lawrence killed himself before he could explain.

He pulled Pearl into the house just as Amy ran up the road, past the cops who tried to stop her, until she found me. She called me a fucking idiot several times between gripping hugs while she walked me inside.

CHAPTER 30

◆◆◆

AMY HATED SWIMMING, but she went to the pool with me anyway. We brought a bottle of Perrier Jouët and drank it between laps and chats. Even after the world's longest shower, I felt the DNA of Lawrence Wilson embedded in my skin. I rubbed my forearms and scrubbed the memory of the thick, sticky splatters.

"I can't imagine how awful that must feel, honey." Amy hadn't called me that since the first time my husband cheated on me. Later, after the champagne and exhaustion kicked in, I lost it a little bit. "I want to go home." I sobbed. "I miss my kids and my bed, and I want my closet back. I miss my life."

Amy watched me from her lounge chair. "You miss Jack?"

"No." I cried harder. Home was a warm kitchen floor on a sunny winter morning or summer parties in the garden, but rarely my husband. "Jack leaves the house at six-thirty in the morning, and he goes to the gym after work and usually gets home at nine or ten during the week—unless he's out with the new hire or dining with the London team—then it's even later," I said. "On the weekends, he wakes up and goes to the gym for three hours. I showed you his texts with the married whore, right?"

Amy's face contorted. "God, no. But why do you sound angrier with her than him?"

I pondered the question on the walk back to the room. "I hate them equally," I said. "What kind of person betrays their partner

like that? Get a fucking divorce if you're unhappy. Jesus, she's practically a newlywed."
Soon, I was drunk as well as angry. I smoked on the patio, relieving the anger, but not the drunk. Erik showed up in off-duty jeans and a black T-shirt. "You're yummy," I said when I saw him.
"I'm going home." Amy had been looking for an excuse, and it walked right in.
"Please don't go back there," I said.
"I want to sleep in my bed." She'd already gathered her bag and walked toward the hall.
"Tomorrow is another day, my friend. See you in Goose Hollow. Don't worry about Ellen. She won't say a word to you while I'm there."
"What about Henry?" I asked.
"You think that fucker will mess with me?" she asked.
"I don't know, Amy. That's the thing." I took her hand. "Please stay."
"I know you know what it's like to want your own bed," she said.
"Call me when you get home," I yelled as the door shut.
"You're afraid of Ellen?" Erik couldn't stop smiling. "The woman wouldn't hit five-three if she wore stilts."
"She's bribing her clients to commit murder," I said. "She's the maestro." It felt like an exaggeration, but I wasn't sure.
Erik smiled. "You okay?"
"I'm keeping myself medicated." I poured him a glass of champagne, filling it to the top. "How are you holding up?"
"Not on my list of favorite days," he said. "Plus, I hate paperwork. They want to talk to you tomorrow."
I nodded my drunken head. "I don't want to talk about it."
He leaned back on the counter. "Fine with me."
"You look amazing in those jeans," I said.

He smiled and took a sip of his champagne. "I feel like I have some catching up to do."

"Three years of catching up," I said.

"I mean the alcohol. You sure you're okay?"

I leaned against the counter, feeling sexy in a tank top and tiered skirt, and wished him toward me.

He didn't come.

"Are you not going to fuck me because I'm drunk?" I asked.

"Because I'm not that drunk. There are a lot of bubbles in these bottles. More bubbles than booze."

He took a deep breath. "Trust me. There's nothing I want more."

"But?" I jumped up on the counter as I'd always told my kids not to and willed him toward me again.

He lowered his glass and stepped between my legs, pulling me close enough to feel him rock hard under his jeans. "But, when I fuck you, I want you to be sober so you remember it."

"I'm not that drunk," I said.

He laughed. "We'll have to agree to disagree on that."

I wrapped my arms and legs around him and made it as impossible as I could before he broke away.

"Are you hungry? I'll order in," he said, taking two steps away from me to pull out his phone.

"I've never been so hungry in my life." I smiled. "For food, I mean." I poured myself another drink.

We ordered enough sushi for six people and sat on the patio after eating. The streets below us were alive with night walkers and bar hoppers, and we watched silently. I tried to quiet the day, but it crept back in clips and streams. "I know I asked that we don't talk about Lawrence, but I can't help it."

"It's your rule, so go ahead," he said.

"He said, 'He gaslit me,' after he saw the mask. That thing set him off."

"Do you think he meant Henry?"

"He meant Henry," I said. "But how do we prove it?"

"That is the problem."

"Maybe Henry scared them off the road somehow. With the stag," I said. "Somehow played on Lawrence's fragile mental state,"

"Are you excited about tomorrow?" This was his polite way of letting me know he'd give up nothing on Lawrence, even now that he was dead.

"I'm a little nervous Ellen will hit me in the temple with one of her Christian Louboutins," I said. "I'd bet that tiny demon could stand on one shoe and kill someone with the other. You should see her climb into Monster."

He smiled for the briefest moment. "Who's Monster?"

"That's what Ellen named her gigantic SUV," I said. "If she were a man, I would wonder if she had an issue with her maleness. Wait, is she a woman with masculinity issues?" I confused myself and let it go. "Imagine someone trying to break all records for speed behind the wheel of a tank and while wearing three-thousand-dollar shoes," I said. "She may not even be able to see over the dashboard. Her driving makes a lot of sense if that's the case."

Erik laughed. "Is that the car you think bumped the Wilson car?"

"No. I don't believe that anymore."

He turned toward me. "Why not?"

"I just don't," I said. "Are you interrogating me? You are. You're watching my eyes while I answer. You don't even know you're doing it, Detective."

"Are you going to share what you know?" he asked.

"Are you?" I asked. "Tell me something, and I'll tell you something."

He thought for a moment. "Okay. There was rear damage to a rear taillight on the Wilson car—evidence it had recently been hit."

"Lawrence said he killed Charlotte. It's like he just realized it when he saw that stag mask," I said. "If someone bumped him off the road, wouldn't he have said?"

"Maybe they were fighting, and he crashed on purpose," he said.

"He was definitely unstable enough to do something like that, but on the way to their new house." I wondered. "It doesn't make sense.

"Alright, let's talk about something else." I leaned into him, but he disappeared, staring out the window into the night.

"Were you a serious baby?" I asked.

"Cranky, from what my mother says."

"You still have a mother. How nice."

"She's a good one—very Catholic, but the good kind—social justice and all that. You'd like her," he said. "Poor Mom. She had a kid every year for six years."

"Why stop there? Why not seven?" I asked.

"I've never asked," he said.

The poor woman's uterus probably fell out, I thought. "Do you have a father?"

He laughed. "I have a father. He's a retired cop turned commercial fisherman."

"Cool," I said. "Beats sitting around." My eyes felt heavy, but I fought it. "Are you going to leave if I fall asleep?" I whispered.

"I'll stay but must leave early to feed the girls."

"The girls?" I asked.

"My chickens," he said.

I lifted my heavy head. "You have chickens?

"Yes."

I laughed. "I'm sorry. I would have thought you'd be a large dog guy."

"They came with my house. Have you ever eaten fresh eggs?" he asked. "They're so much better than store-bought."

"That's so Portland," I said. "I don't know anyone in Forest Glen who raises chickens. It's probably illegal, like multi-family zoning."

I snuggled back into him.

"What's your favorite album of all time?" he asked.

"That's impossible. It depends on the year."

"Best album made while you were alive," he asked.

"Rumors," I said. "I love anything Fleetwood Mac."

"Good one."

"Yours?" I prayed he wouldn't say anything by The Who.

"Harvest Moon," he said. "Neil Young is a god."

I raised my head from his chest. "Thank you for not saying Rush. Thank you."

"I like Rush," he said.

"Oh, don't ruin it." I settled back down into his chest. "Next question. How old were you when you lost your virginity?"

"Sixteen. High school sweetheart."

"What was her name?" I asked.

"Stephanie," he said. "She went to Mercy, and I went to Saint Ignatius."

"A Mercy girl." I knew the all-girls school well. "What happened to her?"

"She dumped me for Eddie Cox. They have a small tribe now."

"What a fool!" I said.

"I probably deserved it," he said. "I was a dick. Who was your first?" he asked.

"I don't remember his name. Ivan or Alexi or something—a visiting Russian ballerina."

"Of course he was," Erik said.

"I was seventeen, at a frat party in Berkeley. You should have seen him on the dance floor."

"Is it weird that I'm jealous?" He traced my face with his finger until I purred.

"I remember the dancing more than anything if that helps." It became harder to speak as I fought to stay awake.

His laugh was the last thing I remembered before passing out.

CHAPTER 31

◆◆◆

I WOKE UP with the sun and thoughts of Lawrence Wilson's brains on my lips. My head hurt like someone jackhammered my temples. Whatever kind of magic had protected me from grief the night before abandoned me. I slinked off Erik's warm chest to start the coffeemaker and smoke a bowl.

Erik came out, fully dressed. I put the bong on the floor under the table. He smiled, handing me a cup of coffee.

"It's just soon for you to see my dirty bong," I said.

"The only thing I see is that black number you're wearing."

I smiled and untied my robe, letting it slip off one shoulder.

"You're killing me," he moaned. "But if I don't feed Gladys, she'll take it out on Ida."

"It's good that you have to go. I need to get my act together. You're a distraction. I haven't even ordered furniture yet."

The thought of sleeping in an empty house made me sad. "Amy said she'd bring an air mattress." I covered up because it was cold, and what was the point?

"Locked out," he sighed.

"Go before your chickens eat each other."

He asked if he could come by the Goose Hollow house to get a read on Ellen. We agreed to meet there at eleven-thirty. Amy took the morning off to see the house.

I chugged water, showered, and slipped a baby blue dress on. It might have been too cheery for Portland, but the fluffy, tiered skirt brought me feminine joy despite my throbbing head. It had been weeks since Lawrence started stalking me, and I couldn't shake the feeling that someone still watched.

When I arrived at the house, I found Ellen had parked Monster in the driveway and a small moving van blocking the entrance.

"That's my new home," I told the driver. The house rose to three stories above the garage. Whoever built it liked symmetry. Big windows balanced the front in neat rows, and the trim was Edwardian—intricate without too much frill.

Inside, Ellen stood on a stool, about to hang an abstract picture over the fireplace. A thick white carpet lay on the wood floors, and a small velvet sofa sat on top. A trendy coffee and side table were already in place.

"A little more to the left," Amy said.

Ellen struck a thumbtack with a hammer and balanced the unframed canvas.

"What's going on?" I asked.

The tiny broker stepped down, shook her hammer, and left the room without acknowledging me.

"She rented some furniture for you as a surprise closing gift," Amy whispered. "For two months."

"That is nice," I said.

Amy looked me up and down and shook her head. "I hate you for being so tall," she said. "If I wore that dress, I'd look like my grandmother's crocheted toilet paper cover."

"Thank you?" I frowned.

"You don't look glowy or anything—kind of the opposite. How did it go last night?" she asked.

"Thanks again," I said. "But you're right. I feel like roadkill. And the detective said I was too drunk to fuck last night. Not in those words, but...."

Amy laughed hard. Once recovered, she said, "I must admit his decision impresses me. You were fat-tongued when I left, and that can't lead to anything good."

"And I opened another bottle. Thank God, it was only half empty this morning because I added martinis."

Amy pointed toward the kitchen. "She's furious about the witch thing. You'd better talk to her."

"I thought you were here to protect me?" I asked.

Amy shrugged. "I heard her side."

I rolled my eyes.

Ellen busied herself reorganizing a toolbox in the kitchen. The sound of footsteps came from above. "They're setting up beds," she said without looking up. "Jack ordered you mattresses."

"Wow," I said. "That was nice. Thank you for all of this. I thought I'd have to stay in the hotel for two more weeks."

"Are you going to tell me why you and your little protégée terrorized my clients?" she asked.

"Getting right to the point. I like that," I said. "You knew Sheila killed her father. Why didn't you report her to the police?"

Ellen looked up, her voice cracking with indignity. "I knew what?" She paused to collect herself. "I suspected, okay? That's not knowing."

"I have suspected since I sat next to you and Eloise in the café. You knew. I knew you knew," I said. "The way you cleaned your glasses so meticulously—it gave you away."

"Well, you're just a regular Columbo, aren't you?" she said.

"Columbo?" I asked. "Would Columbo wear this dress?"

"Listen, I sell sixty houses a year. Do you know how many of those people are completely nuts? Sheila isn't even close to the worst of them."

"Answer the question, Lee. Do you know how many of my clients are completely insane? If they weren't nuts before they bought real estate, they become so during the process—including you. You fell over a goddamned wall, for god's sake."

She looked around for Amy, and we both noticed Erik had walked in. Without blinking, she said, "You know what I love about real estate? Every day is unique." She wasn't finished with me yet. "You knocked on my client's doors and could have given Eloise a heart attack. The woman is fragile."

"You should have told her what happened, so she knew it wasn't some kind of dark magic," I said.

She raised her manicured finger and aimed it my way. "You have violated my client's privacy, and I am certain you committed fraud. You're no Wiccan."

"You're right, Ellen. I'm sorry. I should have just asked you what it was about."

She leaned back, indignant. "I would have said it's none of your business. I have a fiduciary responsibility to keep confidentiality for my clients."

"That responsibility does not include covering up for murderers," Erik said.

Ellen turned around. "Sorry. I don't think we've met."

"I'm Erik Healy, a detective with the Portland Police Bureau."

Ellen looked him up and down over the top of her glasses, raised her eyebrows, and turned to me. "I see."

I blushed. The woman saw right through me.

"Look, I don't like talking about my client's business. I'm their priest and psychiatrist during the transaction. I learned about their marital issues and financial matters. I know it all. After we close, they may decide I've seen too much and never speak to me again. Maybe I knew embarrassing secrets like their kid punched holes in the walls, or maybe they were divorcing or murdered a parent. I'm successful because I don't talk about any of it." The whole thing seemed to exhaust her. She sat down at the table, resigned. "I did suspect Sheila from the start, though."

"Why?" Erik asked.

"I knocked on the door that day after Eloise and I drove by to follow up."

Amy and I looked at each other and rolled our eyes.

"I'd known Buck for years. He was a cranky alcoholic who would never leave that house, even if it did leak in a dozen spots."

No one moved, afraid she'd stop talking.

"Well, Buck told me to stuff it, so I left. Halfway down the drive, Sheila ran out and gave me her email contact, saying Buck was sorry and wanted me to see what he could get for the place. I sent her a market analysis, and a week later, he was dead."

She turned to Erik. "It did occur to me that it was rather convenient, but what was I supposed to do?" Ellen shrugged. "She'd had him cremated."

"That worked out well for you," I said.

Ellen stared at me for way too long. "Do you think I encouraged her?" she asked.

She scared me a little, but I spoke up anyway. "I think you suspected Sheila murdered her father and sold her a condo anyway."

Ellen rolled her eyes. "If I only sold to people I approved of, I'd do very little business." She tossed a folder on the table. "Here's a plan for the kitchen. A friend of mine drew it up for you."

I opened the glossy folder and glanced at the plans, shocked she could get so much done in a week and annoyed she wouldn't let the kitchen thing go. "Thank you, Ellen."

She rose from the table and smoothed her skirt. "Is my interrogation over?"

"I'm only here to see the house," Erik said. "But it is an interesting story."

"Are you going to pursue Sheila?" Ellen asked.

Erik shrugged. "It's not my case."

She was halfway out the door when I shouted, "Lawrence Wilson killed himself yesterday."

"The husband? How sad." But then she chuckled. "I guess that's my fault, too?"

Erik interjected, "If you know anything about the Wilson car accident, I ask you not to discuss it here. We can meet at the station, or I could come to you. It's an ongoing investigation."

Ellen turned around, looking genuinely surprised. "Why would I know anything about a car accident?"

Until then, Amy had leaned against the door jam, politely looking at her phone and trying to appear invisible. Now, she watched closely.

"We're still calling it an accident, but some new details have come up about events leading up to the crash, so we'll be looking into it further." He handed her his card. "If you can think of anything significant, ring me?"

Ellen studied the card and then locked eyes with Amy.

"I have some information that might clear things up."

I jumped out of my chair and shouted, "He just said not to talk about it."

"I just want it out there," Amy said.

I tried to shove her out of the room, but she pushed back. "Stop it."

"Want what out there?" Ellen asked. But she knew. I could tell by her smirk.

"Erik, just go." I lunged toward Amy. "I'll show you the house later."

Amy pushed back harder this time. "Knock it off, Lee."

Erik wasn't sure what to do. "What's going on?"

"I hit the Wilsons! I hit their car with Monster," Amy shouted. "But I didn't kill Charlotte, I swear."

◆◆◆

The four of us sat down at my kitchen table. Amy leaned on her elbows and held her head in her hands.

"Start from the beginning," Erik said.

"The first time I saw Charlotte, she was chatting with Pearl over the fence." Amy took a deep breath. "Do you remember, Ellen? It was before the Open House."

Ellen shrugged.

"You don't forget a woman like her. I mean, she had legs like a giraffe and perfect olive skin. Later, I bumped into her on the landing, and she apologized like it was her fault. I don't remember Lawrence at all."

"Ellen convinced me to sell my condo before I bought anything and loaned me Monster to move furniture into a storage unit before we listed. It was the morning of the Wilson home inspection, and they were parked a few units down from mine, unloading some boxes. I heard them talking about the inspection. Lawrence was concerned about the deck, and Charlotte assured him it would be fine.

"I shook with anger—another fucking couple beat me out of a house. Do you know how many couples I'd lost to?" Amy didn't wait for an answer. "And she got my dream house.

"They were inside their unit, so I crept Monster forward to get a look at them and ran right into the back corner taillight." She winced and broke into a cry. "And I drove off."

She reached out to Ellen. "I thought Monster was fine, I swear. And when I returned the car to you, I was late. Do you remember? You had someone else waiting for it. It didn't occur that I'd hurt Monster until later that evening. But when you called, it was to tell me about the accident, and all I could think about was Charlotte."

Ellen cut the silence that followed. "I was sure the hippies did it."

Erik shook his head. "It seems coincidental that you were both at the same storage unit."

"Not really," Ellen said. "Most of us send our clients there because the first month is free."

"Am I going to be charged?" Amy asked. "I looked it up. It's a misdemeanor. Plus, they died. What if it was my fault?"

He chuckled. "I'm a homicide detective, Amy. And as far as I know, no one is serving time for breaking a taillight that was never reported as broken. But coming forward with this information might have helped the case if I'd known it earlier."

Amy's face relaxed, and I heard her take a deep breath.

"Who had the car next?"

"Either Astral or Henry," Ellen said. "They were still planning on moving then."

Lawrence Wilson's words seeped into my thoughts, and I whispered, "*He gaslit me.*"

"Who gaslit you?" Amy asked.

"When did Astral and Henry decide not to move?" I asked.

Ellen thought back for a moment. "The day after the accident." She left after that, leaving a note on the fridge to call for furniture pickup—a clear message not to contact her again.

When Amy left the house, she hugged me instead of punching me and returned to work. Erik and I were alone in a strange house with strange furniture, and we were strangers, too. Nothing in my life felt familiar.

"If Ellen were a dog, she'd be a miniature pincher," I said.

"I need to get into the station. So do you," Erik said.

"I know. Can I bum a ride?"

"Sure," he said.

"Are you mad I didn't tell you about Amy?" I asked on the way there.

He took his time answering. "I understand keeping secrets for your friends. But what about keeping secrets from them?"

"Mates before dates, dude. But honestly, I didn't know. I just suspected something was off with her." The short, silent drive felt like an hour. "If I were a better friend, she would have told me, but it's been all about my problems."

Erik must have agreed because he didn't say a word. "I'll get out at the hotel and walk over," I said.

"You don't have to," he said.

But I insisted.

CHAPTER 32

◆◆◆

JUSTIN SAT AT the rented dining table just off of the kitchen. A Vietnamese feast spread out before us in take-out containers. I didn't have silverware yet, so we used the bamboo sporks included with the delivery.

"I don't get it," he said. "You completely furnished my condo before I moved in, and you don't even own a water glass here?"

I held up an Ellen Robinson Real Estate mug. "Cheers!"

He raised his. "Cheers."

"They've been useful." I'd already used the mugs for coffee, wine, and beer, each time silently thanking Ellen. She'd been a great agent for a murder maestro.

"Where are you sleeping tonight?" he asked.

"The hotel." For reasons I hadn't figured out, I couldn't bring myself to purchase things as simple as bath towels or pillows.

"Why don't you bring some stuff from the condo here?"

"I've brought toilet paper from the hotel, and now I have leftovers. What more could a girl need?" I smiled and began clearing the mess from my rented table.

"Maybe you should hire Whatshername to do it. The one who helped you with my apartment?"

My brain hummed since the shooting. The idea of putting the house together felt like climbing Mount Everest without oxygen, but Justin didn't need another adult to worry about, so I perked up. "I'll get to it," I said. "Let's walk up the hill and take the stairs into the park."

"If you don't want to talk about it, I understand, but where do things stand with Henry?" Justin asked.

"Henry the wood-chopping, gaslighter?" I asked. "Henry, the fucking poser? Henry, who is afraid to leave his gate? Henry, who knows what happened but lawyered up?"

"Right on, Lee. Let it out." Justin laughed. "That Henry."

"He's arguing squatter's rights on the blood-drenched shed. It's city property, but he's been in it continuously for ten years. He wanted to press charges against me for trespassing. Can you believe it? He's ruined the Henley shirt for me forever."

"What's with the stag cult? Why were those two so into antlers?" he asked.

I could barely breathe from walking the steep trail at Justin's teenage pace, but I managed to shrug. *Stag Cult.* My mind began to wander.

"Maybe he's hung like a buck," Justin said.

I rolled my eyes, wondering why men always seemed to return to their seed spreader. Justin talked endlessly about his first days on the job. His excitement, plus the narrow, winding trails, broke the hard edges from troubles.

We bumped shoulders in front of my house to say goodbye. "I'm so glad you came over," I said. "Lawrence Wilson's brains haven't flashed across my mind in hours. Want to spend the night when I get the beds made up? Maybe I'll have a slumber party before I leave."

He dug his hands into his pockets. "How long are you going to be gone?"

"The plan is to drive across the country with Jack Jr. in August, drop him at college, and bring his car here. I'll fly back and forth and do school holidays and summers in Portland. You'll see lots of me."

He rocked on the sidewalk, staring at his shoes.

"I'm coming back," I said. "And you and the boys will be great friends."

"Do you think?" he asked. "What did you tell them about me?" Sometimes, I could feel Justin's pain. He was the most alone person I knew. "I told them they'd love my new friend who works with Amy and could show them around Portland. The condo situation is none of their business." He sighed.

"Everything is going so well. You're doing great," I said. "Can I hug you?"

Tears filled his eyes, and he shook his head instead of speaking. I held him tight, letting him decide when to let go. He caught his breath and pulled away. "It's cool." He gave me a brave smile and walked toward his home.

❖❖❖

My to-do list stretched a mile long, but my focus was nearly zero. I wandered streets, spending the most time at a shop full of handmade items for the more masculine-minded, leaving empty-handed because my favorite things were living wall sculptures, and I wouldn't be home to water them.

I found an artisan carpet shop and a handmade furniture store in the Pearl District. It felt delightful to put two new carpets on the credit card, knowing it would trigger Jack, I called him.

"What's wrong?" he asked.

"I'm fine. Everything is fine."

"Have you moved out of the hotel yet?"

"No," I said.

"Lee," he sighed. "You're eating into our kid's futures."

"What?" I yelled. "My kids can build their futures."

"Why are you keeping the room? You already have two houses there."

"I like the view," I said. But my breathless last word gave me away, and he was keen for an opening.

"Honey, you hate sleeping alone." He sighed. "I've learned my lesson, I promise. What happened in Portland can stay there."

There were a thousand things he could have said to soften me while I was emotionally skinless. Instead, he infuriated me further. "I only called to let you know I've been purchasing some basics for the new house. Just in case you get an alert on the credit card." I hung up and let the tears fall from behind my sunglasses.

All I could pick out were white towels and sheets after that. He'd killed my decor muse. My plan for the rest of the day included cocktails, season three of Magnum, and an early bedtime. I wandered into a bar and watched a guy with a handlebar mustache make a complicated drink behind a big round bar.

Erik texted, "Where are you?"

"Not that far from you," I typed back. "About to have a cocktail at the Teardrop Lounge."

"I'll be over in a few."

The bartender worked magic on my Manhattan, stirring it in a crystal shaker before pouring it into a glass. He pulled a dark black cherry from a jar and dropped it in a martini glass before placing it on the bar top. I felt my hair to ensure there weren't tangles and reapplied lip gloss, then thanked the closet gods I'd changed out of my hiking clothes and into a long black tank dress and sandals.

Erik came in as I finished my first drink and set a file folder before me. "You aren't going to believe this." He ordered a beer while I flipped through pages of a list with the same two phone numbers. "What am I looking at?" I asked. "Henry's calls to Charlotte?"

"No, Charlotte calls Henry. The earliest record was a year before the accident. Six months before her death, they began to communicate regularly.

"It looks like he didn't answer most of the later ones," Erik said.

"But here, look." I pointed to a short period where their calls were longer, and Henry had phoned back. "Maybe they had a brief affair or something? Reunited?"

Erik pointed to the date, three months before her death, when the calls became one-sided. "Maybe Henry cut her off? He and Astral have a kid. They're family."

"I can't believe it. Astral told the truth," I said. "She accused Charlotte of being the obsessed one. Why?" I made a face because Henry freaked me out. "And why are you sharing this with me when you're always so…"

"Professional?" he asked. "Because you were right about two murders in one week. There's no evidence or motive, but we both know Henry had something to do with the Wilson accident."

An unconfined smile spread across my face. "Tell me I'm right again. I like it."

He smiled a little, then grabbed my barstool and pulled me closer to him until I fit between his legs. "I'm pretty sure you were right about the Wilsons," he whispered into my neck.

The bartender broke the spell by delivering water. I never got to hear how right I was about the Buckwoods.

"Why did Charlotte call Henry so many times? If she'd always loved him, why not return to him?" I asked. "Did you search Lawrence's house? Maybe he kept her hostage."

He raised an eyebrow. "Yes. Oddly, there were no signs of Charlotte and barely a sign of Lawrence. Everything was sterile. You were right about something else. Lawrence has a history of mental illness. He was fragile before the accident."

"Can you talk to his doctors? Have you searched his studio yet?" I asked.

Erik laughed. "No to both. Wilson's been off work since the accident, and no one is getting back to us from the hospitals in LA."

"My source tells me he showed up at the studio late at night," I said. "And we know he claims to have signed in the night Amos died."

Erik's phone buzzed before he could speak. He read a text and stood up. "I have to go," he said. "Body under the Hawthorne Bridge." He threw down too much cash before I could protest and left me with his half-full beer.

The rest of the afternoon was spent trying to understand Lawrence Wilson, the man, instead of the terrible, sick person before me in the shed. It always went back to Henry. If I could find out what Charlotte wanted from him, I could find out why she and Lawrence were dead.

CHAPTER 33

◆◆◆

ON THE TELEVISION show Darkened Forest, a group of traveling carnival workers were cursed for cheating the wrong witch's grandson. Banished to a place astonishingly similar to Forest Park, they fought to survive among other tribes of magical creatures.

Justin and I zipped through every episode to learn more about Lawrence Wilson's work. The campy show thrived on its rustic art direction and rich, green scenes of Portland. In the third season, a man with a face like a lizard wore a trench coat like the one found after Wilson tormented me at the pool.

"Is that what we were looking for?" Justin asked. "Because trench coats are a dime a dozen in a rainforest."

"We're looking for anything that tells me who he was. All that's left of him is his work."

In the first two and a half seasons, Lawrence lived in LA. His creations were beaver-faced warriors and whimsical talking trees. I liked *that,* Lawrence. Halfway through season three, the effects changed from charming to haunting.

"This is the first episode that doesn't suck," Justin said. "Maybe there's a new art director."

The Internet told me otherwise. "Lawrence changed when he got to Portland," I said, fast-forwarding past the cheesy dialog and slowing down whenever another ghostly creature dropped, bone-faced and blood-eyed, from the trees. Unlike the other mystic beings on the show, this one had no roots in the living.

"They look so much like the stag mask in the shed," I said. "But which came first? Astral said she made the lion mask for Pearl's birthday in March."

"Maybe Lawrence saw it in the store, and it inspired him," Justin said.

"I don't know." I paced the room. "We've got to get into that studio tonight."

"How are you going to do that?" Justin asked.

"There is no Y in team," I said.

"What?" he asked. "That makes no sense."

"Whatever," I said. "Let's go. Erik will get there before us otherwise. It was my idea."

"Now?" he asked. "How are we going to get in?"

"I know a guy who said it's a breeze." I crossed my arms and raised my eyebrows.

He got up. "Okay, okay," he said. "I got your back. It'll be easy."

"Get me in and leave, okay?" I asked. "I'm not afraid of being arrested, and it's not like the police will shoot a middle-aged white woman."

"They rarely arrest females," he said. "You wouldn't believe what girls get away with on the streets."

"Let's hope that's true tonight."

❖❖❖

Portland sidewalk life thrives in the summer. We walked past blocks of crowded streets full of diners, moviegoers, and hipsters drinking it up in the endless row of bars and restaurants lining the Northwest neighborhoods. The blocks became dimmer after passing bright marques, and soon, warehouses replaced restaurants. Darkened Forest's sets were inside a block-long warehouse under the creeping hills of Forest Park.

We walked around the building once, surveying for cameras. Justin climbed a brick flower box, then a tree, until he connected to the fire escape and climbed onto the roof. Several moments later, he opened the door to the lobby and let me in.

"Thank you. Now go." I tried to push him out the door, but he dug his heels into the floor.

"No way. You think I'm leaving before I explore every inch of this place?" he whispered.

The Sasquatch over the desk watched my every move. I didn't want to be alone. "Don't break, touch, or steal anything."

Justin went down the dark hall first, opening each door to reveal another sterile office. Finally, we tiptoed to the end of the corridor through a set of doors leading to a giant warehouse and crept past props and equipment using the dim light from Justin's phone.

"Look," he whispered. A sign on a door read, "Make-up." Inside, the room looked part morgue, part beauty salon. Something lay on a table wrapped in a tarp. I pulled a corner over, and the giant burrito rolled off the table and splat onto the floor, exposing a gelatinous human torso, all extremities ripped—not cut—off. Stringy guts spilled out of the gaping hole in the stomach. An involuntary whoop came out of my mouth as I jumped back to avoid the thing landing on my feet. Justin stared closely before poking at it.

"Fake," he said. "Fucking amazing."

"Shit. Fuck." I pranced in place, trying to figure out what to do next. "Help me get it back up," I said. "Turn a light on."

"You sure? The ceilings are open to the warehouse. What if there's a security guard."

"He surely would have heard the body splat or me shout, right?" I asked.

Justin found a switch. After some cajoling, he put the guts back into the body cavity. Justin sniffed his finger and then took a lick, which made me want to gag. We were both a mess when we got the torso back up on the table. I washed my hands in the sink when someone opened the door. A leathery older man held onto his flashlight, ready to draw.

"What are you doing in here?" he barked.

I'd prepared for this scenario. "Working late," I spoke with confidence. "What are you doing in here?"

He hadn't expected this and furrowed his brow.

Justin's hands were deep in the body cavity, where he froze. I dried my hands on my jeans.

"We're shooting tomorrow," I said. "So, this has to be done tonight." I rolled my eyes. "Last minute touch-ups since Lawrence isn't here."

Erik appeared behind the man with a smug smile. "What do we have here, Sam?" he asked.

"I don't know," he said. "I never know what the hell is going on in this place." His disappointment showed in deep frown lines. "Sign in next time."

"Sorry, Sam," I said. "My team is still getting used to things around here. We'll do better."

He grumbled a little and walked down the hall. "Come on, and I'll show you Wilson's workshop."

When they were far enough away, I whispered, "Stay here," and tiptoed out, following the two men across the warehouse.

"This is Wilson's workshop. Barely touched since he was put in the loony bin," the old guard said.

"When you say barely, what do you mean? Who's been in here?" Erik asked.

"Lawrence Wilson, who do you think? It's his workshop—but only at night. He came in twice on my shift."

"Can I look?" Erik asked.

"Sure," he said. "Have a go."

"Thank you, Sam. I'll give you a shout if I need you."

"Well, I can help if you need."

"I'm good," he said. "Better make sure someone else didn't sign in while you showed me around."

"You got that right." He shook his head. "They never want to sign in."

We both waited until Sam's keys could no longer be heard jingling in the dark. "You can come out now," Erik said. I stepped from the shadows into the doorway. Shelves of furry creature heads lined the walls.

"Lawrence was a freak," I said.

"What are you doing here?" he asked.

"What are you doing here?" I asked, stepping in. "It was my idea, remember?"

He sighed. "Do not touch anything." He sighed again and handed me a pair of rubber gloves. "Put these on, at least."

"Is it weird that I find it hot when you're mad at me?" I asked.

He searched a drawer, laying the contents on a worktable. Sketches of human-faced animal creatures spilled across the table."Yes."

Justin texted, "Where are you?"

"Searching Lawrence's workshop," I wrote. "With Erik. Where are you?"

"I found the Cedar King's bedroom," he wrote back. "Never leaving this place."

"Find the tree demon. I don't see anything like it in here."

I sat down at Lawrence's desk and searched the drawers. I ran my gloved fingers under the desktop, took the drawers out, and turned them upside down, feeling for something underneath, and pulled the tape off what turned out to be a disturbing sketch of a demon-faced stag so vivid I could almost hear it screaming. It was virtually identical to the stag mask we found in the shed. Scribbled below were the words, "God help me."

"Why'd he hide this?" Erik asked.

"Maybe he didn't want anyone to know he was insane." I had a nagging feeling there was more to the haunting of Lawrence Wilson. "He'd certainly seen that stag mask before, though. This proves it."

"I found the tree ghosts," Justin texted. "There's a rack of them in the far eastern corner."

We wandered toward the back of the warehouse. A rack of shredded linen ribbons hung to the ground; their bony faces contorted in different versions of horror and agony. The camera might not see it, but I noticed the glue, nails, and lack of patience. The pieces were sad copies of the artistic braiding and beadwork done on the stag from the shed, although the influence was evident.

"They aren't the same." I shook my head. "But definitely inspired by the original."

The lights in the warehouse went on, and soon, Sam stood before us. "What do you want with those creepy things?" he asked.

"Do you know anything about them?" Erik asked.

"Just that Mr. Wilson was as unpredictable as a rabid raccoon last season. Anything that happened spooked him. I say he got afraid of his own creations."

"Don't the writers make the creatures?" I asked.

"Not that season. One of the writers saw the mask Wilson made in his workshop and wrote the whole season around it."

"Was it a stag's head? That first one?" I asked.

Sam scratched his head and pondered. "I can't remember."

"I'm finished for now," Erik said, handing the security guard his card. "If you can think of anything else, here's my number."

We stood outside on the sidewalk. The chilly air made me shiver.

"What were you thinking?" Erik asked. "The last thing Justin needs is a breaking and entering charge."

"You wouldn't even be here if it wasn't for me," I said.

He sighed. "I'll give you a ride home."

"I feel like walking." After twenty years of marriage, I didn't feel like being bossed by anyone.

Erik watched me go down the block before getting into his car. On the way home, I passed six breweries, a girl holding the hair of another back while she threw up, a homeless encampment with six tents and a dog, a psychotic guy mumbling to himself, and several dozen men dressed like loggers. No one glanced at me as I puffed away on my joint. I liked Portland, the dark side and all.

CHAPTER 34

◆◆◆

THE PORTLAND SKYLINE didn't disappoint, gifting me another cool, blue morning on the balcony. The night before, I'd strolled down quiet, tree-lined streets across busy intersections and up the hill to my new house in Goose Hollow. I stood across the street, watching the lights go off one by one on the block, excited to move in. But now, staring at the view from the hotel's balcony, with Mt. Hood promising me everything like a giant diamond, I wished I could stay longer.

Jack called, and I felt soft toward him and answered. After some small talk, he asked if I was packing. Code for moving out of the hotel. I lied to appease him.

"What kind of trouble are you getting into today?" he asked.

"I'm going to visit Astral's shop," I said.

"Did you forget to buy dream catchers for the kids?" he asked.

"Very funny," I said. "No, I just want to see if I can pick up anything for my new place."

"Hmm." Jack knew Bohemian wasn't my thing. "Please don't get yourself killed."

"I'll be fine," I said. "It's just a visit to the store. Maybe you're the one who wants a dream catcher."

"I miss you," he said.

"Bye." I hung up.

◆◆◆

The door to Celestial Beads was propped open, my entrance muffled by the high-pitched giggles coming from the back of the store. A low table hovered over the pillow-covered floor where Astral usually rang bowls. Tween-aged girls surrounded the table, hands stringing and knotting, tongues busy chatting. Astral took her place as queen of hippy mermaids, allowing me to sneak by while she gave directions to one of her guests.

I searched tables and baskets and rows of brightly painted masks, strings of colorful beads, rolls of twine, rope, and chain, but didn't recognize anything resembling the materials used on the stag. A long, woven banner hung from the office door where the lion once hung. I opened the door, and a ribbon of bells rang from the other side. The lion mask sat on a chair, its braided, frayed, and beaded mane hung to the floor. I picked through the ribbons, recognizing the work at once. I snapped a few photos before noticing a calendar on the desk. I fingered backward through the book until I reached the accident date, January 6. The hours between noon and four were empty. I was leaving the office when Astral found me.

She watched me shut the door, her hand on one hip. "Can I help you?"

"Hey, Astral," I chirped.

She softened a bit. "Lee. Hey. I didn't know anyone was in the store."

"I didn't want to disturb you with the girls," I said. "Looks like so much fun."

My hand still held the doorknob. "What are you doing in my office?"

"I was looking for the lion mask," I said. "I noticed you moved it. I'm obsessed."

Astral stared at me with a den mother's gaze. I knew that look, and it said, "Don't fuck with me and mine."

"Do you have you any more like it, Astral? Maybe another animal?"

"I'm in the middle of a party, Lee." She pulled a key from the pocket of her floor-length skirt and locked the office door before walking me to the front of the store. "You carry dark energy today. You're scaring my muse." She held the door open, and when I stepped out, she locked it.

CHAPTER 35

◆◆◆

CLOUDS BLOCKED THE sun, leaving the city damp and chilly. I walked to Amy's house from the village, my feet sore from the long stroll the night before.

Justin phoned.

"Where are you?" I asked.

"In the Cedar King's nest." He practically squealed in delight.

"Oh my god!" I yelled. "You slept in there?"

"Best night of my life. What time is it?" he whispered.

"It's noon!" I yelled. "Get the fuck out of there."

"I gotta pee so bad, Lee. There are people everywhere down below," he whispered. "I'm gonna have to make a run for it." He hung up.

Amy and I had plans to spend the day together. The silence of her road left me cold. There was no sign of Pearl or Henry. Astral might have warned them off.

"Good morning, Sunshine," Amy said from her porch.

"Good day, Sunshine," I sang back. "You look marvelous at your front door."

"I still love the house," she said. "You haven't ruined it for me yet."

"I am so glad." I hugged her. "I was worried you'd have dreams of Lawrence Wilson climbing out of the ravine like a no-faced zombie."

"Thank you, Lee. Thanks so much." She held the door for me to pass through. "What kind of danger do you have planned for today? Visit a serial killer in jail? Break into someone's pot farm? Pretend we're prostitutes and hang out at a truck stop?"

"Honestly, Amy, I just want to return to the park. If I don't, the last memory will be the only one that sticks."

She closed one eye and focused on me. Convinced I told the truth, she agreed. "On one condition," she said. "We re-baptize the park as the magical place it is. No talk of dead people."

"Perfect," I said. "Look what I brought." I held up two pre-rolls. "One for each of us. And I know just where to smoke them." Amy put on her sneakers, and we went to the trailhead.

"I think I know who killed Charlotte," I told her. "I'm saying it now before we go into the park. I don't know how, though."

"Surprise me," she said.

I followed her down the switchbacks that brought us to a bridge. We crossed over the log and walked along the familiar trail, more worn than a deer path after the emergency workers trampled through.

"Are you sure it's okay to come back here?" Amy asked.

"It's technically city property. At one point, they bought it from a farmer who died without heirs--back taxes and all that. The city uses it as a floodplain. That's why no one knew about the shed. They don't come down here unless there's a major flood, which hasn't happened in decades."

Someone had carved into the stag with a knife, destroying the image.

"Jesus," Amy said. "Angry much?"

"Come on." I pushed through the brush and climbed up to the rock shelf. "Welcome to the grotto," I yelled.

She joined me on the rock, and we lay on our backs, smoked our joints, and watched the clouds make animal shapes.

"That's a puppy, and it's coming to your house because pretty soon you won't have any kids to take care of, and your dogs are dead," Amy said.

"Bicoastal dog. Sounds cruel. You should get a dog; I'll be its fairy dog mother."

"I have a pet spider on my living room ceiling, and I worry she won't survive the winter. That's enough pressure."

We both dozed off at some point. I awakened to a crashing noise in the bushes. I sat up, startled and vulnerable, but a buck flew from the brush before I could stand. The magnificent creature looked me in the eye, snorted, and then leaped over the rocks, down the falls, and toward the path. I stood up.

"Amy! Holy shit! Amy!" I ran after him through the narrow opening that led to the trail and looked both ways. To the left was the meadow, and I couldn't go there alone. I chose the path toward Amy's house. When I reached the bridge, the stag waited, munching on something along the trail. I froze, anticipating his next move. He finished chewing and trotted away up the path toward Garret's Ferry. When I got up to the road, he stopped to look back. His rack was magnificent, with six points reaching for the sky. He carried the burden proudly on a powerful neck.

A sun ray broke through the clouds and worked its way down to the dark road where the stag's antlers and the most muscular parts of his physique glowed golden. Above his head, high in the tree, something else glistened too—something metallic I'd missed before. Another came from the tree across the road.

When I looked down, the stag was gone.

Amy still slept on the rock when I returned. I stood over her and whispered, "Amy."

She didn't move.

"Amy," I said louder. "What the fuck? How did you not hear that ruckus?"

She didn't flinch.

A flash of fear pushed on the door of my mind, but I fought it off. "Amy!" I shouted, my voice cracking in panic.

She wrinkled her face and shouted, "Rahhhh!"

I jumped backward and had to catch myself from tumbling. "You bitch. I almost fell over the waterfall."

"That's what you get for leaving me here," she said. "I woke up and thought the ghost of Lawrence got you."

"It's not very professional of you to shock a person who's already traumatized," I said.

"Don't be a drama queen. You play with murderers all the time. It's your fucking hobby." It took several minutes for my heart to stop pounding. I sat on a rock by the water, thinking of the golden stag.

CHAPTER 36

◆◆◆

AMY PURCHASED HER house because of the tranquil location and had expected a quiet period to follow. We sat in her back room, drinking wine and talking about new restaurants, my crumbling family, a rollicking cello performance I shouldn't have missed, cannabis legalization, and how sorry I was to have disturbed her peace.

"It's nice to know no one is after you. I'm enjoying this place again," Amy said. "You should try enjoying your new place sometime."

The Goose Hollow house represented the end of my family, and I didn't want to talk about it.

"I want a photo of me buying legal weed. Let's drive to Vancouver and get some," I said. "I'm not a criminal in Washington State. Woo-hoo."

"You're still a criminal in the eyes of the federal government, and you're breaking the law if you bring cannabis products back over the bridge. Interstate trafficking."

"So, I must consume anything I buy in Washington and drive back?"

"No. Then you'd be consuming and driving. DWI."

"Can I consume it where I buy it?" I asked.

"No, you can't smoke in a dispensary."

"A Park?" I asked.

"Nope. Technically, it's not outside where anyone can smell it. Not even in front of your own house," Amy said.

"Jeez," I said. "I wish they'd make that rule for barbecues. The smell of cooking flesh is repulsive. So, do you want to go to Washington with me to buy legal weed and then drive back to Oregon with it illegally?"

"Maybe," she said.

I grabbed two joints from my purse and threw one at her. "Want to smoke them on the front porch just to break the law?" I asked.

"No, I don't want Pearl to think it's okay. She already watches her father suck on cigarettes all day."

"Plus, all of that spiritual bullshit Astral exhales. Poor Pearl."

"Pearl is pretty awesome," Amy said.

"If Pearl were a bird, she'd be caged," I said. "Have you seen her around?"

"Now that you mention it, no."

"Do you mind if I invite her to a tea party at your house later?"

"A kid? Here?" She looked around the fluffy white carpet and linen sofa. "Why?"

Amy followed me out to the deck. "What's with the sudden craving for the company of children?"

"I need to talk to Astral and Henry without Pearl there." She stared at me for a long time. I bit my lip anxiously, waiting to see if she would lose patience again.

"Do you think one of those two idiots killed Charlotte?" she asked.

"I think I know what happened." There is no way I'd tell her how I figured it out.

"Which one?" she asked. "Is it both? What's going to happen to Pearl?" Her eyes widened with panic. "Oh no, you can't bring that child here and expect me...no."

"I don't think anyone is going to get arrested. I don't know the laws here," I said.

Amy let out a long sigh, giving her time to think. "What's the point then?"

"If it is one of them, I want them to know I know. Maybe they can't be held accountable, but I know," I said. "Do you get that?"

She frowned and sighed and then finally said, "I do."

Amy called Henry to invite Pearl over, but Henry told her Pearl had gone to stay with his parents. I watched their house from the living room window until Astral's van arrived in the twilight. Henry raced out to the car with several suitcases, and Astral walked right past him without a greeting. Henry shut the van doors, stood at the back of the vehicle, and looked around the neighborhood, stopping at Amy's house. The lights were off in the front, but I moved out of view slowly and went to Amy, who sat at the counter reading her phone.

"They're leaving," I said. "I'm going over there."

She put her phone down. "Not alone, you aren't."

"They're your neighbors, Amy. I don't expect you to get any more mixed up in this than you already are."

She put her phone in her back pocket. "Those assholes almost got you killed. Fuck them. Let's go." She grabbed two pepper sprays from her bowl by the door, handing me one.

I sent Erik a text. "Henry and Astral are leaving town. Going now to stall them."

"I need you to do one more thing, Amy." It was a big ask, but she did it. "Can you call Ellen and tell her you're moving? I suspect a sale is the only thing that will get her here."

CHAPTER 37

◆◆◆

SMOKE ROSE FROM the backyard. Amy knocked on the door while I went around to see who burned what, just in time to catch Astral squirting lighter fluid over the lion mask. She set it ablaze as I joined her, and we watched the strings on the mane burn like wicks.

"I made it for Pearl to go in her jungle room. It came out so well, I made a stag for Henry." Astral poked at the fire with a stick to ensure every piece of the lion disappeared.

"It was spectacular. Mind if I add a log?" I asked. "It seems like you have plenty." The stacks of wood reminded me of a settler's fortress. Henry was a century too late. Astral shrugged and chuckled, a tear dripping down one cheek. I picked two logs from the closest wall and placed them over the charred lion. "I'm surprised how cold it gets here in the evenings," I said. "New Jersey summers are warm and humid, and the mosquitos rule the world at night."

"Pearl hated the lion—it gave her nightmares." She spoke to the flames.

Henry busted out the back door. He watched us momentarily before marching down to the yard where we sat. Amy came down the driveway shortly after.

"We're burning an offering to Astral's muse," I said. "Can you see any magic in the air?"

Astral looked up at Henry, tears streaming down her face. "She knows."

"Just shut up," he said. His eyes reflected the rage from the fire, and it scared me.

Astral stood up. "Don't fucking talk to me like that. What have you done? What have you done to our family?" She broke down into sobs. "Oh my god," she cried. "My baby girl."

"Shut up," Henry yelled. "Shut the fuck up!"

Amy and I stood between them faster than either could blink. Amy was at least a foot shorter than Henry but pointed her spray can at his face.

"Back off, Henry." When he didn't move, she poked him below the ribs. "I said back off."

Astral sobbed. I sat down and wrapped an arm around her, hoping Amy would spray Henry.

"Sit down," Amy said. "We just came over to talk." He reluctantly sat on one of the many stumps around the fire.

I stalled while the flames lapped at his thoughts, hoping to hear Erik's car. "Why don't you start at the beginning, Henry?" I asked.

"The beginning, huh?" He shrugged. "I remember the beginning. I was eight when Charlotte was born. Even then, she was the most beautiful baby anyone had ever seen. I was eight years older, and everyone thought it was funny when Charlotte invited me to her birthday parties. She'd always said she'd marry me when she grew up. Neither of our parents could have imagined what came next.

"After Charlotte's mom died, Charlotte disappeared for three days. I didn't think she'd survive living there without her mother. The house belonged to her mother's family, but now it belonged to her father, and he'd soon run it into the ground, racking up a huge tax bill along the way."

"How old was Charlotte then?" I asked.

"She was fifteen when her mother died," he said. "Sixteen when we started our relationship—almost seventeen. And I was twenty-four. We hid it from everyone." He sighed heavily. "When my mother found out, she called it incestuous."

"Maybe she feared you'd get arrested," Amy said.

"I'm a human being. The girl was six feet tall at sixteen. And she loved me. Me!" He looked over at Astral. "I'm sorry, Stargazer."

Astral rolled her eyes. "Beautiful Charlotte. That's what I've heard for the last six years. She was beautiful. What did her beauty get her? Beaten by her father, used up by her neighbor, and kept hostage by that creepy husband."

"Whoa," Amy whispered. "Astral. Think about what the girl went through."

"It's true, though. It's all anyone ever says about her," I said. "I can see why you'd be upset with Charlotte, Astral. She left her child behind and became the beautiful, missing Charlotte. That's what happened, right? Charlotte had a baby in the shed. And Pearl is that baby."

I'd seen Erik's car pull up on the street and breathed relief.

"She's *my* baby," Astral said.

"When Charlotte returned and asked to see her, it couldn't have been easy for you," I said.

"I told her no!" Henry yelled. "She made her decision when she left Pearl alone in the shack. She fucking left Pearl there."

"She was a traumatized, seventeen-year-old girl, Henry," I said. "Can you imagine the trauma of having a baby in that ravine? How could she possibly know what to feel? Charlotte was a child when she gave birth. Legally and emotionally. But you knew that.

"That's why you didn't register the baby's birth. That's the reason she's home-schooled. It's not because you're such hippies but because there is no record of Pearl on paper," I said. "So, you decided to kill Charlotte. She had to go."

He snarled. "Fuck you. I didn't do anything to Charlotte."

"What's going on here?" Ellen walked down the driveway wearing jeans and sneakers.

"Ellen, hi," I said. "Glad you could make it."

"Make what?" she asked. "Why am I here, Amy?"

"We were just getting around to the sad story of Charlotte Wilson," I said. "And I think you will enjoy your part in this story."

"I'm disappointed, Amy," Ellen said.

"It was your idea, Ellen. You are the maestro," I said. "Why not stay and hear me out."

Ellen's eyes lit up in flames. "Have you ever thought of getting a job? Maybe if you weren't so bored, you'd have something to do besides start trouble like a saggy old Nancy Drew."

"Ellen!" Amy said. "What the hell?"

She took a breath and started again. "Me? You two consider yourselves some Cheech and Chong duo, fucking my clients over. Are you trying to ruin my reputation?"

"What did I do?" Amy asked.

"Her!" She pointed at me, frothy with anger. "That's what you did."

Erik and a uniformed officer stepped out of the shadows. "Enough," Erik said. "Mr. Gates, where's your daughter?"

"That's none of your business. Do you have a warrant? You're not permitted on my property." Henry said.

"Would you rather we talk more formally at the station?" Erik asked. "Or should I request a welfare check on a minor? We can be here all night if you want."

Henry looked to Astral, who shook her head. He poked at the fire with a large stick.

"This is Officer Sanchez. I'm Detective Erik Healy, and if you don't know already, we are from the Portland Police. Do you mind if we sit?"

Henry shrugged.

"Where is Pearl?" Erik asked.

"With my parents. You can call them if you want." He handed over his phone, but Erik rejected it. "What do you want to know?"

"Start at the beginning," Erik said.

Henry stared into the flames. "I moved back in with my folks after being laid off from my IT job. After Charlotte's mom's suicide, Charlotte went missing for a couple of days, and I found her in the meadow. I walked her home, and after that, we'd meet regularly while her dad was at work. She felt safe with me, and I wanted to make sure she was okay."

I helped him get to the point. "And when Charlotte's father caught you in the basement, you were twenty-four and Charlotte sixteen, and he threatened you with jail."

He was so uncomfortable I almost felt sorry for him, but finally he answered. "Yes. We had a plan. I restored the shed, and we had a dry place to sleep by winter."

"She looks just like her mother, doesn't she, Ellen?" I asked.

"How would I know?" Ellen asked.

"You saw Charlotte and Pearl talking over the fence and knew."

"You forget, Charlotte wasn't my client," she said. "Why would I see that?"

"Because you waited outside for Amy to arrive so you could show her the house, and during that time, you met Charlotte outside. You saw her talking to Pearl at the gate, and you knew. It's impossible not to see it—they were clones."

"You're cracked," she said.

"When you and Amy lost the house, the agent told you it was because the original owner's family wanted it. Amy didn't get outbid, did she?"

"I don't see what that has to do with me." She looked toward Erik. "Do you?"

Erik shrugged. "What happened next?"

Astral stood up. "I can tell you what happened next. Ellen called me and said her buyer missed out on the house across the street. 'The old owner was moving back in."

Ellen shrugged. "I mean, who wants to live across the street from their husband's ex?" she said. "I had no idea it would lead to murder."

"Well, you'd have to have some idea that real estate leads to murder, Ellen, because Craig Buckwood had just died, like so many around you often do."

"I don't have to take this from you." But she stayed.

I turned to Astral. "That story about how you met Henry. There is something you left out. He had Pearl with him. He hid her from Charlotte's father. He'd have known at first sight."

"Henry told me Charlotte died in childbirth. The two were pathetic, so I stayed in Portland because I believed they needed me." She laughed through tears. "I should have known because he never let her call me Mommy." Tears became sobs.

"When did you learn Charlotte was alive?" Erik asked.

"Ellen told me, and then Pearl confirmed she'd met Charlotte at the gate," she said. "But when Amos showed up and told my daughter Charlotte loved her... I mean, what good could that do her? The woman was dead."

Henry could not hide the surprise. "Why didn't you say anything?"

"How could I?" she cried. "You were already gone. Do you think I didn't notice you sneaking off every chance you got? The obsessive jogging that led you into the night?"

"It wasn't what you thought, Gazer."

"Don't call me that. Don't you dare," Astral cried. "When I met you, your parents were paying your rent. No wonder they loved me. I took over for them. I raised your infant daughter and fed and clothed you because you were some grieving cowboy who couldn't hold a job. I fucked you like a good little whore after I worked all day to pay our bills. And you lied to me the entire time—you and your fucking parents. You let me love Pearl, knowing she could never really be mine."

"Astral, honey." He moved toward her, but she flinched and leaned away.

"You lied to me daily and disappeared for hours. You stopped touching me, calling, or visiting at work—no more surprise lunches. You were obsessed with Charlotte. I saw the phone calls, and then I saw the grief when she rejected you."

"Is that why you ghosted her, Henry? She didn't want a package deal. Just Pearl," I said.

"No! That's not what happened," he yelled. "You shut the fuck up!"

I wasn't afraid of him. "So, then you started tormenting Charlotte's husband. Trying to drive him mad. You scared the hell out of the man with that mask, a man who already knew his wife was slipping away." I kept my cool, even though inside I rattled.

"Then she died, and knowing he'd return to the scene, you burned a stag on the tree at the crash site. She was already dead, Henry. Did you have to take it that far?"

"You're so wrong," he said. The blood vessels on his temples bulged, and his face turned scarlet with anger.

"You haunted him. Charlotte must have told you he was fragile during those long calls you shared. She wouldn't leave him for you because he was so fragile. You must have hated that."

"He was a fucking freak!" he yelled. "You saw what he did. He was paranoid."

The thought of Lawrence still gave me shivers.

"Here's where Ellen comes in. She called the homeowner and asked if they had a solid deal—as you did for me on Southwest Terrace, right, Ellen?"

Ellen crossed her arms and frowned.

"And the homeowner told you the inspection was on the seventh of January. So, you called the house and told Astral or Henry. Which one?"

"No, I told them once the inspection happened, it would be a done deal," Ellen said. "Not because I wanted her to murder the woman. Jesus. I thought she'd list her house, that's all. I'd already lost one deal, and the house was perfect for Amy."

Amy shook her head in disagreement.

"Who? Who did you tell?" Erik asked.

"It was months ago. I don't remember," Ellen snapped.

I wondered if she told the truth or still held on to her code of silence.

"Let me guess," I said. "Astral told Henry, and he decided to scare the hell out of them on the way to the inspection."

"It was Astral, if I remember correctly."

"Why do you keep talking?" Henry lunged at me.

Erik rose from his chair, but I put my hand out to stop him.

"And then you dropped the mask down over their car, and it caused them to swerve off the road, just like you wanted. Only you killed the wrong Wilson, didn't you?"

"What are you talking about? Is that what happened to Charlotte?" He looked at Astral, and for a moment, something crossed between them.

"You'd been after Lawrence for weeks. You knew Charlotte kept her secret from him, and she'd already contacted you daily, begging you to let her see Pearl. All Lawrence knew was that his wife had behaved oddly since they'd arrived and that he seemed to be seeing things--a mysterious and horrifying stag face in the woods by their condo."

"No," he said.

"The stag from the shack is yours, Henry. The one with the blood dripping down its face, the bones you added for eye sockets, and now the brain matter of Lawrence Wilson after you drove him to suicide."

Henry shook his head no, repeatedly.

"I found hooks in the trees on Garrett's Ferry. You should have removed them."

"Hooks?" He looked at Astral. "I don't know anything about hooks," but something about the statement slowed him down. "You know what? Get off my property." Henry stood up again. "All of you. Go, now."

"You knew he'd be susceptible to that kind of thing. You gaslit him."

His anger made me scoot a few stumps away, but he sensed my fear and stomped at me like a bear. "Everything was fine until you fucking showed up."

"What have you done, Henry?" Astral asked.

Her voice calmed him down. "Let's put this fire out and get going." He stood up. "All of you need to get the fuck off my property."

"I'm not going anywhere with you," Astral said.

"You don't trust me?" Henry's face melted in grief. "I didn't do this."

I almost believed him, but Astral stared at her feet, ignoring his pleas to leave.

"No, Henry. I haven't trusted you since you started sneaking off to restore your love nest in the meadow—since your exuberance turned to sorrow—since she died and your grief became a firewood maze in my yard." She sobbed into her hands.

Henry knelt at her side, suddenly softer than I'd thought possible. "Don't cry, Astral. Please don't cry. I didn't do this. You have to believe me."

"What did you do to us?" she asked. "What have you done to our daughter?"

"Stop now. Enough," Henry whispered. "We'll talk on the way to Pearl."

I only had one chance to keep them from leaving. "Did you pick Astral because she could pass as Pearl's mother?"

Henry snarled, then jumped across the fire pit like a jackrabbit, the big stick still in his hand. I stood up to run, but he catapulted me backward. My head cracked against the ground.

Amy jumped on his back and clawed at his face like an eagle.

Henry yelled, "Get her off me," as they tumbled down the lawn.

"Lee!" Erik knelt over me and held his hand against my pulsing scalp.

"Can you arrest him now?" I asked.

Henry continued to scream. "She's biting me!" While spinning around with Amy on his back.

Sanchez jumped into the action, wrestling the two apart.

Erik's voice cracked when he called for an ambulance.

I felt a heartbeat in my head before everything went black.

CHAPTER 38

◆◆◆

TWELVE STITCHES IN my head, and one night in the hospital later, I moved into my new home. Justin stayed with me while I recovered. He grilled many cheese sandwiches and made me watch bizarre cartoons.

The District Attorney declined to charge Henry with fourth-degree statutory rape. Mainly because Pearl was missing, and her birth mother was dead. The tormenting of Lawrence Wilson would also go unpunished. But Henry's assault on me would result in jail time.

I knew Henry hadn't done anything to Lawrence. The more I thought about the look on his face when I accused him, the more I was convinced my accusations confused him.

Astral left town before the police car holding Henry made it to the station. She picked Pearl up from her grandparent's house in eastern Oregon and disappeared. I pictured them dancing in the woods, celebrating their new freedom in a field of wildflowers and hippies swinging rainbow ribbons. But I could also see the dark side of Astral, and threatening their family will turn most women into wolves.

Ellen walked away unscathed, with three commission checks thanks to my two and another when Henry's parents listed the house across from Amy's. Soon, she'd have a new neighbor, and it would be a new era, and the tragedy would wash away in the winter rains.

Things had been strange between Erik and me. My injury caused us to think about what we were to each other, but we didn't discuss it. Amy slept by my side at the hospital, and she and Justin were always at the house. It wasn't the baptism I'd hoped to give the new place.

Once my headache faded, I asked Erik to take me to the meadow.

"The city deemed the structure unsound and destroyed it," he said.

"I don't care about that creepy shed. I want to find Charlotte down there. Find what she found, you know? There is forest magic down there." I'd never told him about the stag because he'd say it was the weed.

The mountain reappeared that day, and its pointed glacier reflected light pink until noon approached. A sporty black wrap dress with a slightly twirly skirt had arrived in the mail—part of a long retail therapy week I had while recovering. I slipped it on and added brown sandals.

Amy was at work when Erik and I pulled up in his car. Henry and Astral's house sagged with loneliness—even the brightly shining pinwheels and rainbow banners in the garden couldn't cheer it up. A tree behind the sad cottage creaked in the breeze. We walked single file along the trail. Erik kept asking if I was okay.

"Please, stop treating me like I'm fragile," I said.

"Are you kidding me? You took a blow to the head to keep the bad guy from escaping. You're disinvited to the fragility club after that move."

"There's a club?" I asked. "Do you have to cry in public to get in?"

"They won't take you. Don't even try," Erik said. "I hear they named a room after you at the Reckless Club." He stopped on the bridge above the brook, where the water's crystalline chime echoed up the steep hills and filled the air.

"I have a flight home in two days." I felt shy, but he put his hand out for me to come to him, and I obeyed. He pulled me close, and everything else but his body fell away.

"Can I make you dinner at my house tonight?" he said.

"Sleepover?" The thought of finally seeing his bed sent a warm pulse. "Sounds perfect."

Our kiss became urgent until a teenage dog walker came down the path.

"Meadow," I whispered.

We climbed the log, ignoring all warning signs, and stopped at the burned-out stag on the tree.

"This never made sense to me. The quality and patience don't fit Henry the Wood Chopper." I ran my finger over the knife gashes. "These look more like Henry. When you searched, did you find any wood carving instruments?" I asked.

"Nothing. He's not an artsy guy," Erik said. "Not much of a carpenter either. More of a lumberjack."

"What about Astral?" I asked.

"What about her?"

"She makes rainbows out of ribbons, Erik. She's a fucking craft master. Did you find the materials? Antlers? What about bones? Did you find bones?"

"Nothing like that. The guy is a vegan. He doesn't even wear leather."

"He's an angry vegan." I touched my partially shaved head. Thank God for ponytails—you could hardly tell. "Maybe Astral made them. Maybe she wanted to torture Henry. Pay him back for not telling her Charlotte was alive."

We strolled along slowly so the day wouldn't end, passing the entrance to the falls until coming to the meadow.

I closed my eyes and pressed the moment of Lawrence's suicide out. When I opened them, the field lay before me, smaller somehow. The shed lived like a ghost above the remainder of a stone foundation. The ancient blackberry bush that once engulfed the roof lay nearby, ready to spread over the blood-stained ground.

A stream carved itself through the ground, snaking back and forth to find a shallow path. A giant cedar kissed the woods and dominated the meadow. The tree wore a hoop skirt of fan leaves draped to the ground.

I wandered past the shed without looking and made a new path in the grass. I parted the flat-leafed branches and stepped into a pillowy room of red earth and smooth, snaking limbs, some touching the ground like elbows to keep the giant balanced.

Erik followed me in and sighed. "I love that smell."

Branches spread like stairs for climbing, some low and perfect for sitting. Above us, trunks sparkle in gold as the afternoon sun shined, lighting thousands of tiny sap droplets in amber diamonds. I leaned against the soft fur of the trunk, and he came to me as if I were something delicate that he didn't want to break, kissing me everywhere until I begged him for more.

He, too, was golden in the sunlight.

◆◆◆

Erik didn't seem like a chicken guy, but his yard had a large poultry apartment house freshly painted pumpkin orange. He introduced me to his chickens, Gladys, Ida, and Agatha, swooping up a little fluffy black one that settled into his arms.

"This is Agatha. She's my best girl."

"Who named them? Your great-grandmother?" I asked.

"The ladies came with the house, and I had to have the house." He softly stroked Agatha's back. "She's an amazing girl." The chicken closed her eyes in bliss while he stroke her chest.

The inside of his house was as neat as I'd imagined, with a surprising amount of natural wood and minimalist accents. "I hope it's not too soon to introduce you to the girls."

"We can keep the kids separate, except for Justin. I need you to share him with Amy and me while I'm gone, okay?"

"My chickens like me much better than he does." He tossed a big bowl of lettuce in a metal bowl and cut an avocado like a true Californian, sprinkling perfect cubes over the salad.

"Justin likes you," I said.

"You're a terrible liar."

"He hasn't had great experiences with cops, and it would be a great time to win him over," I said.

"I'll give it my best," he said. A long silence followed.

"So, what will happen when you get to New Jersey?" he asked.

I felt like twelve stitches in my head excused me from this conversation for a while, but the way he looked at me—so crystalline—I wanted to be clear, too.

"I'm going to make life as normal as possible for the kids. I'll get Max ready for his school year; then I'll drop my son at his college and drive across the country with his car since he can't have it in his first year and keep it here."

"Will you stay in the house with Jack until then?" he asked.

"Well, yes. It's my home." I spoke too quickly. "I hope you don't...I don't know how to explain it. I never quite understood home until I lived in my house in New Jersey. It's full of light, and I raised my babies there."

"And your husband lives there," he said.

"Yes. Jack lives there." I looked at my shoes. "He's always going to be family, regardless of what happens."

He poured more wine into my glass and set the bottle down. "I've never been the other man before, Lee."

"I'm going to work it all out," I said. "I just don't know what that means yet." I stared into my glass of wine. My brain hurt, and I could not work on the future when I barely grasped the present. "But Jack and I are over. It's the one thing I do know."

He pulled a tray of lasagna from the oven and set it on the stove.

"That smells delicious," I moaned.

Erik removed his oven mitt, walked around the counter, and lifted me off my chair. "You're delicious," he said.

I took a deep breath of relief.

We ate dinner late that evening.

CHAPTER 39

◆◆◆

ON MY LAST day in Portland, I sat under a sunspot in a rented kitchen chair on my empty brick patio. I'd had my coffee here every day since I came home from the hospital. A mix of evergreens and Japanese maples swayed in a slow breeze. I hadn't even left Oregon and already wanted to return to its perfect summer. At the same time, my heart ached for my kids and the easy familiarity of home.

Amy and Justin took me to the airport in the afternoon. On the way, I counted bridges and homeless tents to keep from crying.

Justin stepped out from the back seat at the airport. He hugged me for the first time. "If angels are real, you're mine," he whispered.

"I'll be back before you know it." I let the tears fall. "Or you could come out for a long weekend."

He nodded the way people do when they don't believe you.

A cop ushered Amy on. "I love you!" She yelled out the window as they drove off. I watched until they disappeared.

Just as I buckled into my window seat, Erik sent a text. "The warrant to search Astral's store came in. Guess what we found in the basement? Stags. Stags, and more Stags."

"You're welcome," I typed. The flight attendant came by and asked me to turn off my phone.

THE END

The Lee Harding Mystery Series

AVAILABLE AT AMAZON
AND
YOUR LOCAL BOOKSTORE

I WOULD LIKE TO THANK:

You, the reader. I hope you had a fun trip.

Thea, Jessica, Ashley, and Greg from the Wednesday group for listing, reading, editing, and honesty.

Nancy Rachel, for her incredible insight and for letting me talk constantly about Lee on our walks.

Naomi Gamorra, thank you for telling me exactly what you think with the most love possible.

Deborah Kaplan for creating my cover concept.

Edel Rodriguez for continuing to make art representing my and the nation's mood. You're a genius.

My darling husband, Glenn, for allowing me to live in an alternate universe while writing and giving me space to find my muse when I've lost her. For reading, rereading, and listening to me read. For putting up with my endless delays and for being the best human I know.

Lilli Gurney for her brilliant hawk eyes.

Made in the USA
Monee, IL
01 March 2024